PRAISE FOR JAMES TUCKER

"Gripping from its opening lines, *Next of Kin* is a white-knuckle page-turner, where ruthless power, murder, and crimes hidden for generations create an intricate, utterly absorbing tale. The life of a vulnerable young boy hangs in the balance, and Detective Buddy Lock must find the killer before it's too late. Simply a fantastic read."
— Marya Hornbacher, Pulitzer Prize–nominated author of *Wasted*, *The Center of Winter*, and *Madness*

"Terrific plot! And Buddy Lock is a cop protagonist that's a delightful departure from the norm. I'm wholeheartedly recommending *Next of Kin*."
— Mike Lawson, author of the Joe DeMarco thrillers

NEXT

OF

KIN

JAMES TUCKER

Text copyright © 2017 by James Tucker
All rights reserved.

Published by Thomas & Mercer, Seattle

www.apub.com

Amazon, the Amazon logo, and Thomas & Mercer are trademarks of Amazon.com, Inc., or its affiliates.

ISBN-13: 9781542045667
ISBN-10: 1542045665

Cover design by David Drummond

Printed in the United States of America

for Megan

Chapter One

Ben heard shattering glass. He pictured the bottle of champagne his father had been holding, now lying in shards on the oak floor.

His father's voice boomed from the living room. "What are you doing? *What are you doing?*"

He froze.

He was in the walk-in pantry at the back of the house, looking for a chocolate bar.

He listened for an answer to his father's question, but only heard him groan loudly. His mother screamed.

Then she shouted: "Run, Benjamin! *Run! Ru—*"

Silence. Her voice had been cut off.

A shiver passed through him. His hands began to shake.

He stared at the columns of shelving. If he could keep his hands steady, he might be able to get out. But what about his sister, Ellen-Marie?

She cried once, a pitiful burst, and the house again grew quiet.

Then he heard footsteps on the oak-plank floor, moving toward the back of the house, toward him.

Slowly, quietly, as only a ten-year-old can do, he moved to his right, to the farthest segment of shelving, the one he'd accidentally pressed against the previous June. He pushed on the section of shelving holding the jars of olives, just as he'd done last summer, but it wouldn't budge. He put both hands on the vertical planks and pushed. Nothing. He wondered if his father—who'd told him never to mention the secret doorway—had nailed it shut, to keep him from exploring.

The footsteps again. They were in the long hallway now, perhaps fifteen yards from him.

He brought his shoulder against the shelf, leaned into the wood, and shoved as hard as he could. He strained and his slippers began to slide on the floor, but then he heard the faint snap of the catch.

Now he pulled on the heavy shelf, grateful it made no sound as it swung into the pantry. He saw the stone steps leading down into darkness.

The footsteps grew closer and came faster.

He moved onto the stairs, balanced precariously, and turned to pull the pantry shelf closed behind him. He did so carefully. When he heard the catch snap into place, he stood on the top stair, perfectly still.

The footsteps entered the pantry. He heard them cross from one end of the generously sized room to the other and back again. Then they ceased. There was no sound. Yet Ben hadn't heard the footsteps leave. He held his breath. Someone knocked on the pantry walls. One wall. Another wall and another. Not six inches from his face, a knock on the fourth wall. Startlingly loud. He shook involuntarily and swayed backward. He hoped the shelving sounded solid. For thirty seconds he heard nothing. He shivered with fear and cold. He was dressed in a thick cotton bathrobe over his pajamas, but his hiding place was frigid and he was thin as a reed. Even the pantry had been cold.

Now he heard breathing on the other side of the shelves. He listened carefully but kept still. There was no sound other than the person's calm, full movement of air in and out of his—or her—lungs. An unusual scent, one he didn't recognize, passed through hairline cracks in the shelving. New leather mixed with lemon and something else.

And then, all at once, the footsteps retreated from the pantry.

A moment later he sensed a change in the air, followed by the sound of the house's front door opening and closing, but he couldn't be sure. And because he wasn't sure, he knew that he remained in danger. He couldn't go back into the house.

He drew his bathrobe more tightly around himself and eased down the steps into the darkness. It was farther than he remembered. When he reached the tunnel's soft earthen floor, he began walking. His hands guided him along the left concrete wall into the unknown. He went much farther than he had last summer. His teeth chattered and his hands tightened with cold. He thought he had to get out or he'd die.

After a while he stumbled upon another set of stairs. These he climbed carefully and at the top of them, touched the wooden surface he found. At first it seemed to be the back of another hidden pantry door with no discernable latch, but he was relieved to find a typical round knob.

Turning it, he pushed open the door and walked into a pantry that was much larger than the one in his parents' house. He knew he'd reached the lodge. Recessed lights burned low, illuminating shelves of spices and juices, canned goods and cereal, flour and wheat, syrup and sugar. On the floor he saw bushels of potatoes and winter squash. At the edge of a green marble countertop was a telephone. Beside the telephone was a pile of folded wool blankets.

Without alerting anyone in the lodge to his presence, he picked up the telephone and dialed 911.

"Someone killed my family," he whispered when the dispatcher answered. "Please help me."

Chapter Two

Three days later, Buddy's cell phone rang in the silent, brittle cold. He considered not answering. He was standing at his mother's grave in Kensiko Cemetery north of New York City—his mother who'd died of cancer twenty-one years ago today. He'd been close to her and didn't want to be distracted. But a feeling of duty welled up within him. He was a detective first grade with the New York City Police Department, and his job was nearly all that mattered to him. He reached into the breast pocket of his navy-blue overcoat and pulled out the phone.

"Lock here," he said.

"Detective Lock, this is Ray Sawyer. I'm an attorney for a member of the Brook family."

The names weren't immediately familiar. "Yeah?"

"Detective, I need your help solving murders."

In the faint light—it wasn't yet seven in the morning—Buddy shook his head, annoyed this stranger had called him. He said, "I'm with the NYPD and I don't moonlight. You'll have to find someone else to work the murder."

"*Murders*, Detective Lock. Three of them. Almost an entire family. Upstate, at a great camp in the Adirondacks wilderness."

Now Buddy made the connection. He'd read about the crime in the *Gazette*. Many hints about the murder of a rich family at their estate up north. No arrest, he recalled. Hardly any information. Not even a statement of how the family had died. And some of the details he'd found didn't add up. For example . . .

No, he told himself. *Goddammit, no. Stop thinking about it.* He turned from his mother's grave and said, "Mr. Sawyer, I'm assigned to the Nineteenth Precinct in Manhattan and normally don't have jurisdiction anywhere else. Aren't the State Police handling it?"

"Yes, but they're lost," Sawyer told him. "And this is a *Manhattan* crime. I need you, Detective Lock," Sawyer pleaded. "I need you or I wouldn't have called."

Buddy stopped. Turning, he looked at his car, the only one parked along Lakeview Avenue. "What do you mean, a 'Manhattan crime'?"

Sawyer said, "Camp Kateri is owned by the Brooks. Four houses arrayed around a main lodge, one house for each branch of the family. In the winter there's nobody up there except the caretaker and one or two of the staff. But a few days ago the entire family was gathered for the New Year's holiday. Somebody entered one of the houses and killed Alton Brook, his wife, Brenda, and their daughter, Ellen-Marie. The murders are Manhattan crimes because all the family live in Manhattan."

"And the staff?" Buddy asked.

"They may be local, but why would they do something so awful?"

Buddy thought of a number of reasons as he headed back to his car. He wanted to end the call with Ray Sawyer and get down to the precinct before the worst of the morning traffic. He also wanted to quash the interest in this case that had formed in his gut. He couldn't get involved, but at the same time he wanted to know more. A bad sign. A sign of an addiction he recognized all too well, one that tallied his clearance rate against the breakup of his family. He'd long ago chosen to focus all his energy on work, the organizing principle of his life. Work helped him blot out his misfortunes. It helped him move forward and was the key to his survival. For years there had been nothing else. Until he'd met Mei on a case the year before. Now his world had two suns that eyed each other warily. He said, "Mr. Sawyer, you said *almost* an entire branch of the Brook family was murdered."

"That's right."

He came to a monument in the shape of a cross. With his free hand he brushed off the snow and looked down at the name: Sergei Rachmaninoff. Here lay the great Russian composer who'd been one of Buddy's inspirations when he was on the concert circuit as a young man, before he'd failed in the most public way possible, at Carnegie Hall.

"Detective Lock? Are you there?"

"Yeah, I'm here," Buddy said, touching the headstone once, then turning from the grave and hurrying down the hill toward Lakeview. "Who survived?"

"Their ten-year-old son, Ben. I'm now his guardian."

Jesus. Buddy closed in on the last thirty yards between him and the unmarked Dodge Charger. "Was Ben at the camp that night?"

"Yes, but he escaped. We don't know how, and he won't tell us."

"Where is he right now?"

"He's with my wife at our apartment on West End Avenue. We're afraid to put him back in school until we know he's safe."

Buddy reached the Charger, opened the door, and dropped into the driver's seat. He closed the heavy door and started the car. "The remaining family won't take him?"

"Ben's parents were very clear in the family trust documents. They didn't want him living with his aunts and uncles. They thought his uncles were unethical in business and in life, and that his aunts spoiled their children so much those children didn't need to work. Ben's parents hated their laziness. And I won't allow these people custody of the boy, especially when a family member might be the killer."

Buddy said, "And you think Ben is safe at your apartment?"

"I think so."

More and more questions filled Buddy's mind, but he stifled them. He bit down on the insides of his cheeks and tasted blood. His left hand gripped the steering wheel. Years as a piano prodigy had taught him to see order in a thousand notes, and he thought this skill would help him find clues invisible to everyone else. His relentlessness would lead him to the killer. And yet he knew the job couldn't be his. Forcing his voice to be calm, he said, "Mr. Sawyer, I can't take over an investigation upstate. But I'm going to refer you to someone who might be able to help."

"Who?" Sawyer asked, his voice betraying disappointment.

"His name is Ward Mills. He has the time and money this case will require."

Buddy gave out his half brother's telephone number, wished Sawyer the best of luck, and ended the call.

He thought of why—why Ben Brook had lost his mother, why he couldn't help the boy or his family. In frustration he pounded the steering wheel with his heavy fist.

Chapter Three

Not long after he'd sat down in his cubicle at the Nineteenth Precinct building on East Sixty-Seventh Street between Third Avenue and Lexington, his brother Ward had called him.

"Can't do it," he'd told Ward.

Ward's cultured voice was smooth and cajoling. "What is it you can't do?"

"Work the murder up north."

"All right, Buddy. But why don't we look at the crime scene? Just for an hour or two."

Buddy drank from his large Dunkin' Donuts coffee. "Can't. Not my jurisdiction, and I have cases to work."

"So what? Take a vacation day. You probably have two months in the bank. I'll pick you up in an hour at the South Street Seaport."

"We're taking a boat?" Buddy had asked, stalling as he calculated his vacation hours, which came to about four months.

"The lakes in the Adirondacks are frozen, and I want to see the crime scene while it's fresh. So we're taking a bird."

Buddy didn't like helicopters. He said, "The murders were a week ago. Nothing's fresh."

"Whatever, Buddy. Are you in or not?"

He was in. His irritation had only grown after he'd left the cemetery. His mind had begun turning around the details of the case, and he'd been powerless to stop it. After calling Mei at Porter Gallery, he'd finished his coffee and taken the subway down to the Seaport.

Now he was sitting next to Ward in the plush rear seat of the Sikorsky helicopter his brother had chartered for the day. Taking off—rising up as Atlantic winds buffeted the machine—unnerved him. He liked to be on firm ground. But once they'd left South Street Seaport in Manhattan and were flying rapidly above the trough of the Hudson River Valley, he breathed easier.

But not easy. He was preparing for the puzzle he'd find when they landed.

He said, "Who are the Brooks? The *Gazette* mentioned they had piles of money but not much else. Ray Sawyer didn't explain."

Ward had dressed in dark-wash jeans, Sorel boots, and a black-collared ski sweater with a zipper. His sandy-colored hair was brushed back perfectly. His handsome face showed an easy confidence that at times slipped into arrogance. He was forty-one, two years younger than Buddy. Ward said, "Sawyer didn't think he had to explain."

Buddy didn't appreciate the runaround. He said, "Give me a straight answer."

Ward's blue eyes didn't turn away. "The family owns Brook Instruments, which makes high-end lenses used by Hollywood, the US military, and most consumer product companies on earth. BI is privately held by the four children of Walter Brook, the founder's son who died about five years ago. They're four brothers: Alton, Bruno, Carl, and Dietrich, oldest to youngest. So when someone murders part of the Brook family with a hatchet, we're talking about murder *and* money. A lot of money."

Buddy was silent as they followed the snaking Hudson between its bluffs covered in white snow, outcroppings of rock and evergreens flecking the landscape. It seemed quiet and lonely below, away from what he considered civilization: skyscrapers and crowded streets and ambulance sirens. He said, "Sawyer mentioned but didn't explain the Brooks' compound. Called it a 'great camp.'"

Ward nodded as he gazed at the land below. He said, "Wealthy families built compounds in the Adirondack wilderness. Started in the late eighteen hundreds but really hit its peak in the first couple decades of the twentieth century. Often there's a lodge with a large dining room, fieldstone fireplaces, and a library. The families would come up to the great camps for the summers, and they'd bring their servants and provisions and it would be a grand old time. Boats kept in wooden boathouses with cedar-shingled roofs. Everyone water-skiing and canoeing in the afternoons, and nights around campfires with stories and lots of gin. To do it right takes staff and a lot of money. But usually this time of year, the camps are closed."

Buddy thought about the killer's use of a very unusual murder weapon. To be sure he'd heard right, he said, "Ray Sawyer told you it was a hatchet?"

"That's per the State Police, and the coroner agreed."

"They have the weapon?"

Ward shook his head. "No. But it wasn't a knife. The damage was too extensive."

Buddy said, "What does that mean?"

Ward looked at him. "Sawyer told me what happened to Ben's family was brutal, even medieval."

Chapter Four

As the pilot set the helicopter down on the frozen lake, Ward opened the door, letting in the frigid wilderness air. Buddy followed him outside.

A strong northwest wind blew across the expanse. It was cold and biting down to the bones. Upper Saranac Lake formed a vast empty whiteness. The ice spread out before them under a gray sky, and the land bordering it rose from the shore and extended away beneath the cover of spruce and other evergreens. Here and there were stands of oaks and maples barren of leaves. Buddy tried to imagine the lake populated by people water-skiing, paddleboarding, or swimming out to rafts anchored to the lake bottom. But he couldn't.

For him this place was strange and forbidding. At this time of year, there were no neighbors for safety. No grocery stores or hospitals or much in the way of law enforcement or fire protection. Out here you were on your own—something that hadn't worked out so well for the Brooks. He turned around to see the camp.

In the center stood a lodge that resembled a chalet in the mountains of Switzerland. It had second and third stories that extended over the first, with numerous gables and carved wooden ornamentation at the roof peaks and under the eaves. On either side of the lodge stood two houses in close proximity to each other. The houses shared the lodge's architectural themes, including cedar shingles, large double-hung windows, and wide screened porches.

A man in his early seventies was walking down the stone path to the edge of the lake. The man waved to them. He wore a camel-hair overcoat and dark-brown leather gloves. A scarf in tartan plaid encircled his neck and was tucked firmly into his coat. He had thin gray hair and a pale complexion except for the touch of pink the cold had given his cheeks.

Buddy guessed the man wasn't accustomed to the world of multiple homicides, but Buddy was. In the few moments he'd been on the ice, he'd noticed things the old man would probably never see:

A pair of snowmobile tracks running in all directions, even near the camp.

A broken window on the upper story of the house immediately to the right of the lodge.

The face of a young woman in the lodge's third-floor window.

"Ray Sawyer," the man shouted over the noise of the Sikorsky's rotors. "Thanks for coming."

"Detective Lock, NYPD," Buddy said. "And this is Ward Mills."

Sawyer's face brightened. "I'm so glad you decided to work the case, Detective."

Buddy shook his head. "I'm here to look around. That's all."

The helicopter pilot cut the engines, and the rotors began to slow.

"Come with me," Sawyer said. "I'll show you where it happened."

He turned and led them up the fieldstone staircase to a wide path made of pavers, cleared of snow, that curled in a semicircle to the house immediately north of the lodge—the house with the broken window on the third level. When they'd reached the front porch, he pulled open the screen door and held it for them. Once they were on the porch with its stone floor and lack of furniture, presumably stored for winter, Buddy examined the brass doorknob on the house's heavy front door. No obvious evidence it had been picked. Nothing on the brass or the wooden door indicating forced entry. On New Year's Eve the door had been unlocked, he thought, or the killer had been invited in.

Buddy grasped the knob, twisted it, and pushed open the door.

They filed into the foyer, breathing warm air, unbuttoning their coats.

Buddy had thought the crime scene would be stale, but he was wrong. Evidence of butchery remained on the floors, walls, and furniture. The scene looked much as it had on New Year's Eve, minus three bodies.

Buddy had never seen anything like it. Copious amounts of gore mixed with shards of glass from a smashed crystal tumbler. Some footprints left by the paramedics and the local police. Sprays of scarlet extending over the oak-plank floors. Ten feet here. Eight there. Only three there—the little girl, he guessed. Easier to kill her, less blood to flow from severed carotid arteries on each side of her neck or from the diminutive chest cavity.

Buddy closed his eyes and imagined the scene in all its horror. The family's confusion. The fury of the hatchet and the swift blows. He sensed it then—the loss of a mother and father and child. It was the young girl's death that hurt most. He'd made a mistake last year and a girl had died. His chest tightened and he fought off the hardness of the loss with a single deep breath.

Then he opened his eyes.

Regained his focus.

Experienced his own anger.

He said, "Why?"

Ray Sawyer and Ward were standing to his left, facing the long hallway that led past the living room where the murders had been committed, past the kitchen, to the back of the house. They looked up at him.

"We know what happened," Buddy explained. "Someone came to this spot and killed three people. The killer either opened an unlocked door and entered unexpectedly, or was invited in by a family member.

The problem we need to solve is not how the family died, but *why*. Mr. Sawyer, do you have any thoughts on motive?"

Sawyer shook his head. "God only knows."

Buddy gazed again at the dried pools of blood and decided Sawyer was wrong. Given the proximity of the lodge and the other houses, he thought someone did know. He thought it might be a family secret.

Chapter Five

"Buddy?" Ward asked.

"Yeah?" Buddy woke from his thoughts and noticed the two men standing by him, watching as he stared at the dried pool.

"Did you see the broken window upstairs?" Ward asked.

Buddy met his brother's lively blue eyes. Ward knew more than he did about almost everything, including deviant psychology. But he couldn't read a crime scene the way Buddy could. Ward was ethereal, floating in the air like a brilliant hummingbird. Buddy was a plow horse working the mud. Buddy got his hands dirty. But his familiarity with dirt made him effective and allowed him to spot possibilities—or dead ends—that others couldn't see. He said, "Why don't you take a look? See if there are footprints on the roof. I'll work this floor."

Buddy walked down the hallway to the back of the house, Sawyer following him. The hallway was long and wide, with wainscoting stained dark brown, almost black. Above the wainscoting the walls were beige and on them hung family photographs, some dating from the late eighteen hundreds.

He stopped and examined one of the more recent photographs. He saw four pairs of adults and several children, some in their teens. The youngest—probably Ellen-Marie—might have been one or two years old in the photograph. The teenagers and the adults were attractive.

He saw that all were dressed for summer, in bathing suits and Bermuda shorts, and the boys and some of the men without shirts. The women and girls in bikinis. Lots of skin. A surprising amount of barely concealed private parts for a multigenerational family photo. Buddy wondered if it meant anything.

After a moment he turned from the photograph and went farther along the hallway. To his right was a small bathroom. He went inside and closed the door.

No window.

No exit.

Nowhere to hide.

Then he opened the door, crossed the hallway, and entered a rustic master bedroom. Sawyer followed him as he looked around. The bed was made and the toilet seat and cover in the master bath were down. There were no clothes on the floor. The windows were closed and, more importantly, further insulated by storm windows inside the exterior windows, each screwed into steel plates nailed into the wooden window frame. Touching the storm window screws, he found that none were loose.

Emerging into the hallway, he turned left and a few paces farther walked into a medium-sized pantry. Enameled white shelving from floor to ceiling was laden with soda cans, jars of hard candy, chocolate bars, waffle makers, canned goods, mixers, spices, and industrial-grade pots and pans of all varieties.

Buddy said, "Maybe the boy was back here during the murders."

Sawyer shook his head. "He couldn't have been. He'd have been trapped and killed."

Buddy turned to the gentleman lawyer. "But he was close enough to hear what was happening in the living room?"

"That's true. He told the police that his father said, 'What are you doing?' Then he heard screams. His mother's last words were a shout.

She told him to run. He must have run. Or something. But he got close to the killer and told me there was a distinctive scent in the house."

Buddy said, "What kind of scent?"

"Cologne, maybe. Aftershave. Deodorant. He couldn't be more specific."

Buddy searched the shelves for chests, cabinets, or sacks of food where a boy might have hidden, but there was nothing large enough. He said, "You still think he was upstairs?"

Sawyer shrugged and said, "What if the killer didn't have time? Maybe with the screaming and shouting, he left the house and didn't have time for Ben."

Buddy thought the killer would have taken as much time as necessary for the job. No, something else had happened.

Sawyer added, "Ben told us he heard what happened in the living room, but he didn't see anything. He's very bright and he listens to his parents. Those qualities saved his life."

Buddy turned three hundred sixty degrees within the pantry, but there was no second doorway and no window. He looked up and saw that Ward had joined them. Buddy raised an eyebrow.

Ward shook his head. "The broken window upstairs is in an attic, and there are storm windows inside those windows. The storms are screwed into the frames. No way the boy removed them to get outside. Also, no footprints on the roof. I checked the second floor as well. Two children's bedrooms, one for a boy, another for a girl. Plus one guest bedroom. Those windows also have storm windows inside. None removed."

Buddy nodded and said, "The killer knows Ben is in the house. He takes out Alton, Brenda, and Ellen-Marie in the living room. Then he comes down the hallway into this pantry. Ben must have been right here. How did he escape?"

Ward said nothing.

Sawyer said, "I don't know. But when the police arrived, they found him in the kitchen storage room in the lodge, dressed in his cotton bathrobe and slippers, shaking with cold, his lips blue."

Buddy thought about this for a minute, imagining the boy shaking and suffering the beginnings of hypothermia. He asked, "Isn't the lodge heated?"

"The lodge *is* heated," Sawyer said. "So Ben must have gone outside. That's the only way to explain how cold he was."

Buddy paced back and forth along the pantry shelves. He ran his hands on the shelves and the vertical pillars, and began pushing on them to test their sturdiness. In the northwest corner he stopped.

He moved a waffle iron and a bag of potatoes to the left. Then he held up his hands against the paneling behind the shelves. He constructed the house's floor plan in his mind. "Is the master bedroom behind this wall?"

"I think so." Sawyer nodded.

Buddy knew it wasn't. "This is it," he told them, turning around. "This is how Ben escaped. How he noticed the unusual scent."

Ward laughed. "You're bullshitting us."

Buddy stepped aside and pointed.

Ward approached the shelves and held his palms against the back panel. The oak was cooler than the room. Buddy watched him examine the shelving. This particular section didn't fit together as the others did. The oak panels weren't flush but slightly, ever so slightly, apart. With his elegant but strong hands, Ward took hold of the shelf's vertical pillars. He pushed and pulled, but the shelf remained immobile. Then he tightened his grip and used the weight of his shoulders to push against the shelf.

Click.

They heard the sound of a metal latch releasing. A three-foot-wide column of shelving swung outward into the pantry.

Buddy looked behind the door. He saw a fieldstone staircase that led down into blackness.

Chapter Six

Ward peered through the opening and then walked down the steps. He stood in the darkness. "A room of some sort," he called. "Maybe a cellar?"

Buddy said, "It's a tunnel." He followed his brother down fifteen steps until he reached a hard-packed dirt floor. He blinked in the cold blackness, waiting for his eyes to adjust. He heard a rustling from Ward's direction, then Ward switched on the flashlight feature of his cell phone.

They found themselves in a passage with a low concrete ceiling and cinder block walls. As Ward's flashlight swept back and forth across the space, they saw that it contained nothing but cobwebs. It was barren of furniture and visible rodents. Yet beyond the reach of the flashlight lay only more darkness.

Buddy looked back and saw Sawyer standing on the top stair, hesitant to join them. "Maybe you should stay at the door," he told the lawyer, "to make sure Ward and I aren't locked in here."

Sawyer's face showed relief. "If you insist, Detective. I'll wait right here."

Buddy turned and followed his brother. He imagined a terrified ten-year-old boy making his way blindly without a flashlight. He wondered if Ben had known where the passageway led, and thought the boy had more courage than most adults.

Ward moved quickly, following the white glare of the flashlight. The space before them was perfectly straight. It went on for about thirty yards and ended at the base of a second fieldstone staircase. They walked up fifteen steps leading to a narrow door with a brass knob.

For a moment Ward spun the flashlight beam around the door's perimeter. Seeing nothing unusual, he reached for the knob and turned it.

While the side of the door facing the stairs was only a door, a column of pantry shelving—just as in the house they'd left—camouflaged the face of the door in the bright room beyond. Buddy wondered to himself how many people knew of the underground connection.

Switching off the flashlight, Ward went through the hidden door, Buddy a pace behind. They emerged into a well-lit food-storage room, several times larger than the one in the house they'd just left. Buddy assumed the tunnel had led them to the lodge, where the staff would have served meals to all four branches of the family.

"Who are you?"

Buddy and Ward turned toward the storage room entrance. They saw a black-haired woman pointing a shotgun at them.

Chapter Seven

Three hundred miles away, in Manhattan, Ben Brook waited for Nan Sawyer to become absorbed in her television show.

He missed his parents so much he almost couldn't stand it. Most of the time he was able to keep himself from crying, but not always. Compared to his home on Seventy-Fourth just east of Central Park, the Sawyers' apartment was small. It had floral-print sofas everywhere, and the small bedroom Mrs. Sawyer had given him had silk curtains printed with pink roses. Everything was worn out and boring. Nothing was fun or cool.

He didn't care how old she was, and she smelled like wet sweaters and tea.

And yet Mrs. Sawyer had told him never, ever to leave the apartment.

But he didn't care what the Sawyers told him. They weren't his parents and he wasn't a prisoner.

So he waited, watching a movie on his iPad in the spare bedroom they'd given him. From there he could hear the television Mrs. Sawyer was watching. After a while he put down the iPad and peeked out into the living room. She was sitting in a wingback chair, a maroon quilt over her legs, her head tilted to the side, her eyes closed, her breathing regular. He backed away, stood silently in the hallway, and texted his friend Trevor. Like Ben, Trevor went to Browning, the boys' prep school on Sixty-Second between Madison and Park. Ben told Trevor he'd meet him a block south of Browning, at Sixty-First and Madison, if Trevor could sneak out of school. He thought Trevor would find a way, since Trevor seemed to do whatever he wanted. In the past year they'd played hooky three times: for a movie, for a visit to a video arcade, and to check out the skateboards at Modell's.

A moment later he put on his peacoat, scarf, and gloves. He unlocked the front door to the apartment and peeked outside.

A single lamp on an oak table lit a dim path to the elevator. The doorways to four apartments faced the hallway. He saw nothing dangerous.

He closed the door behind him and walked along the dark-gray carpeting. In the small elevator lobby he pressed the button on the wall. As he waited, he thought about what to do with Trevor. Maybe they could go to the movies. He had enough money. When Mr. Sawyer and the police had taken him to his home to pack some clothes and his school-books, laptop computer, and iPad, he'd gone into his parents' bedroom. In the top drawer of his father's dresser, he'd found a stack of money and taken all of it. He wasn't a thief. He knew the money was his.

A minute later he left the building's main-floor lobby, absently waved and said hello to the doorman, and walked out into the bright sun and the January cold. He stood on the sidewalk along the wide sweep of West End Avenue and looked both ways, but saw nothing strange. Then he gazed at the people on the north side of Sixty-Sixth Street.

Nobody seemed to be watching him.

He turned east toward Central Park. As he crossed West End, he sensed that he was being followed or at least observed.

He stood against the building on the southwest corner of the intersection at Amsterdam Avenue and looked to the west, the direction he'd come from. He studied the pedestrians. He saw a mother pushing a stroller, a gray-haired businessman who was dressed in a gray suit and carrying an attaché case, and teenagers holding hands. The teenagers wore blue jeans and Converse All Star sneakers, and they ignored him as they passed on their way to the park. He saw other people walking and a few joggers. Nothing seemed out of place among the throngs of people looking at their iPhones or moving to the beat of their earbuds.

Yet he was afraid.

Determined to escape this unseen and unknown person, he waited for the "Don't Walk" light at the intersection to blink six times, and then he pushed off from the building wall behind him, sprinted across Amsterdam Avenue, and ran as fast as he could toward Central Park.

Chapter Eight

"Ma'am, please lower the gun," Buddy said, slowly but firmly. "Or I'll have to arrest you."

The young woman didn't catch the irony in Buddy's order, but she did as he asked. She had long black hair, dark eyes, a sturdy frame. And a hostile expression.

Buddy moved to her left. "What's your name?" he asked.

"Onata."

"That's a nice name. Native American?"

She nodded. "Iroquois."

As she turned her head to follow Buddy's movement, she didn't see Ward approaching from her right. With a single motion he grabbed the shotgun away from her. Drawing back in surprise, she watched as he opened the breach, emptied the single shell into a waiting hand, and carefully set the gun on the green marble countertop. Yet she appeared docile and less frightened than when she'd had them cornered. She watched as Ward pulled his phone from an interior pocket of his parka and dialed.

"Mr. Sawyer?" Ward said. "The tunnel led to the lodge. We're at the back in a food-storage room."

Ward hung up. Buddy, Ward, and Onata stood quietly. Nobody spoke.

Buddy listened for other sounds in the lodge but heard nothing. The place was eerily calm. He looked at Onata. "Did you know about the tunnel?"

"Nah." She shook her head.

"How long have you worked here?"

"Three years."

He asked, "Were you here on New Year's Eve?"

"Yeah."

"Did you see or hear anything unusual?"

She hesitated.

Buddy said, "Please don't obstruct a murder investigation, Onata. That wouldn't be smart."

Her eyes flickered. "After the family had their champagne and omelets around midnight, I heard nothing until the sirens. The boy must have called for help."

Buddy leaned back against the counter and shoved his hands in his trouser pockets. He tried to be relaxed and put the young woman at ease. "What happened *before* midnight?"

She shifted her weight from one foot to the other. She said, "They were fighting."

"Fighting?"

"Well, not really fighting. Not with fists or anything. Arguing, more like."

Buddy nodded slowly. "About what?"

Onata said, "About money."

Chapter Nine

"I'll pay," Ben said.

Trevor hesitated. "Movies are boring."

They were standing at the corner of Sixty-First and Madison, high-end stores and office buildings around them. Trevor was an inch taller than Ben, with blond hair and blue eyes. Dressed in his school uniform of khakis, a white Brooks Brothers button-down, and a navy-blue blazer under a gray overcoat, he looked as if he were headed to work in a law firm. But he'd done plenty of illegal things already, and he was only ten.

Ben knew this, and knew that he needed to convince Trevor to play all afternoon with him. Because even now, even as they stood on the busy corner of Madison Avenue, he sensed that someone was watching him.

Ben said, "I'll pay for the tickets and popcorn. Sodas and candy, too."

Trevor's eyes narrowed. "Why do you care about the stupid movie?"

Ben said, "Come on. Nobody will find out."

After a moment Trevor shook his head, turned away from Ben, and looked around. "Let's go to Starbucks."

Ben tried not to let his disappointment show. Or his confusion. Trevor had always wanted to play with him, not just in the city but also during their summers in Sagaponack. Their parents had been close, and Trevor's little sister had been Ellen-Marie's best friend.

They walked a few blocks to Starbucks, both pretending the winter winds didn't bother them. Trevor ordered a hot chocolate, and Ben ordered a second and paid for both.

They found a table by the windows. Ben took off his gloves, unbuttoned his coat, and loosened his scarf. He watched to see if Trevor did the same, but his friend kept his gloves on and his overcoat buttoned.

Ben said, "Did you get the new Star Wars video game?"

Trevor nodded. "Yeah. Pretty cool." With a gloved hand Trevor pushed a lock of his blond hair out of his eyes.

"What level did you get to?"

"I dunno. Four, maybe."

"I'm at level six."

"I'd be there, too, if I didn't have school."

Ben didn't respond.

Trevor said, "When are you coming back to school?"

Ben saw his hands begin to shake. He put them in his lap. "Soon, I guess. But maybe a different school."

Trevor nodded. "Yeah. Don't come back to Browning."

"Why not?"

"You can't."

"Why does it matter?"

Trevor stared at him. Then he looked away and took a sip of his hot chocolate.

Ben said, "Why does it matter where I go?"

Still, Trevor wouldn't meet his eyes.

"Why?" Ben asked again.

At last Trevor looked at him and said, "Wherever you go, bad things will happen. My mom told me."

Ben felt his face warm. He wanted to argue with his friend but didn't know what to say.

Trevor got up from the table and peered down at him. He said, "My mom told me I should stay away from you. So I shouldn't even *be* here. Not with you."

Ben watched Trevor walk out the door and disappear up the street. As he sat there alone at the table and alone in the world, he faced out the window so no one could see him cry.

Chapter Ten

"Ben?"

Nan Sawyer had woken in the living room, surprised that she'd slept during her soap. Taking care of a young boy had tired her more than she expected. Putting aside the quilt, she stood carefully and walked toward the small bedroom.

"Ben?" she called again.

Perhaps, she thought, he was napping. Didn't young boys take naps? She didn't know. She and Ray had never been able to have children.

Yet Ben wasn't in the spare bedroom. He must have gone into the kitchen for a snack, she decided, and padded quickly toward the kitchen. She hoped he'd found the orange juice she'd bought for him, the cheese and crackers.

"Oh!" she said when she entered the kitchen. "Who are you? Why do you have that . . . ? *What are you doing? No!*"

Chapter Eleven

Ben returned to the Sawyers' apartment building after he was able to stop crying at the Starbucks. It had taken a long time. He'd drunk all his hot chocolate and many times wiped his eyes. Wiped his nose. Tried to keep other people from hearing him sob. One of the employees, a young woman wearing a green apron, had heard him, come over, and asked if he was okay.

"Yes," he'd said, "just a cough."

She'd eyed him carefully for a moment. "Would you like me to call your mom or dad?"

He'd felt as if he was going to be sick. Unable to speak, he'd turned his whole body toward the window. Then he'd begun to shake, and was afraid the woman would call the police. So he got up and averted his face as he pushed past her and out onto the sidewalk. The bracing air outside made him feel a little better, but not much.

Now, for the first time, he'd be glad to see Mrs. Sawyer.

"Good afternoon, Ben," said the doorman.

"Hi," Ben replied.

He walked into the lobby and pressed the button for the elevator. As he waited, he turned around and faced the full-length mirror opposite the elevator doors. He saw his red eyes. He wished his hair were long enough to hide his entire face. He wished it were brown instead of black. He wished that he were taller. Mostly he wished that everything were okay and that his mother and father and Ellen-Marie were alive.

Sometimes he'd pretend they were away on a long holiday. Ellen-Marie would dress up like a princess and order everyone around, her long hair flowing over her shoulders and a tiara on her head. His mother and father would be near her, laughing along and holding hands.

Yet he knew these were only wishes and dreams. He knew his family was dead. On New Year's Day the police hadn't allowed him back into his family house at Camp Kateri. But he'd guessed the details of what they found. He'd overheard one of the local police say, *Must have been an ax or a hatchet.*

When he thought of the last few moments of their lives, his mind seized up and he found himself staring at nothing, having not moved or thought about anything he could remember for long periods of time. Except he'd develop a stomachache and his hands would be damp with sweat.

As the elevator chimed and the doors opened, he turned from the mirror and walked inside. The doors closed and a few moments later opened onto the fourth-floor hallway. As he was stepping out of the elevator, he stopped.

There it was.

The scent.

The same one he'd noticed on New Year's Eve when he hid in the tunnel to the lodge. Suddenly, he couldn't breathe. His eyes focused on the Sawyers' door. It was no more than twenty feet from him.

He reached behind himself and put out his hand to prevent the door from closing. Never taking his eyes off the hallway, he backed into the elevator. Then he looked at the buttons and pressed the one marked "L."

Only when the door closed and the elevator began descending did he bring air into his lungs.

A moment later he burst into the lobby. Running to the doorman standing on the sidewalk outside, he shouted, "Help! Mrs. Sawyer isn't okay! Something is wrong!"

The doorman looked down at him with a kindly, imperturbable expression. "What do you mean, young man? What's she doing?"

"I didn't go into the apartment, but I just know something is wrong."

"And why do you think so?"

"What? No. No!" Ben walked around so that he was staring straight at the doorman. He sensed that his face was flushed and that he was crying, but he couldn't be calm. "Please call the police. *Please!*"

The doorman's face showed his annoyance. "No, I won't call the police. I'll just ring the Sawyers' apartment. If there's no answer, I'll go upstairs to check on things."

"Please, hurry."

Lumbering through the glass doors and into the lobby, the doorman leaned over his small desk and picked up the black telephone. He dialed the Sawyers' extension and waited. After a minute, he set down the receiver and turned to Ben, who was watching him expectantly. "There's no answer."

Ben said, "She's hurt. She's . . . she's . . ."

The doorman sighed and stared at the ceiling. "All right, Ben. I'll go check on Mrs. Sawyer. You stay here."

Ben waited by the desk. He feared that the man or woman who wore that distinctive scent would come into the lobby and kill him. He picked up the telephone receiver and dialed two digits: 9-1. Holding a trembling index finger above the 1, he waited to see who came around the corner.

He heard the elevator chime. Then footsteps moving rapidly. His stomach tightened and he gripped the telephone.

The doorman hurried into the lobby and over to his desk, his face pale. His eyes were wide and he appeared shaken. "Give me that," he said to Ben, and took the telephone from him. He saw that Ben had dialed 9-1. He pressed the final 1.

A moment later he nearly shouted, "I need to report a murder!"

Chapter Twelve

Buddy said, "An argument between whom?"

Onata knit her muscular fingers together. "Alton and Bruno and Carl."

"Alton Brook who was killed?"

"Yeah."

"What about Dietrich Brook?"

"I'm not sure about him. I think he was drinking champagne, listening to his older brothers."

Buddy said, "What were they arguing about?"

"I heard only a few words. The adults—the four sets of parents—were having drinks. I was bringing in another bottle of champagne when I heard them."

She paused.

Buddy added, "I understand you weren't eavesdropping. What were they arguing about?"

"The company they own."

Before Buddy could ask another question, they heard rushed footsteps and turned to the main door to the storage room.

"You made it," Ray Sawyer said, slightly out of breath. "That must have been how Ben escaped."

Ward nodded. "One mystery solved, at least."

Sawyer unbuttoned his overcoat and unraveled his scarf, revealing a Harris Tweed sport coat over an ivory-colored shirt with no tie. It was then he took note of Onata. "Hello there. I'm Ray Sawyer, Alton Brook's lawyer. I've asked Detective Lock and Mr. Mills to help with the case."

Onata was quiet.

Buddy took a step closer, trying to engage her. "Onata, would you tell us everything you heard Alton, Bruno, and Carl arguing about?"

She shrugged. "I didn't hear much. I just went into the room with some champagne and left quickly, taking a couple of empty bottles with me."

"But what *did* you hear?" Buddy pressed.

She looked at each of them in turn as she said, "Carl wanted Brook Instruments to be sold. Alton and Bruno wanted the family to keep it. They kept talking about the price they could get, but that was all, except . . ." Her voice trailed off.

Buddy waited a moment. When she didn't speak, he prompted, "Except what?"

After a long moment Onata said, "As I was closing the door, Natalie told Rebecca, 'You already borrowed my husband. Why do you have to take the company, too?'"

Buddy held up a hand. "Remind me—who is Natalie?"

Sawyer said, "She's Bruno's wife."

Before Buddy could ask another question, Ward said, "Thank you, Onata. But I'd like to be sure I understand. Ben's aunt, Natalie, was upset about the potential sale of Brook Instruments. And she was angry with Rebecca, her sister-in-law, for having an affair with her husband?"

Onata turned to him. "That's how it sounded."

Buddy was going to ask more about the goings-on in the Brook family, but Ray Sawyer's mobile phone rang.

"Hello?" the older gentleman answered. "What?" Sawyer pressed the phone more tightly against his ear. "Yes, this is Ray Sawyer. I'm not hearing you very well." He put his free hand over his other ear and stared downward in concentration. "What?" Sawyer repeated, and then listened intently.

Buddy and Ward glanced at each other. Buddy feared he'd been proven right and Ben was dead. He watched Sawyer carefully.

Sawyer's hands began to shake. "The boy is all right?" he said into the phone. "But my wife . . ." Sawyer was quiet. His free hand moved uncertainly over to his eyes, covering them, pressing on them.

Buddy knew what was happening. He'd delivered that message before. Ward's face showed empathy. Onata's hard exterior softened. She took a step toward Sawyer.

At last Sawyer removed his hand from his eyes, which had filled with tears. He saw Buddy and Ward, and yet didn't see them. Red splotches formed across his face. Slowly he sat down on the floor. "No," he said, dropping the phone. "My poor Nan. My poor, poor Nan. My sweetheart. My darling."

Buddy went to the older man, knelt down, and put his arms around him. Didn't say anything. No words would have helped the old man's pain. Sawyer seemed to shrink, to reduce in size as he was overcome with the terrible news. He cried and wept and said no over and over and over again. There was no way to comfort him.

Buddy felt awful for Sawyer but also spurred on. As he held the older man, who shuddered in his arms, a new resolve formed within him. He needed to act, quickly and decisively.

When Sawyer grew quiet, Buddy picked the phone off the floor and spoke into it, identifying himself and getting the name and precinct of the officer on the other end of the line. Then Buddy moved away from him, stood, and handed Sawyer's phone to Ward. Onata reached down, took Sawyer's arm, and helped him up. She murmured something in his ear. She led him out of the food-storage room and into the lounge beyond.

Ward went with them, but turned at the doorway. "Sawyer can return with us. I'll have someone drive his car down to the city."

Buddy said, "Give me twenty minutes."

Ward nodded.

Buddy waited a moment, then began his search of the lodge. Without a search warrant, he couldn't enter the three nearby houses owned by Bruno, Carl, and Dietrich Brook.

In the lodge and in Alton Brook's house, he found nothing.

This told him he was dealing with someone very lucky or very good. Or maybe with a professional.

Chapter Thirteen

The crime scene at Ray Sawyer's apartment.

Buddy sensed an electric current in the air, as if a powerful thunderstorm were coming right at him.

His muscles tightened. He held out his hand, half expecting a shock from static electricity, but found only air.

The murder, the scene—they were fresh.

That morning he'd seen gore but no body. The killer had been long gone. But that wasn't true here.

The killer was nearby.

The killer had known Ben was staying at the apartment.

The Manhattan location gave Buddy jurisdiction. Mike Malone, chief of detectives, installed him as lead detective on the case, even if Nan Sawyer's murder occurred on the West Side in a different precinct. He'd joined the roving Special Crimes Unit that, with Malone's approval, could work anywhere in the five boroughs and reported only to Malone. It dealt with high-profile homicide cases, especially serial murder. This status brought with it the pressure of responsibility but also a grim satisfaction. Now *he* would make the decisions. He was going to grab this case and not let go. He believed he had only one extraordinary quality: relentlessness. He wasn't the smartest or the nicest, the most handsome or the richest. Except for the piano, he had no hobbies. But to solve a case, he'd work all day and all night. He'd never give up, never yield.

He stood in the building's lobby. It was cramped and had a dim, tired décor. Nothing like the Carlyle Residences, adjacent to the famous Carlyle Hotel, where he lived with Mei. Mei's wealthy parents had given her the family apartment when they moved to Palm Springs and bought a small pied-à-terre a few blocks away. He'd lived in places much worse than this one, and he felt comfortable here.

He saw the doorman's desk with the scratched brass surround. He saw the scuffed terrazzo floor. Behind the desk, staring at his hands and refusing to look up at the commotion made by the police, the residents, and the detectives from CSU—the Crime Scene Unit— sat the middle-aged doorman. His face was pale and his shoulders slumped. Buddy assumed it was the first time he'd seen the victim of a murder.

By the lobby windows was a low bench upholstered in brown fabric. On the bench sat a young boy. He was handsome, in need of a haircut, and slender. His navy-blue peacoat was unbuttoned and his striped scarf spilled out messily over his chest. His hands were in the coat's side pockets. His large, expressive brown eyes watched the activity in the lobby. His black hair, falling over the right side of his face, looked a lot like Buddy's, though Buddy's was cut short.

Buddy walked over to him and said, "You're Ben Brook?"

The boy looked up. "Yes, sir."

"I'm Detective Lock," Buddy said, not offering his hand. And though he didn't want to be overly familiar, he squatted down and added, "You can call me Buddy."

The boy's nervous dark eyes fastened on his.

Buddy said, "I'm in charge of this case. So when you talk about what happened today and what happened on New Year's Eve, who will you talk to?"

Ben watched him.

Realizing the boy was stunned or in shock, Buddy said, "I'm your guy. Do you understand?"

Ben nodded as his eyes filled with tears.

Buddy said, "We need to get you out of here. Did anyone talk to you about where you might go?"

"No," Ben said, his voice wobbly with uncertainty. "I don't know what to do."

Buddy thought quickly. "Would you like to stay with any of your aunts and uncles?"

"Please, no!" Ben pleaded, his voice rising. His eyes showed real fear as he reached out and put a hand on Buddy's forearm. He lowered his voice to a whisper. "They're going to be killed."

Buddy leaned in. "Who's going to be killed?"

"Everyone. Everyone in my family will be killed."

Buddy asked, "Why do you think so?"

"Nobody's safe. If I have to be with my aunts and uncles, I'll die."

Buddy said, "How can you know that?"

"I know it, sir. I just know it!" Ben said, seemingly relieved that Buddy was taking him seriously.

"All right," Buddy replied, silently conceding that the boy might have a point. And not only his aunts and uncles. It was clear Ben had seen something, or knew something, or *was* something the killer wanted extinguished. Buddy said, "If you don't stay with your aunts or uncles, where would you go?"

Ben's eyes left his and moved to the phalanx of policemen standing outside the lobby on West End Avenue and then back to the interior and the CSU team going in and out of the elevator. Strands of his hair hung down over his forehead.

"Where?" Buddy asked again. As he crouched down to be at eye level with the boy, his shoulder holster became visible.

Ben brought his attention back to Buddy. He stared at Buddy's shoulder holster, which held a Glock 19. Then he raised his eyes to Buddy's. "If you don't let me stay with you, I'm going to die."

Buddy wanted to argue with the boy but said nothing. He thought the boy was right.

Chapter Fourteen

"Is it possible for me to meet him before we decide?"

This was Mei, over the phone from her office at Porter Gallery on East Fifty-Eighth Street.

"There isn't time," Buddy explained. He was standing in the darkening street outside Ray Sawyer's apartment building, never taking his eyes off Ben Brook, who hadn't moved from his seat by the lobby window. Next to Ben stood Buddy's partner, Detective Jonas Vidas, who was young and ambitious, tall and pale, with brown hair and angular features. Buddy thought he was still green but in time would be a great detective. Through the glass Buddy could see Vidas talking with the boy, trying to comfort him.

Ben looked vulnerable, tired, and afraid, on the verge of giving up whatever had enabled him to survive his family's massacre. He'd swiveled around on the bench, away from Vidas, and was watching Buddy carefully, though he couldn't hear Buddy's conversation.

"Mei, I'd like him to stay with us," Buddy continued, softening his voice so it didn't sound commanding. "I realize Ben can't stay longer. We'll call it protective custody—I got the okay from Ray Sawyer, his guardian. But I'm asking you for three days."

"Three days," she echoed. "But what if we like him . . ."

Her change in position surprised Buddy, who said, "You want him to stay longer?"

There was a long silence on the line.

Buddy thought the connection had been lost. "Hello?" he said. "Mei?"

"I'm here." Her voice, slower now. "Maybe having a boy . . ." Her voice trailed off. Then she said, "I . . . I think we should try for a child of our own."

Buddy felt a lump form in his throat. He didn't know how to respond. He'd never thought seriously of being a father. They hadn't discussed having children, except in passing. At last he said, "I don't know."

"We should talk about it, another time."

"Yeah," he said, feeling the shock of her suggestion ease. "Another time."

A moment later she said, "If Ben comes to live with us, would we be in danger?"

Buddy recalled the scene at Camp Kateri and Nan Sawyer's body—what was left of it—in the building in front of him. He said, "We'd have to be careful, but we'd be all right."

"You don't think anyone would try to get into our home?"

Buddy thought of Schmidt, the doorman for the Carlyle Residences. He thought of the card-key access to the elevator and the elevator lock on their floor. He said, "We'll be safe."

Mei hesitated a moment. And then she said, "Three days."

Buddy put his phone in the breast pocket of his suit coat. He looked at the boy on the other side of the lobby glass and waved him out onto the sidewalk.

Chapter Fifteen

Jessica, Mei's coworker who sat at the desk next to hers, stiffened. Mei sensed it. Something had happened. She looked over at Jess, who was tall, blonde, thin. Too thin, Mei thought. But a nice girl from Montana and, like her, unmarried, though currently dating a finance guy with a condo in the Village and a country house.

Jessica said quietly, urgently, "He's *here*. And he has eyes for you."

Mei looked up from her desk and saw that her last appointment of the day had arrived. She stood and straightened her black dress with sleeves to the middle of her forearms and orange half-moons running down one side.

She said, "He's just a client."

Jessica whispered, "He wants to be more. And when I get back from vacation, I expect details of your romance."

Mei laughed at this idea, which she immediately discarded, saying, "You know I'm with Buddy."

Jessica raised an eyebrow. "A girl should have options."

Peter Armitage stood in the center of the large space, a handsome figure above the smoothly polished concrete floors. Peter had begun visiting the gallery when they'd hung several of Gentileschi's paintings. He studied the Baroque master's colorful canvases based on biblical scenes and Greek and Roman mythology, but glanced over at Mei and smiled at her as she rose from behind her desk.

As she approached Peter, she couldn't help but admire the way he was put together. Just under six feet—shorter than Buddy—he was trim, and his carefully tailored suit made him appear trimmer yet. She noticed the Savile Row cut of his clothes, the rich-looking walnut-colored English shoes. He had an affable face with a square jaw, two days of stubble, blue eyes, and a tan even in the winter. She smiled and offered her hand. "Good afternoon, Peter. Thanks for your continuing interest in Gentileschi's work."

Peter Armitage returned her smile. His hand took hers and held it for longer than she expected. "Hello, Mei. Wonderful to see you. Glad you're free to have a working happy hour."

"Of course, Peter. Let me just get the—" She began to turn back to her desk to pick up the exhibition's catalogue and price list.

Peter interrupted, "No need for all of that."

"But—"

He laughed. "I've been here several times. I know the work and you've already given me the price list. Come on!"

"All right," she said.

A few minutes later she and Peter were seated at one of the better tables at Le Cirque on East Fifty-Eighth Street. The top of a golden circus tent ostentatiously hung over the room. Peter smiled while ordering a bottle of Taittinger.

She began to feel miserable. For Peter was not only a potential client but single and the managing director of a private equity fund. She realized now this business happy hour was anything but. He didn't want to buy a painting. No, today he wanted something else.

She sat up straighter. She began to wish she'd put on makeup this morning. She was reed-thin but perhaps she hadn't worked out enough the past month. Was her stomach bulging, just a little? Did her face look too wide? She sensed her own discomfort. Recognized it for what it was: the idea she wasn't good enough for Peter Armitage. She wished away this nonsense, and yet it wouldn't go away.

"How great to see you outside of work," Peter began.

"Yes." She nodded politely. "You as well. Is there a particular piece in the new show that interests you?"

Smiling, he reached over and touched the back of her hand. "Work again," he said, not unpleasantly. "Why don't we discuss other things? I'd like to learn more about you. I hear you're single and"—he almost winked—"so am I."

Her spirits dropped to the floor. Jessica had been right and she hadn't seen it coming. Hadn't wanted to believe it. She shook her head. "I'm seeing someone, Peter."

His expression showed disappointment. "Is it serious?"

She recalled her conversation with Buddy about children and how he hadn't responded with the enthusiasm she'd expected. "Possibly, I'm not sure yet."

She heard herself say these words, and yet to her it was as serious as any relationship could be. Sitting across from Peter Armitage as the waiter set out two champagne flutes and popped the cork from the bottle, she knew she loved Buddy. With him she didn't need to prove anything. His respect and encouragement helped her to grow stronger rather than weaker. He was confident in his decency, and never arrogant. He'd never see her as a contestant in a beauty pageant or matchmaking game. He'd never abandon her.

And now he was bringing a young boy home with him. Whatever would happen with that boy? Whatever would happen with Buddy? She knew she wanted to marry him, but they'd been dating six months and living together for only two. It was still very soon to make that decision. Despite Peter's money and good qualities, her heart pulled firmly in Buddy's direction.

Peter raised his glass. "To new beginnings."

She did the same. "To new beginnings."

They drank. She savored the champagne. And then she said, "I misspoke, Peter. My relationship is quite serious."

He frowned. "So there's no room for negotiation?"

She shook her head. "I'm sorry."

Peter Armitage leaned forward. "But may I check in with you in three months? In case something has changed?"

She hesitated but in the end agreed. "Three months," she said. "But not before."

Chapter Sixteen

Buddy held the elevator door open for Ben, and they walked into Mei's elegant apartment.

As Buddy watched him standing in the foyer, he knew something had changed. And it wasn't his having to care for a child. He was completely unprepared for that endeavor but had confidence that he and Mei could make it work, for a few days. No, the biggest change was having to protect a boy whose life was in mortal danger. Only now did the responsibility hit him. Only now did he see the apartment differently. It wasn't, he decided, all that safe.

He sensed Mei's presence. The trace of her perfume. The faint sounds coming from the kitchen.

He turned to the now-closed elevator doors. After turning the wall switch to "Locked," so that the elevator wouldn't open into the apartment, he decided that electronic protection wasn't enough.

"Ben?" he asked. "Would you help me?"

Ben turned around. His face was less drawn. His eyes were calmer. "What should I do?"

Buddy rested a hand on an antique Chinese medicine cabinet against the wall to his left. "Help me move this chest in front of the elevator doors."

Ben slipped his backpack off his shoulders and set it on the herring-bone oak floor. Then he went to the other end of the medicine cabinet and waited. The cabinet was about his height and four feet wide. He asked, "Won't this be super heavy?"

"Yes, and that's why we're going to put it in front of the door."

Understanding immediately, Ben put his hands on either side of the cabinet and tried to lift. The cabinet didn't move.

"We can't lift it using our arms alone," Buddy told him. "We'll have to put our shoulders into it." The truth was that Buddy could probably move the cabinet by himself, but he wanted Ben to feel active rather than passive. "Watch how I do it," he said. He bent at the knees, gripped the sides of the cabinet, put his right shoulder against the black lacquered wood, and looked over at Ben. "Try it this way, okay? On the count of three, we'll lift it."

Ben crouched and then leaned against the cabinet. Buddy saw his small hands grip the cabinet edges, though the boy's face was obscured.

"One, two, three," Buddy said. He lifted and began to move backward, trying to carry at least eighty percent of the cabinet. Yet he was surprised by how much of its weight the boy had taken.

They moved the cabinet about five feet, setting it down where it would block anyone from entering via the elevator. It wouldn't block anyone, exactly, Buddy admitted to himself, but it would give him time to react. He'd booby-trap the cabinet so that if anyone tried to move it, some glass or metal item would crash to the floor. By that time he'd be awake and alert, Glock at the ready.

The cabinet in place, Buddy faced the boy. He'd prefer to stop this conversation before it started, but he had every reason to believe the killer of Ben's family would make a third try for the boy. He needed to push the conversation forward one more step, to prepare Ben for what he feared would happen. He said, "When your family was attacked at Camp Kateri, you hid and ran away, didn't you?"

Ben's expression changed to one of doubt. He seemed unsure if hiding and running away were good in Buddy's eyes. "Yes," he admitted.

Buddy said, "That was the right thing to do, okay?"

"Okay."

"If anything happens ever again, hide. If you can't hide, run. Because if you have to fight a large man, you'll have a tough time, won't you?"

Ben nodded.

Buddy knelt down, met Ben's eyes. He said, "But what happens if someone gets to you, captures you? What will you do then?"

Ben shrugged. "I don't know."

"You'd be in a tight spot," Buddy said. "So here are a couple of ideas. First, you kick or punch the guy in the balls. Okay?"

Ben's face reddened. "Okay."

"Second idea," Buddy continued. "What if you can't kick him? Maybe he's too far away, maybe he's too close, maybe you can't get your feet up because you're in a car or something."

Ben watched him carefully.

Buddy said, "You know what the hardest part of the human body is?"

Ben shook his head.

"It's the bone just above your forehead, right by your hairline." Buddy held out a hand and lightly touched the boy's hairline over his forehead. "So you wait until the guy is close to you, real close, and then you push yourself—you drive your head—right into the other guy's nose or mouth." Buddy put his hands on Ben's shoulders and pretended to head butt him. He said, "You push forward at the other guy with everything you've got, and you clobber him with your own head. Got it?"

Ben nodded. "Yep."

Buddy wasn't sure Ben did, but he stood as he heard someone behind him.

"Why are you moving the furniture?"

They turned to see Mei standing in the hallway. Her black hair shimmered under the recessed lights. She wore a pair of dark-blue jeans, knee-high leather boots, and a cream-colored silk blouse.

Buddy thought she looked rich and gorgeous and wondered, as he did each day, what she was doing with an oaf like him. Despite having made love to her more than a hundred times and having entwined their lives, he was hesitant to propose marriage. He simply didn't deserve her. And if she agreed to marry him, he'd ruin things somehow and wind up alone. Things worked well as they were, he'd decided. It would be too risky to push for more. He smiled and said, "We moved the chest in front of the elevator doors for safety. We'll move it back in the morning. Hope that's all right."

"Yes." She nodded.

"Mei, this is the boy I've told you about. His name's Ben Brook."

Despite the imposition of having to care for a young boy she'd never met, she smiled warmly at Ben and strode into the foyer. Though Mei wasn't tall, she bent over and offered her hand to the boy. "I'm Mei Adams," she said. "I'm glad you'll be staying with us for a few days."

Shyly, Ben took her hand. "Hello," he said.

Mei straightened up. "May I take your coat?"

He nodded, slipped it off, and handed it to her. She took the coat and then held out a hand for his scarf, which he gave her.

She hung the coat and scarf in the foyer closet and then turned to him. "I'm sautéing some chicken breasts. Is that something you'd like?"

"Yes."

"Are you hungry?"

He nodded.

"Good. Would you take your backpack to the guest bedroom? Just go down this hallway, and it's the second room on the left. Then if you'd wash your hands in the guest bathroom, we can have dinner right away."

After only a moment's hesitation, he nodded, picked up his backpack, and walked into the hallway. His footsteps sounded faintly on the oak floors.

Buddy asked, "You all right with this?"

She smiled at him and whispered, "Yes, it's all right for a few days. Maybe even longer. Come here."

He leaned down, kissed her, and hugged her tightly. God, she felt good. He never tired of coming home to her. "Thank you," he whispered.

"Darling," she said quietly. "The coat Ben gave me is from Prada. Is he one of *the* Brooks? The people murdered in the Adirondacks?"

"Yeah, he is." Buddy glanced back at the elevator door and said, "We'll be all right, but I've booby-trapped the cabinet with a water glass for advance warning."

"The lock works, you know. Who could get past it?"

Buddy stared at her. Where and how to begin the story of the Camp Kateri massacre? Or the murder of Nan Sawyer? But then he heard Ben's approaching footsteps. He said, "We can talk it through after dinner."

She looked at him uncertainly. "All right, Buddy. But I'm trusting you on this."

"I know. And I won't let you down."

Chapter Seventeen

"Are you Chinese?" Ben asked as he finished dinner.

Mei took a sip from the tumbler of Jack Daniel's over ice that stood next to her water glass. She raised an eyebrow. "I'm American," she told him. "My parents are also American, but they adopted me when I was six months old. Before that I lived in an orphanage in Beijing."

Ben lowered his eyes. "I'm sorry," he said.

"It's all right."

"Would you tell me how to spell your name?"

"M-E-I. But it's pronounced 'May,' like the fifth month of the year."

He nodded yet appeared regretful. "I shouldn't have said anything."

She smiled. "Don't worry about it, Ben. It's good that you're inquisitive."

"My mother always thought . . ." His voice faltered. "My mother . . ."

But he couldn't speak. He stared at Buddy and Mei in turn through wet eyes.

Mei pushed back her chair, walked around the table, and stood behind him. She put a hand on his shoulder.

Leaning away from her, he said, "You're not my mother."

She knelt and looked up at him. "I can't be your mother. But I'm glad you're here. I'm so glad you're here."

Ben turned to her. He began to cry.

"It's all right," she told him, again putting her hand on his shoulder.

He shook his head, but he didn't pull away.

She said, "Why don't we turn in for the night? If you'd like, I can read to you, stay with you for a while."

At first he didn't respond. Then, slowly, he got up.

She led him into the hallway to the bedrooms. Buddy thought Mei had handled the difficult moment far better than he could.

His reverie ended when his mobile phone rang. He pulled it from the breast pocket of his suit coat. "Lock here."

"Chief Malone."

"Hi, Chief."

"Everything okay with the boy?"

"Yeah. No problems."

Malone said, "I need you to come out tonight."

Buddy felt himself tense. He said, "That's not a good idea. Ben would be unprotected. And my girlfriend."

Earlier he'd told the chief that he'd take care of Ben for three nights. The chief knew this was a violation of many rules, but as a favor to Buddy he'd agreed to call the boy's stay with Buddy and Mei "police custody."

"I'm sending two street cops to guard them," Malone said. "But you're coming up to East Seventy-Ninth Street. It's just a few blocks from where you are."

Buddy paused. He was tired and didn't want to leave Mei and Ben alone, no matter how many cops were posted around the building at street level. "Orders are orders, Chief. But are you sure about this?"

Chief Malone grunted. "We have a bigger problem than the boy. How many branches of the Brook family are left?"

Buddy thought of Bruno, Carl, and Dietrich, the remaining of Walter Brook's four sons. He said, "Three branches."

"Wrong. After tonight, there are two, plus the boy."

Chapter Eighteen

"Was it a hatchet?" Buddy asked.

He and Chief Malone climbed the stairs from the first to the second floor of Bruno Brook's palatial town house. On the walls lining the ten-foot-wide staircase hung large paintings and tapestries with scenes of battles featuring castles, rivers, cavalry. A Persian runner covered most of the staircase's treads, and the polished mahogany banister was at least eight inches wide.

Despite Malone's having waited for Buddy outside, where the temp was fourteen degrees Fahrenheit, sweat covered his domed forehead. The big chief seemed to boil over with anxiety and frustration. His face was redder than usual, his tie looser. Buddy wondered how often Malone entered a town house like this one, which Buddy guessed was worth $50 or $60 million.

Malone panted and grunted as he said, "Not as bloody as a hatchet, but effective as hell. Their housekeeper discovered them and went into shock."

Buddy's nerves jangled at this information. He said, "No sign of forced entry at any of the doors?"

Malone shook his head. "None. And no picked locks. First thing we checked. Security system was off, too. Nobody tripped the alarm."

Buddy said, "The killer was invited in?"

"Probably. Either known to the family or a delivery person or some such."

Known to the family, Buddy thought. *Or maybe a family member.*

Similar to the situation at Camp Kateri.

On the second floor they walked into a hive of activity. CSU was on-site. They wore navy-blue windbreakers and blue booties over their feet. He saw they'd set up bright lights on stands, and knew their first task would be creating a photographic record—before anything was examined, touched, or moved. They'd begin with photographs taken from each corner of the room toward the center.

He and Malone slipped booties over their shoes and latex gloves over their hands.

"This way," Malone said, and led Buddy down a wide hallway on the building's north–south axis. Malone gave him the names and ages of the children.

As they entered the master bedroom, they could see the bright lights brought in by CSU. The team noticed Malone, and they backed off so he and Buddy could pass through to the bathroom. The chief stopped at the open doorway. Buddy looked over his shoulder.

He saw one CSU detective taking video of the scene. Another detective was drawing the scene on a sketch pad, using a tape measure to record on the drawing the distance from each body and piece of evidence to a wall, bathtub, or other reference point. A third detective would take photos: panoramic, middle-range, close-up.

Malone growled, "Everyone out of here."

Two members of CSU filed out of the master bath. When the room was clear, Malone extended an index finger and pointed once at Buddy and once toward the doorway.

All day he'd felt worse and worse. First the dried gore at Camp Kateri. Then Nan Sawyer.

Now an entire family.

His heart raced. His hands grew damp in the latex gloves. He felt light-headed, but he couldn't sit down or show weakness. Not with the chief so close to him.

He coughed twice, into his arm, buying time to settle down.

Then, slowly, reluctantly, he walked through the French doors and stood on the gray-and-white marble tile.

Four bodies lay at the other end of the enormous bathroom that included a daybed and a wall-mounted television that was switched off.

Lucy—sixteen years old, dark hair, attractive—seemed to be reaching for the daybed covered in gray suede. She lay on the floor, her wide-open eyes rimmed with blood and staring up at him. Her lips were caked with vomit and white mucus that also was spewed onto the marble near her head. She had no visible bruises.

Bruno, Natalie, and their son William, age seventeen, with a goatee, were dressed casually, except for Natalie, who wore a pink bathrobe. They lay in the far corner, near the vanity.

Buddy sniffed the air. He couldn't smell anything and guessed the family had been injected or made to drink poisoned food or water. He went over to the bathtub and looked down.

Empty. But perhaps Natalie had been getting ready for a bath. He looked over at her and saw that the robe barely covered her torso. She'd been beautiful, and her body showed no visible marks of struggle. Except for the same blood-red eyes and the vomit and mucus on and around the mouth.

Buddy walked around the gray daybed to the girl. He squatted next to her and looked carefully at her skin. No visible puncture wounds or marks from a needle. A slender river of redness, like syrup, running from her ears.

He took a deep breath, stood, and turned to Malone, who'd remained in the doorway. "Cause of death?"

"Poison. Or gas."

Buddy pointed to the corner. "There's a radiator. Where would the gas come from? Not from the stove all the way down in the kitchen."

"CSU set up their mobile lab in the living room downstairs. They found traces of a powder in the bathtub."

Buddy said, "Stuff for a bubble bath?"

"Maybe."

Buddy returned to the bathroom doorway, Malone behind him, and faced the CSU team in the bedroom. He addressed all of them. "Time of death?"

"Five to six p.m.," a young man said. He wore thick green eyeglasses and a black turtleneck sweater under his windbreaker.

Buddy said, "Two hours ago?"

"More or less."

"Track marks? Anything to indicate use of a syringe?"

"No."

"Administered orally?"

"Possibly. We'll wait for the results of the toxicology screen."

He turned from the CSU detective and returned to the master bath, Malone a step behind him. Standing there quietly, he thought the bodies were perfect statues, pale under the bright lights of the laboratory the room had become. Strangely peaceful now, but their deaths had been wrenching torture.

A commotion in the adjoining bedroom pulled at his attention. Soon one of the CSU team, a guy about fifty, entered the bathroom. He had graying black hair and clear plastic goggles over brown eyes. His mouth was covered by a surgical mask.

"Detective, please come out of the bathroom," the man said, his voice high-pitched with excitement. "You, too, Chief."

"Why?" Buddy asked.

"There could be gas in the air. It might not kill you at this point, but it might damage your lungs or heart. Please. Come with me."

The CSU guy rushed Buddy and Chief Malone into the master bedroom.

"Farther away," the man with the surgical mask told them, pointing out to the hallway. "Let's go downstairs, away from the bathtub."

The group hurried along the hallway and down the enormous staircase, Chief Malone and the man from CSU bringing up the rear. As if they'd made a plan, they gathered with several other members of the CSU team in the grand foyer. There, the functional casement windows had been cranked open.

Buddy felt desperate to get outside, into the frigid air, away from the scene of death—the third one today. His stomach frothed.

He looked at his watch: 8:30 p.m. Focusing on the guy from CSU, he said, "What's your name?"

The man removed his mask. "I'm Detective Gonzalez."

"Tell us what you've found."

The man stared. "We need to be sure the murder weapon remains confidential. If it gets online or into the *Gazette* or the *Times*, we'll have a real problem."

Malone pointed at the man. "Tell us now. Is it bubonic plague or something?"

"Nothing like that," Gonzalez snapped, his hair shiny under the recessed lights. "Now, are we agreed the cause of death doesn't go beyond the people in this room?"

Buddy nodded, as did the others.

"Okay," Gonzalez said, relaxing a little. "What we found in the bathtub are remnants of hydrogen cyanide. When pellets of the product the killer used are exposed to air, they vaporize into gas and the cyanide component is released. At the right concentration, it kills everyone who breathes it, and it takes a couple of minutes to fifteen or twenty." After this explanation, Gonzalez looked at each of them, as if they were certain to grasp his meaning.

Chief Malone said, "So the murder weapon is cyanide gas. The killer must have some background in chemistry or taken some science classes. So what? Why should it be confidential?"

Gonzalez stiffened once again and glared. He didn't blink. His mouth crimped on one side, as if they'd disappointed him. "It wasn't just cyanide gas," he explained. "It was mixed with a stabilizer to prevent further reactions, as well as . . ."

"Come on!" Chief Malone interrupted. "Speak English, okay? What do we need to know?"

Gonzalez was silent for a moment, his face purple from the way Malone had shut him up. "You need to know, Chief Malone," the man said, his voice dropping almost to a whisper, "the killer used a gas called Zyklon B."

Two members of the CSU team gasped. Malone's faced showed only puzzlement.

Buddy thought he'd heard the term before but wasn't sure where. At this point he didn't mind admitting he was lost. He asked, "What's Zyklon B?"

Gonzalez turned to him. "It's what the Nazis used in the gas chambers at Auschwitz."

Chapter Nineteen

Buddy turned from the small group and walked off by himself. He ignored the activity around him. He needed to think, needed to make order out of confusion.

First a hatchet.

Now Zyklon B.

Strange ways to kill, unless . . .

He put his hands together and absently studied the lines of his skin, the single small mole on the back of his left hand.

He thought the killer was confident, even arrogant. But more importantly, the killer was making a point.

But what was it?

Buddy wondered where the Brook family had come from. He thought maybe, long ago, the Brooks had participated in the Holocaust—the ultimate crime—and now someone was taking revenge.

He separated his hands and turned them over. His palms were large and ugly, he thought. Muscular, unrefined, blocklike. As he looked, he thought of two possible killers, one who used a hatchet and was motivated by money or love gone bad. And a second killer who wanted revenge for a nearly century-old crime.

He stuck his hands in his trouser pockets, forced his mind back to the facts. To the scene here at Bruno's town house. The deaths upstairs were the obvious things, he decided. But there was something else—something like a hidden musical note. It was so faint he was sure nobody else heard it. He tried to block out the commotion and focus on that muted sound.

Standing in the foyer, he imagined the events of earlier that evening.

Someone had gotten into the house, or been invited in, then forced the family upstairs and into the bathroom. *How do you make a family go upstairs?* he asked himself.

Threats backed up by violence.

And muscle wouldn't be enough.

The force had been applied right here, in order to gather and move the family.

Quietly he circled around the group that included Malone. He walked aimlessly, almost in a trance, not thinking but only observing. He stopped and stared at the hallway leading to the back of the town house's main floor.

Hanging on the walls on either side of the hallway entrance were two old paintings. They were a kind of pair: two portraits of European royalty, at least that was what Buddy assumed. Both about three by four feet. Dark backgrounds with fair-skinned nobles in the foreground. One a young brunette in a light-blue dress and with pearls in her hair. The other a man with a short beard and a dark uniform with red and gold ribbons. Buddy continued to stare. The portraits were so similar, and yet there was something strange about the portrait of the woman in the blue dress.

For a moment he couldn't figure out what made it unique. Then he realized what it was.

Her right eye twinkled. The painter had applied a fleck of white paint mixed with varnish to give that illusion.

But the left eye was lifeless black.

He went over to the portrait and examined it. Craning his neck forward and up, he had a better look.

His pulse jumped.

Placing his gloved hands on either side of the portrait's ornate gold-colored frame, he gripped carefully and lifted it off the wall. Holding it off to the side, he looked at the wall section that had been behind the painting.

He saw a small hole in the plaster. A hole made by a bullet. Small, low caliber.

Terrifying to the family.

Buddy's imagining of the scene gained new detail. The killer had entered the house. The family hadn't been sure they wanted to follow the orders to go upstairs to the master bathroom. The killer had fired a single bullet, to show they couldn't refuse or they'd die right here in their foyer. He'd fired at a painting instead of a blank wall, either to damage the art in general or maybe that painting in particular.

Buddy said, "Detective Gonzalez?"

In a moment Gonzalez was at his side, following his glance, and understanding. Gonzalez took the painting from him and set it down, then summoned another of the CSU detectives.

Chief Malone joined them. His face had gone white at CSU's mention of the Third Reich's most notorious death camp, but was now regaining its color at Buddy's discovery of the bullet in the wall.

CSU was already searching the floor for the shell casing.

Malone put a hand on his shoulder. "Nice job, Buddy. And keep working the case while it's fresh. The next few hours might make the difference." The chief stared at him, to underscore the point that Buddy wasn't to go home and sleep. He was to work all night.

Then Malone returned to the CSU team.

Normally Buddy wouldn't have hesitated to be gone from home. But this time he was leaving Mei and Ben exposed.

He walked into the living room, took out his phone, and dialed Mei's number.

"Buddy?" she asked. "Is everything all right?"

He thought of the dead family upstairs, but there was no need to open that door. "Yeah," he said. "We just came across some . . . some information about the Brook family. That's why I'm calling. The chief needs me here, so it's going to be an all-nighter. I'm sorry."

For a moment she didn't respond. Then she said, "I understand."

"I'm sorry," he said again. "Ben's supposed to be my responsibility. Are you getting along?"

"Oh, yes. He asked me to read to him, but I have nothing for children. So I found some art books."

Buddy said, "I hope not the ones with nudes."

She laughed. "Impressionists, mostly. Country scenes that would reassure him. And it worked, because he fell asleep right away. Buddy, he's shaken up from everything, but it's nice to have company while you're gone."

Buddy looked over at the bright lights the CSU team had set up as they prepared to cut into the foyer wall for the bullet. "I'd like to be home with you," he said. "Especially since Ben is there. And I want everyone to be safe. But the chief did us a favor and installed two cops in your downstairs lobby. You'll be okay."

"But when will *you* be home?"

"Maybe around breakfast."

"We're fine," she said. "Don't worry about us."

But he did worry. After hanging up, he called Schmidt, the doorman for the Carlyle Residences.

The line rang and rang, but Schmidt didn't answer.

Buddy felt a chill on the back of his neck. "Chief?" he called toward the foyer.

Malone broke away from the group and took a few steps into the living room. "What?"

"Who were the two cops you assigned to guard my apartment?"

"I don't know. I asked Sergeant Jackson to put them in the lobby, one by the elevator and one by the fire stairs."

Buddy nodded and redialed Schmidt's number. No answer. He hung up and dialed the sergeant.

"Jackson."

"Sergeant, it's Detective Buddy Lock."

"Hey, Buddy."

"Mind if I check in with the team guarding my apartment? The chief put me on a case, and I want to make sure everything's solid at home."

"No problem. Let me check."

As Buddy listened to the shuffling of papers, he pulled out his notebook and pen from the side pocket of his suit coat.

"Here we go," Jackson said. "Randy Massey and Debby Bolan." He then read off their mobile numbers.

Buddy hung up and dialed Randy Massey. The line rang four times and then went to voicemail. He then dialed Debby Bolan. Again, the line rang four times and went to voicemail. He hung up and tried Schmidt a final time.

But there was no answer.

Chapter Twenty

Mei pushed open the door to the guest bedroom. In the patch of light spilling from the hallway into the room, she saw Ben asleep, lying on his back, his chest rising and falling regularly. She thought it was delightful, having a boy in her home. She wanted a child of her own, she realized now. And she wasn't getting any younger. Thirty-seven and approaching forty at the speed of light.

She left the bedroom door ajar, went out into the hallway to the foyer, and switched off the light. Entering the living room, she stood for a moment by the windows and looked out over Central Park South and the Plaza Hotel. Thousands of people were down there, living and dining and fighting and making love. But from this distance and height, all were invisible to her. She could see nothing. From her living room the city was often as silent as if she were standing on a remote mountaintop.

At the bar in the corner of the room, she poured some Jack Daniel's into a crystal tumbler. She carried the tumbler over to the glass coffee table, set it down on a coaster, and sat cross-legged on the sofa. This had become her sanctuary. After her parents had given her the apartment, she'd redecorated. White walls with a large abstract painting by Joan Mitchell over the Steinway. Parquet floors mostly covered with a white rug, and leather furniture the color of slate from Roche Bobois. She'd made this her home, and had removed all evidence of her parents' finicky décor. The fourteen-foot ceilings and molding remained, but she'd changed out everything else. She'd known for years that she was nothing like them.

Dressed for bed, she wore black panties and no bra under a white terry-cloth bathrobe, with warm Ugg slippers on her feet. As Porter Gallery expected her to do in the evenings, she opened her laptop and began to check e-mail.

She responded to a client's request for more information on two of the Gentileschi paintings in the current show. Then she clicked on the Safari browser icon and searched for the Brook family. A Wikipedia entry appeared in the search results, and she clicked on the link and began reading. After going through basic information about Brook Instruments, its estimated revenues and profits, products, and employee count, she reached a section entitled "Founding." This she read with particular interest:

> *Gerhardt Bruch, a chemist and the son of a common laborer and a seamstress, founded Bruch Instrumente in Berlin, Germany, in the spring of 1935. At this time he'd been married to Hilda Mann Bruch for nine years, and they had a three-year-old son named Walter. They had no other children, possibly due to injuries Hilda Bruch suffered during an attempted robbery on the Friedrichstrasse.*

> *Gerhardt Bruch created a new process to dye steel that he called the Bruch'sche Brennen, or, in English, "Brook Burn." Its possibilities for military use brought him to the attention of Reichsmarschall Hermann Göring and to Heinrich Himmler, who ran the Third Reich's concentration camps, where slave labor was used in the application of the Brook Burn.*

Hearing the faint whirring sounds of the elevator moving upward and then coming to rest on her floor, she looked up from the computer screen. *Buddy must be home earlier than he expected,* she thought.

Yet the elevator door didn't open.

In front of the door was the antique medicine cabinet that she and Ben had pushed back in place when Buddy left. Atop it, the glass of water stood, unmoving.

She listened carefully but couldn't hear anything.

After closing the laptop and setting it on the coffee table, she walked across the living room and into the foyer. The elevator door remained closed.

She stood quietly, unmoving, holding her breath.

From inside the elevator came faint sounds, as if someone were taking small steps or shifting weight from one foot to the other.

Buddy had warned her there might be some danger, but that didn't change the fact that she felt secure in the apartment. She was twenty-five floors up. The security lock on the elevator had always worked well. Schmidt was downstairs, as were two police officers.

Buddy must have misplaced his access card, she thought. *He must be fumbling through his clothes, searching for it.* And she knew that when the security lock was set within the apartment, even the card wouldn't provide access. She took a step forward and reached to flip the security switch that would allow the elevator door to open.

But she hesitated, returned her hand to her side. "Hello?" she called.

The sounds within the elevator ceased.

"Buddy?" she said. "Is that you?"

There was no answer.

A sensation like cold fingers crawled up the nape of her neck. She took a step back, turned, and looked into the darkened hallway that led to the bedrooms. She didn't think she should call Buddy. If he weren't in the elevator, there wasn't anything he could do. But should she call 911?

Three firm knocks sounded from inside the elevator.

The noise startled her. She took another step back. She glanced again at the switch locking the elevator door in the left, or locked, position. Someone was in the elevator cab, just a few feet from her. It didn't whirr upward or downward but remained on the other side of the door. She heard shuffling noises.

She stepped forward again. "Who is it?" she called.

Thud! Thud! Thud!

She jumped. The knocking had become a rough pounding. It wasn't Buddy behind the door but someone else—someone who wanted to get into her apartment. The cold fingertips moved down her spine and around her chest—and tightened. She had difficulty breathing and she felt weak.

Boom! Boom! Boom!

She knew she had to move. There was only one choice. She turned, ran into the kitchen, and dialed 911 on her landline.

Five seconds and the dispatcher answered. "What is the emergency, please?"

"This is Mei Adams. I'm in unit twenty-five A of the Carlyle Residences at Seventy-Sixth just east of Madison. Someone is breaking into my apartment! Please send the police! *Now!*"

Boom! Boom!

CLANK!

The sound had changed. Harder and louder. Not a fist or a knuckle against the door but something metallic. The butt end of a knife, perhaps. Or a wrench. Or the stock of a gun.

"Ma'am," the dispatcher said, "are you alone or are there others with you?"

Mei gripped the phone more tightly. "A boy. Ten years old."

"Anyone else?"

Clank! Clank! Clank!

She couldn't answer. She'd run out of time. Leaving the phone on the counter, she dashed along the short hallway from the kitchen to the foyer. The elevator remained closed, but not all the way. A gap had appeared between the elevator door and the wall. The gap wasn't large enough for someone to squeeze through. Not yet.

But it was three inches wide.

Something extended through the gap. In an instant she recognized it. Blunt on one end, sharp on the other. Silvery steel and deadly. Shining dully and being worked to pry the door open. As it moved, she saw that it was slick with blood. It was a hatchet.

Oh my God! she thought. She stifled a scream and sprinted into the hallway to the bedrooms. As she ran, she remembered there was only one way of escape. But she had to reach it in time. Reach and use it. She flicked on the hallway light and pushed open the door to the guest bedroom.

Ben was standing in his T-shirt and boxer shorts, trembling. "What's happening?" he asked.

She took his hand and said, "We need to go. *Right away!*" She yanked him out of the bedroom and toward the far end of the hallway.

Bang! Bang! Bang!

The sound of metal echoed through the apartment. Then stopped. She heard the shifting of the Chinese medicine cabinet, the shattering water glass they'd set on top of it.

Someone had gotten in.

She pulled Ben into the laundry room at the end of the hall and to the right. It was a small room with a sink above a cabinet, a washer and dryer, and racks to hang clothes. The floor was white tile. The walls were white. There was no window. But there was a single door.

The door was to the left of the washing machine and gave access to the fire stairs.

She feared that someone was waiting on the other side of the door. Someone coordinating with the person who'd gotten in through the elevator. But she had to take the risk. Remaining in the apartment would mean certain death.

She swallowed once, drew the dead bolt, and opened the door.

Nothing.

Just an empty concrete staircase lit by a series of dim overhead lights, each protected by a wire mesh guard.

"You go first," she whispered. *"Hurry!"*

He darted onto the stairs and began going down them in his bare feet. Very fast. Faster than she could go, even in her slippers. But not before closing, quietly as she could, the door behind her. Then she took after Ben, skittering down the stairs. She barely landed on each steel-bordered tread before dropping down onto the next, the concrete stairs hurting her feet through her rubber-soled slippers.

After several floors she saw little footprints. At first she thought Ben had sweaty feet. Then she realized the moisture from the boy's footprints was blood. The rough concrete steps edged with metal had cut his feet. Soon he began to cry aloud.

She caught up with him but didn't slow him, didn't ask him to stop, didn't offer to carry him. His comfort didn't matter. Survival was all. And he was faster on his own two feet than if she carried him.

The stairs switched back at every floor. Back and forth in a blur. Some of the lights above had burned out, and Mei and Ben plunged through shadowy sections without slowing their frantic pace. A few times Mei turned behind her and glanced up at the stairs they'd just come down, but she couldn't see or hear anyone else.

They were nearly out of breath, adrenaline driving them on. Her legs felt rubbery and weak. Her lungs felt as if they would burst. But she kept going. And after descending twenty-five floors, they reached the metal door that opened into the lobby.

Ben halted abruptly and waited.

Mei approached the door in slow motion, as if in a dream. Maybe the person who broke into her apartment was waiting for them in the lobby. Just on the other side of the door. With a hatchet. Or a knife. Or a gun.

Her pulse raced and her hand shook. But she reached for the door handle, turned it slowly, and pushed.

Chapter Twenty-One

Buddy tensed when the door opened. He pulled the Glock from his shoulder holster, raised the gun, and aimed at the door. He touched the trigger with the pad of his index finger. He didn't say anything. He just waited. Tried to be calm. He'd jumped into his Charger and driven like a madman the few blocks south from Bruno Brook's town house on East Seventy-Ninth to the Carlyle on East Seventy-Sixth Street. The dead bodies he'd seen upon his arrival sank his hopes. He assumed Mei was dead. The boy, too. His chest tightened with anxiety. He forced himself to breathe, if only to keep the Glock steady.

He knew that if Mei were gone, he'd have no reason to live. He couldn't endure another catastrophic loss. As if in anticipation, the lobby seemed to darken. His body turned cold.

Between him and the fire door lay Schmidt, barely alive, a dark pool of blood forming from a gash at the side of his head. Schmidt breathed shallowly and appeared to be unconscious, but he'd been the lucky one. He might live, unlike the two cops who lay like grotesque statues on the marble floors. They'd been disfigured. With a hatchet, Buddy guessed. He could see where the blade had cut them, the man in the neck and what remained of his face, the woman in the shoulder blades—the bones protruded white and bloody through her uniform. The cops' guns had been drawn and as they'd fallen, the guns had dropped onto the marble. They'd recognized the threat but hadn't been fast enough. And they'd been trained, unlike Mei and Ben.

Thank God. He breathed deeply and lowered the Glock as Mei stepped through the fire door and into the lobby. Her face was damp with perspiration, her black hair disheveled. She tightened the belt of her bathrobe.

"Mei!" he called.

She saw him and began to cry. He walked around the bodies of Schmidt and the two cops and went toward her. She ran into his arms, and he embraced her tightly. He felt the warmth of her skin against his face, the softness of her hair, the lemon scent she wore. Her arms wrapped around his neck, and he closed his eyes for a moment and enjoyed the sensation of her body against his.

It was then he realized that Ben had put an arm around each of them and was hugging them as hard as he could. Buddy reached down and put the palm of his hand on the boy's back. The boy felt fragile and small, more vulnerable even than Mei. As Buddy and Mei separated, he looked carefully at Ben. He saw tears running down the boy's face, perspiration at his temples, his little boy's chest rising and falling, and his bloody bare feet. Buddy knelt down in order to be at Ben's height. He just wanted to talk, but Ben opened his arms and wrapped them around Buddy's neck. Ben pushed his damp hair and tear-stained face against Buddy's cheek with its day-old stubble. Buddy put his large arms around the boy and pulled him close. Ben started to sob.

"It's going to get better," Buddy said. "I'm making that promise to you. All right, Ben?"

Ben said nothing, but after a moment he nodded his head against Buddy's cheek.

Jesus, Buddy thought. *Why did I tell him that? And where can I find a safe place for him?*

And then he knew.

Chapter Twenty-Two

One minute later, thirty cops had surrounded the building where the killer was trapped.

Five minutes later, an ambulance had taken Schmidt up to Lenox Hill Hospital.

Ten minutes later, a CSU team had cordoned off the bodies of the two fallen police. The team began photographing the bodies in situ and checking for prints and fabric and other indicators of the killer or killers.

Fifteen minutes later, Ward Mills was standing in the lobby of the Carlyle Residences.

Ward stood just beyond the yellow tape, his appearance markedly different from anyone else's.

He was dressed in a navy-blue suit with thick chalk pinstripes, a lavender shirt with a purple-and-white-striped tie, and a pocket handkerchief spilling out of its pocket sufficiently to show the image of Botticelli's *The Birth of Venus*. Some might consider him a superficial dandy. But Mei knew those people were wrong. She'd seen his eyes grow cold, his expression harden, his voice become low. Buddy had implied that Ward fought persistent demons—physical and psychological—without offering details. He'd told her of the viciousness hidden by the Brioni suits.

"Ward," she said, "thank you for coming."

She walked over to him, holding Ben's hand and pulling the boy with her. She leaned over the tape and embraced Ward with one hand, air-kissed both his cheeks, and smiled at him as best she could. She wondered briefly how he'd arrived so quickly, as he'd never divulged to her or to Buddy if he had a place in the city or if he stayed at hotels or with friends.

"I'm glad to help," he said, his usually jaunty voice subdued. "Buddy called. Asked for me to take you somewhere safe."

Mei nodded.

Ben looked up at him and said, "Is anywhere safe?"

Mei watched Ward carefully. He didn't smile or condescend or say something like: *Of course, little guy. There are lots of safe places!* Instead he maintained a calm but flat expression. He said, "Yes, you'll be with me. At my country house."

"Why with you?" Ben asked. "Why *your* house? My family was killed in the country, at our house up north."

"The difference," Ward replied, "is that I'm trained to kill people, and I'd kill them before they kill you."

Ben seemed incredulous. "Are you a policeman, like Buddy?"

"No." Ward shook his head. "I'm not a police detective." He didn't elaborate about his occupation, for he had none. But he added, "My house is in the country, in Greenwich, but it has a security system. It also has a service with Rottweilers that patrols the grounds. And I have many guns. There's no way anyone will be getting onto my estate, let alone into my house. Ben, you'll be safer there than anywhere else on earth. Mei will be coming with you, and you can take the bedroom right next to hers. If you agree, then I think we should go. It's clear you're not safe in the city, not even with police guarding this lobby."

Ben turned his head to glance at the fallen officers, who were being lifted by the CSU team onto the gurneys used to transport them to the Manhattan Office of the Chief Medical Examiner. But when Mei put her hands on the sides of his head and brought his gaze to hers, he searched her face and asked, "Do you think it's all right to go to Mr. Mills's house?"

Mei said, "Yes, I'm sure of it. He's Buddy's brother, and Buddy will visit us. Maybe not every night but some nights. We'll be safe while the police catch the person who's doing these terrible things."

"But once the person is caught," Ben said haltingly, "where will I live?"

Mei stopped short. She'd been taught by her parents and by Miss Porter's School to give, at a moment's notice, the appropriate response to any question, especially an inappropriate question. But this one stumped her.

Ward knelt down, reached under the yellow police tape, and touched Ben's shoulder. "A boy as handsome and smart as you?" he said as Ben turned to meet his eyes. "We'll have no trouble finding a good place for you."

Ben seemed unconvinced. He said, "Will Mei be there?"

Ward didn't hesitate. He answered as if Mei weren't standing there holding Ben's hand. "We'll have to see what happens. Remember that Mei just had her apartment broken into, and she can't make a big decision tonight. But she's coming with you to my house now—that is, if you're ready to join us."

Ben waited a moment. His large brown eyes watched Ward. He tilted his head as he listened. Then he turned to Mei and nodded. "Okay. I want to get away from here. To somewhere safe."

Chapter Twenty-Three

Ben walked out of the lobby of the Carlyle Residences, Mei to his right and Ward to his left. He screamed. His bloody feet had touched the icy concrete sidewalk outside. He tried not to cry, but he couldn't stop.

"My God," Ward said.

Mei saw him looking down. Her face crumpled, and she said, "Oh, Ben. I'm so sorry. We forgot to wrap your feet."

And then he felt himself lifted off the ground. Ward picked him up and cradled him with one arm under his shoulders and the other under his knees.

"I've got you, old man," Ward said in a reassuring voice. "No more walking for you tonight."

Now that his feet were no longer touching the cold sidewalk, he could control his crying, and he stopped. He wiped his eyes and saw that they were approaching a silver Range Rover idling at the curb. A driver stood next to the open right rear door, grasping the handle. The driver was of medium height, Caucasian, with a slender build and blond hair. He smiled at Ben, and Ben began to feel more comfortable.

Ward set Ben on the seat, and the driver closed the car door.

The car had thick seats, like the chair in his father's library. The seats were heated and warm. He relaxed into the black leather and watched the driver open the front passenger door for Mei.

She climbed in, the driver closed the heavy door, and she turned in her seat to look back at him. She said, "We'll clean and bandage your feet at Mr. Mills's house."

Ben nodded. He was resting his feet on the car's soft floor mats. He knew he was making the mats bloody but didn't know what else to do. He couldn't hold them above the floor all the way to Connecticut. And his feet no longer burned but throbbed. Even now, when he was warm and at rest, he began to feel his chest tighten with anxiety. He said, "I wish Buddy were here."

"He'll visit us."

"When?"

"Soon."

"But *when?*"

Before she could answer, the driver opened the car's left rear door, the dome light came on, and Ward climbed in beside Ben. Ward said, "Brick, let's head to the country."

The driver nodded.

Ward turned to look at Ben as the door was closed. "Sorry about your feet. We'll patch you up good as new. You'll see."

Ben didn't answer. He was staring at the nickel-plated handgun fitted into Ward's ankle holster.

Chapter Twenty-Four

Buddy stood by the bloodied floors of the lobby, considering how to catch the killer.

Who must be within the Carlyle building.

The killer hadn't left. Nobody had. Not with thirty alert and very pissed-off cops surrounding the property.

"Nobody gets in or out," Buddy said. He spoke into the police radio that the SWAT team, newly arrived, had given him. The building was on lockdown. The killer of ten people was presumed trapped inside. And Chief Malone had gotten the commissioner to give Buddy tactical command.

Detective Vidas stood next to Buddy. Looking around at the gathering crowd, he said, "What's the next step?"

Buddy considered the best way to clear the building. "Evacuation," he said. "It's much of a city block with hundreds of hotel rooms and residences. Plus storage and laundry rooms, kitchens, maid's rooms, linen-storage rooms, and countless other places to hide. Even if we search the entire building, the killer could hang out in a ventilation duct and then slip away. He could say he'd been at the Carlyle Restaurant, at the Gallery Restaurant, at the Café Carlyle, or at Bemelmans Bar—and there's no way to prove him wrong."

"Unless you find prints in Mei's place."

"Yeah," Buddy agreed. "But that's unlikely."

He decided that a partial solution was all he'd get. He held up the police radio. "Evacuate everyone in the building," he said. "Bring them through the checkpoint on East Seventy-Sixth Street. Take down everyone's ID if they have it. Run the IDs through NCIC. If the database shows nothing suspicious, allow the person to pass through the checkpoint. Let's make five lines. One officer sitting with a laptop, taking down the information. One companion officer standing, searching if necessary, keeping an eye on things, making sure nobody gets through without showing ID or giving name, address, and telephone number." Buddy let go of the talk switch on the radio. He heard a chorus of 10-4s.

So he had the killer surrounded. But that wasn't as good a position as it sounded. Because the killer was anonymous and might be impossible to detect. But at least he'd get the names of everyone who exited the building over the next few hours. Even if NCIC, the National Crime Information Center database run by the FBI, showed nothing, he didn't care because he'd have the list.

A key he could use. If not tonight, then soon.

The SWAT team evacuated the Carlyle Hotel and the Carlyle Residences. Every room. The restaurants, kitchens, and those who worked in them: managers, staff, everyone. At Buddy's direction, Vidas joined the team that cleared Mei's apartment and studied the elevator cab the killer had ridden up to her foyer. He wanted someone he trusted to confirm that everything was safe.

Buddy observed the crowds. They walked out onto the sidewalks and were waved toward the checkpoint on East Seventy-Sixth. He stood on the curb about twenty yards to the side of the tent and the card tables. He saw hundreds of people.

Some were dressed in long coats over gowns and suits for a night on the town. Others wore mismatched clothes that had been put on after having gone to sleep or at least to bed. Most were sober, although some weren't. Most were older than fifty, but not all. Some were children, confused or anxious or wild. They milled around in the darkness and then, slowly or immediately, followed the orders of the SWAT and police teams.

A woman on the other side of the police cordon called out to him. "Detective Lock! Detective *Lock*!"

Turning in the direction of the voice—a voice he recognized—he noticed a stunning blonde waving at him. It was Sophie Bardon, the husky-voiced reporter for the *Gazette*.

His rapport with her was cordial, though he had any cop's innate distrust of the press. At the same time he knew she might be useful to him in the future. He walked toward her. She held up a digital audio recorder. He shook his head. Reluctantly she put it in the side pocket of her parka.

"Detective, can you give me some background here?"

"What kind of background?"

She arched an eyebrow and said, "For example, why are you evacuating an entire building late at night? Why were bodies loaded into ambulances, three by my count?"

He said, "You should talk with the press room."

She laughed. "That's bullshit, Detective. Give me background. I won't quote you. I know you trust me."

He stared at her and said, "I don't trust you. But I'll give you background." He stepped closer to her, until he could smell her minty breath. He said, "Multiple homicide."

She nodded. "Identity of the victims?"

Buddy said, "Two cops."

"Names?"

Buddy shook his head.

She asked, "Were they shot?"

"No."

"Detective, how did they die?"

Buddy said, "No comment," and turned away.

She called after him, but he kept going.

SWAT directed people from the sidewalks toward a white tent that had been set up in the northern lane of Seventy-Sixth Street. The street had been blocked to all traffic. The tent had gas heaters and bright lights. Five lines of people led to five police, who stood and checked photo IDs. Those without photo IDs gave their names, addresses, and telephone numbers. Each cop was paired with a second cop who sat at a small card table and first typed names into a spreadsheet on a laptop computer, then ran those names through NCIC. When the databases showed no match to any criminal or suspect in any kind of crime, the cops at the laptops waved the person through.

Each standing cop had a metal detector wand of the type used by TSA screening agents at airports, and used the device to scan everyone between the ages of fourteen and seventy. Once through the checkpoints, people waited on the sidewalk on the south side of Seventy-Sixth Street. Or disappeared into the city. Many waited to get back into the Carlyle, wishing to return to their dinners now gone cold, to their warm rooms upstairs. But the killer would escape if the police didn't finger him now.

Buddy stepped into the tent's interior. At six feet three inches, he stood above most of the crowd. He looked for anything suspicious.

For a few minutes everyone seemed innocent.

Then everyone seemed guilty.

Then he realized he'd lost this battle.

The SWAT and police teams would find nothing. Possibly a name he could cross-reference in the future, when he knew more. But that was all.

He wore his badge on a lanyard around his neck, outside his overcoat. But without looking at it, his fellow officers knew who he was.

The chief had sent all of them a text, and his name would already be familiar. He'd achieved fame as the lead detective who'd stopped the Death Clock Killer the year before. His face had been on the national news and every newspaper in New York.

But there was a problem with being in the spotlight. Any additional murders would be blamed on him.

He could sense failure. It was close. Very close.

Chapter Twenty-Five

At 1:10 a.m., Buddy watched the process wind down. They'd found no murder weapon and no killer. After he'd returned his police radio to the SWAT commander, he stood unmoving on the sidewalk. He was tired, wired, relieved Mei and Ben had survived, but afraid their lives were still in danger. He thought maybe if he'd done things differently, the result of his search might have been different, but he didn't know a better way. He had to trust the data they'd gathered would help his case.

Feeling a hand on his shoulder, he turned and saw Vidas.

"We'll get him, boss," Vidas said, "just not tonight."

"Yeah, I know."

"Buy you a drink?"

Buddy thought maybe a drink would help. "Last call at Bemelmans."

This was the famous bar in the Carlyle. It was hardly a police hangout, but he'd been standing in the cold for too long to go anywhere else.

Minutes later they were sitting in a booth at the back of the bar. He'd been here before and seen, on the cream-colored walls, the murals of scenes from Ludwig Bemelmans's *Madeline* children's books. Early in their relationship Mei had explained to him the character in the story. She'd described a scene in which Madeline and her school friends, dressed in royal blue, walked two by two along a path through

Central Park, with their teacher, a nun, behind them. There was much Mei had told him about her childhood. There was more he didn't tell her about the life he witnessed at work. Only in the past few days was she getting the picture, and he was angry she'd become involved in what he thought of as "real life." He wanted her to live in Madeline's world, not his.

He'd told her there was no Madeline in his childhood, only a piano. And his father sternly watching over his playing. He'd always sensed that his father was comparing his playing with that of another, imaginary boy who was just a little more talented. His father's behavior made sense once he learned of Ward.

When the waiter approached, Buddy ordered a Michelob and Vidas the same.

Buddy looked across the table at his partner, and saw that Vidas had the benefit of youth. The late hour hadn't made him look old. His eyes were clear. His angular face had only the hint of stubble. Buddy knew Vidas lived for cases that moved fast and kept him up late. Buddy did, too, when the cases didn't involve Mei.

Vidas said, "It's only a matter of time."

Buddy nodded. "I know."

The waiter brought their beers. They clinked their bottles together and drank.

Vidas put his elbows on the table and leaned closer to Buddy. He said, "You can't let it get to you."

Buddy gripped the glass more tightly. He took a moment. Looked away from his partner, then right at him. "What do you mean?"

Vidas shook his head. "Buddy, come on. That girl wasn't your fault."

Buddy wasn't confused. He knew his partner was referring to Lauren, the girl who'd died while they were investigating the Death Clock Murders last year.

They'd been pursuing a serial killer who struck every ninety days. The *Gazette* had begun printing the image of a digital clock on its front page, providing a countdown until the next killing. The *Gazette* had referred to the gimmick as the "Death Clock" and to the case as the "Death Clock Murders." Buddy had been lead detective, publicly excoriated every ninety days until he'd discovered the killer's identity. Yet he hadn't enjoyed the praise.

Because he'd killed a young girl.

◆　◆　◆

Twelve years old.

Long dark hair.

Blue eyes.

Shivering with fear.

He'd cornered the killer in a four-room apartment in Harlem. The killer had taken the girl hostage and positioned himself across the small living room from Buddy.

Lauren was tall for her age, about the height of the killer who was hiding behind her. The killer had his left arm around the girl's chest. His right gripped a KA-BAR straight-edged knife.

Buddy held his Glock steady, but he had no clear shot. He needed to buy time.

So he looked at the girl and spoke gently, soothingly. "Would you tell me your name?"

"Me?"

"Yeah."

"Lauren."

"Hi, Lauren," he said. "I'm Buddy. Hang in there. You're going to be okay."

He kept the Glock trained on the killer's hairline and waited for the killer to become annoyed or distracted.

Lauren was crying and shaking as the edge of the knife blade came to rest against her throat. Her eyes on Buddy, she said, "Okay."

The killer had a smug smile on his face, as though he was enjoying their stilted conversation. Yet he didn't move from behind Lauren, didn't take the risk. He was in control.

Buddy knew he had to change tactics. He addressed the killer, hoping Lauren would move just enough for him to have a shot. "Put down the knife," he said calmly, firmly. "There's no way out. You have no choice, and you can't run. So let's end this now. Peacefully. Don't hurt Lauren. She's a nice girl. She's got nothing to do with you and me."

The killer laughed. Loudly, sneeringly.

Buddy watched as the killer's right hand tightened around the knife handle and pulled the silver blade into Lauren's neck. The blade broke her skin, drew a thin line of blood.

Lauren started screaming.

Buddy needed to act. He looked her in the eye and yelled, "Lauren, get down!"

She tried, but the killer was too strong. Her head dropped slightly, giving Buddy a partial shot at the killer's eyes and forehead.

Buddy pulled the trigger.

But as he did, the killer drew the knife across her throat.

She jerked her head up, away from the blade.

And Buddy's shot went through her left eye.

Seeing what he'd done, he froze.

The killer reacted first. Lunged at Buddy with the knife. Knocked the Glock from his hand.

Buddy toppled over backward and gripped the killer's hand that held the KA-BAR.

They grappled on the floor, the killer with the weapon and the advantage. The killer shoved his knee into Buddy's chest. Buddy couldn't breathe. He couldn't hold the knife away. It got closer and closer as the killer pushed the blade's point down toward Buddy's face.

And then Vidas, who'd hurried to the scene to provide backup, rushed into the house. He launched himself from the adjacent kitchen, tackled the killer, and suffered a nearly fatal wound to the stomach.

Buddy didn't remember the next month. He was suspended, investigated, cleared. He stayed by Vidas's hospital bed until his partner could get out of it. Mostly he hated himself. For taking risks, for failing Lauren, for the loss her parents had to live and die with. He considered giving up as he'd given up the piano. Going away somewhere. But he didn't. Turned out he needed the job more than it needed him.

◆　◆　◆

Buddy drank half his beer. The alcohol made him less angry with himself. "Yeah, it *was* my fault."

"We can't work miracles."

"It wasn't a miracle. It was a mistake."

Vidas nodded. "And everyone makes them. Stop beating yourself up over it."

Buddy drank the rest of his beer and put a twenty on the table. Vidas finished his beer.

Buddy stood and walked toward the door, Vidas following him. He was angry with Vidas for offering advice, angrier with himself for the mistake he couldn't forget or forgive.

As they stood in the vestibule buttoning their coats, Buddy said, "I'm sorry. That's still a raw nerve."

"I get it," Vidas said. "But it's not going to happen again. Not with the boy."

In that moment Buddy realized he'd been connecting Ben with Lauren. He was trying to save him where he hadn't been able to save her—trying to protect Ben even to the point of taking custody of him and having him move into the apartment he shared with Mei. That he was already failing in this duty put him on edge. But it would also make him work harder.

He held open the door for Vidas. They stood for a moment out on the sidewalk in the cold.

"Good night," Buddy said.

"Good night, boss."

Vidas patted his upper arm in support, walked to the corner, and climbed into one of the waiting taxis.

Chapter Twenty-Six

Two Rottweilers.

As Ward's chauffeured car pulled up to the mansion's front door, Ben noticed these immediately. A pair of the immensely powerful black-and-mahogany dogs with big heads and muscular shoulders stood on either side of the drive. The dogs were leashed, he was relieved to see. Two men dressed in black each held a leash. In the car's headlights Ben could see the dogs panting, their breath silvery puffs in the frigid air.

When the Range Rover came to a stop, Ward opened his door, came around the back of the car, and opened Ben's door. Ward reached in, picked him up as he'd done outside the Carlyle Residences, and held him close.

For a moment Ward paused and turned to his driver. "That's it for tonight, Brick," he said. "I'll call you tomorrow if we need anything."

Brick nodded and pulled the Range Rover into the garage. Moments later he drove away in a small Volkswagen.

Ward carried Ben up to the front door. Lights shone on the house's exterior, and Ben thought it looked like a giant white cube. He'd been to many large houses, but this one seemed to weigh less, as if it might rise above the ground and hover.

An older gray-haired woman dressed in black opened the door. Ben guessed this was Ward's mother. The woman's face was gaunt and severe, but she smiled and said, "Hello, Ben. My name is Rose Gallatin. I've prepared a tub of warm water for your feet."

He tried to say thank you but only heard himself murmur inaudibly. He felt his eyes closing. He tried to keep them open and to stay alert, yet somehow the warmth of Ward's house, the lateness of the hour, and the low voices of Ward, Mei, and the older woman soothed him.

He awoke once, just briefly, and found himself in a large bathroom with cream-colored stone floors. Mei was holding his right foot over a tub of soapy water and using a large clear plastic cup to pour water over his foot. He raised his left foot and saw that it was dry and already bandaged.

Ward was kneeling beside him, fastening a rubber bracelet around his right wrist.

"You're awake," Ward said. "Good. Pay attention, okay, Ben? This panic bracelet is a tracking device connected to my phone and my computer. I can look on the screen and see exactly where you are. And it has an important feature." Ward lifted Ben's wrist and rotated the rubber bracelet, revealing a smooth square red button. "See this red area here?" Ward asked.

Ben tried to answer, but he just wanted to sleep.

"Ben," Ward said. "*Ben!*"

Ben jerked awake.

"This is very important," Ward told him, his voice no longer soothing but louder and hard-edged. "Do you see this red square on the bracelet?"

Ben looked from Ward's face to his wrist. He saw the red square on the bracelet and nodded.

"Speak out loud," Ward ordered. "Do you see it?"

"Yes," Ben answered.

Ward said, "It's an alarm. If you feel you're in danger, if *anything* doesn't seem right, you press the button. Okay?"

"Okay."

"So let's test it. Would you go ahead and press the red button?"

Ben decided that maybe he didn't like Ward. The handsome man, despite being related to Buddy, seemed stern and severe. Kind but at the same time mean. Buddy was gruff but kind. Hard but soft. Ben couldn't explain it, but he preferred Buddy and hoped that soon he could be back with Buddy and Mei. But this preference didn't mean he didn't trust or respect Ward. He did. And so he moved his left hand, extended his index finger, and pressed the red button on his bracelet.

Almost immediately he heard a siren sound coming from nearby. He watched as Ward removed a mobile phone from a small inner pocket of his suit coat and touched the screen to turn off the siren sound.

Ward asked, "Do you see how it works?"

"Yes."

"You have one, and I'm giving one to Mei as well. Got it?"

"Got it," Ben said.

Chapter Twenty-Seven

Buddy saw what the hatchet had done.

He rode the elevator to the apartment. In addition to the black fingerprint dust on the surfaces, he saw that the cab's oak-paneled left side and rear remained intact, although there were drops of blood on the tiled floor. He knew that many of the drops had been taken up by CSU for analysis. But he didn't need an analysis. He knew the blood belonged to Schmidt plus the two cops who'd died in the lobby downstairs. A shame and a waste and a dreadful injustice, but more motivation for him to crack the case.

As if he needed it.

Glancing up, he saw the brass-colored metal ceiling reflect his image back to him. He looked old and tired, but not as bad as the elevator door on the right side of the cab.

The hatchet had cut through the oak paneling to the aluminum doorframe. The edge of the door was beaten, dented, and bent, exposing the locking mechanism and the wires that connected a plate on the door to the security switch—the switch that, when activated in one of the apartments, would prevent the door from opening at a particular floor. Bending down to look more closely, he saw the wires had been cut.

The blows to the door and to the right side of the elevator, from which the door traveled when it opened, had been blunt and brutal.

Fury, Buddy thought again. Same as at Camp Kateri. Same as in the case of Nan Sawyer.

When the elevator reached the twenty-fifth floor, he pulled the Glock from his shoulder holster and gripped it tightly. Usually he'd have to hold his access card up to the disclike card reader inside the elevator cab. But now the door automatically slid open. He stepped into the apartment. Vidas and the search team had walked the entire building, and especially Mei's rooms, and found almost nothing. Many prints in the elevator cab, as expected for something used by so many people. But would any of them be useful?

Buddy gritted his teeth. "Mei's apartment," he said aloud. "*My* apartment. The fucker."

The black lacquered medicine cabinet had been pushed or kicked up against the wall where it had previously stood. The drinking glass he'd set on the cabinet before leaving earlier in the evening lay on the floor in dozens of pieces, the floor still damp from the water the glass had contained. The cabinet appeared to have sustained no damage, except its normally smooth top was caved in where the blade of the hatchet had come down with force. The top was splintered, mangled. The killer had left the hatchet, CSU had told him. They'd taken it for analysis but told him it was the kind of thing available in any hardware store. Carbon steel head with a three-and-a-half-inch blade, the entire tool no more than eleven inches in length.

Glock in hand, Buddy went room by room, confirming that each was clear. The shock of the attack wore off, and he felt his chest turning hot. He realized how close the killer had come to Mei and Ben. The killer had been a minute, maybe less, from taking Mei away from him.

Buddy pushed the cabinet in front of the closed elevator door, holstered the Glock, and walked out of the foyer and into the living room. He went immediately to the small bar in the corner.

A large Jack Daniel's—Mei's favorite drink—eased his mind. He liked the way it warmed his throat and stomach. After pouring another, he went to the sofa and sat down heavily. He thought he'd never been so exhausted. He looked at his watch. Almost three. It was then he noticed Mei's laptop.

When he opened it, two names caught his eye: Brook and Auschwitz. Mei must have been reading up on Ben's family.

Scrolling up to the beginning of the Wikipedia article, he read the history of the Brook family. About the invention of the Brook Burn that dyed metals. About its use in the Wehrmacht's machine guns, tanks, and submarines. About concentration camp labor, including labor from Auschwitz-Birkenau, used in factories that specialized in the Brook Burn.

Then he read on:

Gerhardt Bruch entered Hitler's inner circle, dining often with Albert Speer, minister of armaments. It was at this time that Bruch, with his new travel permit allowing him to visit metals mines throughout the Reich and even into Switzerland, is believed to have secreted suitcases filled with Reichsmarks to several banks in Zurich. From August 1942 until April 1944, Bruch traveled monthly to Zurich, each time with suitcases filled with money. Financial analysts have calculated that in this way he moved at least $175 million—far more today if adjusted for inflation—into Swiss banks.

Once it became clear that the war was lost, and German forces began their retreat from France, from the Low Countries, from Russia and North Africa and Italy, Bruch used his travel privileges a final time. He hired a private plane to take him and his wife and son on a daring flight to Zurich, where the Bruchs would live until immigrating to the United States in 1949.

After settling in Manhattan, Brook—having changed his name to the English equivalent—and his son, Walter, founded Brook Instruments Inc., building it into the third-largest privately held company in the United States. The Brook family, headed by Walter Brook's four sons, is estimated by Forbes to have a net worth of $24 billion.

A success story, Buddy thought. A story of opportunity seized and a narrow escape. The story of a family starting over—albeit with nearly $200 million—in America, the land of opportunity. But this success story angered him. The Brook family's wealth and position were built on theft and slavery, on the ashes of those who perished at Auschwitz.

He closed the computer, stood, and walked to the windows overlooking the park. He saw the string of lights over the footpaths curving through the darkness. So few lights in the seemingly endless gloom. He sighed wearily. His mind felt as thick as the murk outside. His body ached. In his tiredness he tried to connect Gerhardt Brook's mercenary behavior in the 1930s and 1940s to the murders committed more than seventy years later, but he couldn't do it.

Turning from the windows, he left the living room, padded slowly along the hallway to the bedroom, and lay on the bed. He didn't undress or pull down the duvet. He reached over to the night table and shut off the light. Then he lay in the darkness, listening for someone to break through the elevator door, hearing only his breathing. In the silence his mind wandered. His body grew heavy, and now his bed rested on a melting sheet of ice. The ice cracked slowly, audibly. There wasn't anywhere for him to go. There was no help to be had. And then the ice broke and the bed fell into the depths, the ocean's cold enfolding and drowning him. He tried to breathe, but it was impossible. So he allowed the water to bear him downward to the center of the earth. The frigid emptiness calmed him, lulled him into an endless sleep. Yet he resisted just for a moment. He looked out into the darkness, and was comforted by the Glock in his right hand.

Chapter Twenty-Eight

Mei took off the panic bracelet.

She stood in the guest bathroom across the hallway from the room where she'd sleep. After stepping out of the Ugg slippers she'd been wearing since her escape at the Carlyle, she took off her bathrobe, hung it on a hook to the side of the door, and turned on the shower. For a long time she stood under the hot water, trying to wash off the fear and anxiety of the past several hours. Calm—that was all she wanted right now. It was twenty minutes before she could think of the attack on her home as the past rather than the present. At last she could breathe more easily, relax a little. She stepped out of the shower, dried herself with one of the white towels on the vanity, and brushed her teeth. Then she put on her panties. A small digital clock embedded in the mirror showed the time: 3:04 a.m.

Switching off the light, she opened the door and went across the hallway toward the bedroom. Sensing someone near her, she looked up and to her left.

It was Ward. He was coming toward her. He stopped.

She saw that he was wearing boxer shorts and nothing else. His body was toned and muscular. His shoulders were broad. His hair was slightly disheveled. He gave her an embarrassed smile. Holding up the book he was carrying and a drink in the other hand, he said, "Had to get a drink and a book from my library across the hall. Sorry, Mei."

She held her breath, unable to speak. Instead she crossed her arms over her bare breasts and continued into the bedroom, closing and locking the door behind her. Only then did she exhale. And understand how nervous she felt. And how tired. She climbed into bed and tried to put the image of the handsome Ward out of her mind. She hoped he hadn't seen much of her and that the light in the hallway was dim. She told herself it didn't matter. He was Buddy's half brother and would never be closer to her than that.

As she drifted off to sleep, she remembered that she'd left her panic bracelet in the bathroom.

Chapter Twenty-Nine

Ben liked the warmth. He stood close to the bonfire at the water's edge. In his left hand he held a metal skewer that flashed in the light of the flames. He was holding the skewer close to the heat, toasting the two marshmallows on the end. Careful not to burn them, he glanced to his left and right. His cousins John and Hayley and Ariel were toasting marshmallows. He looked through the flames and saw his mother and father on the other side of the thick branches they'd used to build the fire. His father held the end of Ellen-Marie's skewer with one hand while she held the middle of it with two hands. She kept trying to put the marshmallow too close to the fire, and their father restrained her.

Ben smiled. He knew she wanted to see the marshmallow catch fire and then to fling it at a tree or out into the lake behind her.

His mother sat on one of the enormous logs around the bonfire, eating a s'more, talking with Aunt Natalie. She noticed him watching her. With her mouth still full, she giggled at him and waved.

But no, she was pointing at the bonfire, at the flames.

He looked more closely and saw something dark in the center of the fire. *It must be smoke,* he thought. Dense, swirling smoke that resembled a small version of tornados he'd seen on the television news.

And then the darkness at the center of the fire grew larger, spun faster, reached higher, up into the air. He watched it rise, lifted his head to follow its path, saw it spread out above all of them until it hid the stars and covered the sky in blackness.

He tried to step back from the fire, but he couldn't. He looked left and right. His cousins were laughing and eating s'mores. They hadn't noticed the smoke. Across the fire his mother was still talking with his aunt. His father helped his sister rotate her skewer to brown the underside of the marshmallow.

Ben waved at them, but they didn't see him.

He called out to them. "Mom! Dad! Ellen-Marie!"

Yet they ignored him.

Can't they see the smoke? he asked himself. *Aren't they afraid of it?* And of the fire.

All this time the fire was growing, spreading outward until the flames licked his knees. He smelled something burning and realized his bangs were on fire.

He swatted at his face. He cried out. He tried to lean backward.

But he couldn't move, and the others wouldn't move.

First the smoke enveloped his cousins. And then he watched, helplessly, as the growing fire touched them gently, as if giving their faces the faintest kiss, and then it burned them.

They caught fire, and their skin bubbled and broke open and turned crimson before blackening. Their hair exploded in a white puff and then turned to ash.

"No!" he called out. "No!"

It was then he looked over at his mother and father, at his sister. All three of them were smiling at him, waving.

And then the fire seized them. They didn't fight it. Didn't try to run from the heat.

He shouted at them: "Go into the water! It's just behind you! Jump into the water! It will save you!"

But they didn't move, couldn't move.

He felt the warmth. Looked down. His clothes were on fire.

He struggled to get out of them.

He saw his skin bubble and begin to peel off him.

With all his strength he tried to get away from the heat. He took in the deepest breath he'd ever taken and gave a final shout.

Chapter Thirty

Mei heard herself scream.

The sound was muffled, as if it came from a great distance. Alarm and distress mixed with the most basic of emotions: fear.

Breathing deeply, she opened her eyes and remembered she was at Ward's house in Greenwich, Connecticut. Sitting up on one elbow, she shifted her legs on the soft white linens. Listened to the barely audible sound of the furnace pushing warm air into the room through the registers. Opened her eyes in the darkness to see the clock beside the bed, its digital numerals gray green and reading 4:07 a.m.

Then she heard another muffled cry. Was she still asleep? No. No, she couldn't be. She was quite sure she was awake. And her mouth was closed. No, the cry couldn't have come from her.

Ben.

He was in distress. Of course. The scream and cries were coming from the bedroom next to hers.

She threw back the duvet, put on a T-shirt, and opened the door to the hallway. Nobody there. She went to Ben's door and didn't knock but opened it quickly, closed and locked it behind her, and went over to the bed. Perching on the edge of the mattress, she could see the faint outline of Ben's form. He'd kicked off the duvet. Moving closer, she saw his long black hair against the white sheets.

She put a hand, very gently, on his side.

"Ben?" she said. "Ben, it's all right. Everything is all right."

He writhed for a moment and then was still.

"Ben," she repeated. "You're okay."

She saw him turn. Heard a gasp, a great intake of breath.

"Ben?" she said again.

"Mei?" His voice small, uncertain.

"Yes."

In a quavering voice, he said, "I was having a nightmare."

"I know. But I'm here and you're all right."

"I was *dying*."

She put her arms around him. He snuggled in and pushed his face into the crook of her neck. She felt the wetness of his tears. She said, "It was only a bad dream. You're here with me in Ward's big house."

For a moment he was quiet. Then he said, "There was a fire. It burned everyone and I screamed but I couldn't move couldn't get away couldn't raise my hands couldn't . . ."

He sobbed and held her tightly.

She returned his embrace just as tightly and said, "It's all right, Ben. It's all right. You had a dream. A really bad one. In dreams we can't do what we need to do. But in life, sometimes, we can. Remember how you escaped from the killer and survived. And now you're here with me at Ward's house. There are guards and Rottweilers outside. There's a security system. And Ward has weapons, and you have your panic bracelet."

Quiet for a moment, he rolled onto his back. "But what happens next week or next month?"

She put a hand on his chest. "Buddy will catch the person who did these terrible things and put him in prison forever."

Ben sighed.

She waited.

After a while he asked, "Do you have to go?"

"Go where?"

"Back to your room?"

She bent over and kissed his forehead. "I'll stay right here tonight."

"All night?"

"Yes. All night."

She got into bed beside him and lay quietly. Soon his breathing grew even, and she knew he'd fallen asleep. What a wonderful new sensation it was to be near this boy, to smell his hair and sense his light breath against her skin.

As she lay in the darkness, she thought of Buddy. It was with Buddy she'd decided to have a child—if they married. Although she'd been adopted, she'd never considered it. She hadn't strongly desired children until she'd met him. But here was a child who needed her. Not just anyone, but *her*. Should she, could she, turn her back on that responsibility?

As she in turn fell asleep, she knew she couldn't answer that question.

Chapter Thirty-One

The next morning Buddy left the apartment for an interview with part of the surviving Brook family. He suspected they knew something, but he didn't know if they'd tell him what it was.

After walking over to Fifth Avenue, he turned south and studied the high-end co-op buildings to his left and the park to his right. A few blocks farther, and he looked through the park's black wrought-iron fence at the zoo. He sniffed but couldn't smell the animals. He kept going, taking a right on Central Park South that led him past the Plaza Hotel and the Ritz-Carlton.

He looked down Seventh Avenue and could see Carnegie Hall's ochre-colored façade, which brought back memories of his senior recital there during his last month as an undergraduate at Juilliard, when he'd failed in front of thousands.

He'd begun a difficult piece—Schumann's *Kreisleriana* Agitatissimo—with suitable aggression. In an instant going from silence to maximum volume. The first minute was the most difficult, and he played its rumbling chords with clarity and technical perfection.

But as he'd begun the development section, he'd glanced out at the audience to his right. He'd seen his father watching him, coldly it seemed, sitting next to his wealthy blonde stepmother. And a row behind them, his mother perched on the edge of her seat, alone.

He'd returned his eyes to the keyboard. Tried and failed to keep focus.

Blurring an easy passage, he'd grown conscious of his hands. They'd always been large and muscular but now they seemed chunky and oafish, too clumsy for demanding sixteenth notes, and lacking in finesse.

Having lost his place, he'd lifted his hands from the keyboard.

The hall was silent, and he'd hunched over the instrument in the silence.

Then the notes had come to him, but they made no sense.

He'd detected his father's disapproval and derision, his mother's alarm.

Pushing back the piano bench an inch, he heard the sound echo out into the hall.

He'd put his hands together.

In that moment he hadn't felt his father's disapproval or his mother's alarm. He'd only sensed his rejection of those emotions. A pushing away of them.

A cough had sounded in the audience.

More coughs.

The rustling of programs.

He'd realized that for at least a year he'd been playing for his father, and that he no longer wanted to continue. Didn't want to play the piano. Maybe ever. He'd thought he was a highly trained monkey, performing for his father, the famous Juilliard professor.

Pushing the bench away from the keyboard, he'd stood.

The coughing had stopped. An eerie quiet had come over the hall.

Slowly, Buddy had turned away from the crowd. Then he'd walked off the stage, the roar of the audience's surprise, compassion, and ridicule following him as he went.

The next day he realized that he should have regained his focus and finished the piece, no matter how badly he'd played. He'd come to believe that if he'd finished his performance like a man, his mother would have been proud of him. She'd told him his failure didn't matter, but he knew it did. She'd sacrificed so much for his private lessons and touring, she must have been greatly saddened. During her subsequent illness he'd given up the piano, and her death made all music frivolous. He'd decided never to perform again. Instead he'd become a homicide detective with the NYPD, something as far from Juilliard as possible, but to him, just as magnetic. He'd become a different man, or maybe he'd always been a man who wanted to hunt others, who was attracted to darkness and saw weakness and fallibility everywhere, not only when he looked in the mirror. There was nothing frivolous about homicide.

At the southwest corner of the park, he reached Columbus Circle, a busy roundabout with Time Warner Center, an enormous mixed-used development, curling around its corners. Two towers clad in smoky but partially reflective glass, the right housing the Mandarin Oriental Hotel, the left some of the world's most expensive condominiums. Russian oligarchs and other foreigners had bought many of the condo units, their way of laundering money they'd made in various criminal enterprises. Buddy knew that if he hadn't moved in with Mei, he'd have been priced off the island along with others like him. Now Manhattan served tourists and the rich. Everyone else just visited.

He walked around to the entrance to the condos. After he badged the doormen, one called up to Carl Brook's duplex on the top floor to get the okay, and he was shown to an elevator and began his rise to the top of the city.

His first thought, when the lawyer Robert Kahler opened the door to the condo, was what every police detective thinks when investigating a case: If you aren't guilty, why do you need a lawyer? But of course he knew that a billionaire wouldn't meet with the NYPD absent legal representation. This didn't bother him all that much. He'd get his man no matter how many lawyers were hired.

"Good morning, Detective Cyrus Edward Lock." Kahler was dressed in a conservative navy-blue suit. He wore his graying hair short, and his pale complexion seemed almost white behind the silver-colored frames of his eyeglasses. Buddy had met him before. He'd never liked Kahler, who earned millions of dollars a year defending wealthy criminals.

Buddy didn't smile. He didn't like his given name or Robert Kahler's use of it. "Mr. Kahler."

"Please come in." The lawyer pulled the door farther open and stepped to the side so that Buddy could pass. "The family is ready for your interview."

Buddy walked into a modern foyer with expensive-looking paintings on the white walls, light maple floors, and modern furniture. He looked up at a wide skylight that showed clouds passing not far above. Refocusing on the room, he saw no members of the Brook family. He stopped and turned back toward Kahler.

After closing and locking the large door, Kahler looked at Buddy and said, "Perhaps we should discuss ground rules."

Buddy shook his head, turned, and walked into the living room.

Chapter Thirty-Two

His first thought was that he'd never seen better-looking people. All slender with great facial structure and not an ounce of fat. They wore beautiful clothes. All had dark hair—Carl's graying at the temples—and perfect skin. He felt like he was in an advertisement for Armani. Or some kind of Hollywood casting call for the perfect family. The perfect *rich* family.

Perfection put him on guard.

"Good morning," he said to the Brooks. He didn't bother to smile. "Detective Lock, NYPD."

"Good morning," they answered in unison.

They were sitting on furniture arranged around a low glass coffee table. The furniture was black leather and dark wood. Husband and wife on the sofa. Son and daughter on chairs facing the sofa.

Carl Brook stood up and crossed the floor toward Buddy. He was fifty years old but looked younger, despite his eyeglasses' thick black frames. His tailored white shirt underscored his skin's healthy glow and the expensive-looking dark-wash jeans. He was well built, with broad shoulders and muscular arms. He offered his hand. "I'm Carl."

They shook hands. Carl's grip was firm, strong.

Carl said, "This is my wife, Rebecca, our son, John, and our daughter, Ariel. We're anxious to be of help, because we want justice for whoever killed my brothers and their families."

"Thank you," Buddy said. "I'm sorry for your loss."

"Losses," Carl corrected him.

"Yes." Buddy looked him in the eye. "Losses."

Kahler appeared to Buddy's right. "Shall we begin?"

Buddy ignored him. "I'd like to interview Carl, Rebecca, and Ariel together. But I'll start with John, alone." He turned to the young man. "You ready?"

John was shorter than his father, about five feet eight inches and thicker in build. All-American in appearance with dark eyes and a square jaw. Could have been—maybe was—a model. Despite the family tragedy, he had a pleasant demeanor edged with a confidence that bordered on entitlement.

Buddy thought he recalled John from the photographs that hung in Ben's parents' house at Camp Kateri. He said, "Where can we speak privately?"

Kahler said, "Detective Lock, I object to your interviewing John without me or his father present."

Buddy kept his eyes on John. "You have something to hide?"

John stood up quickly. "Nope. That's fine, Mr. Kahler. I'm not worried about it."

"You're sure?" his father asked.

A moment later Buddy and John were sitting at each end of an oversized tan leather sofa. It was a large den with a flat-panel television mounted to the opposite wall that must have been at least seventy inches. Below the screen were two ottomans that matched the sofa. Buddy opened his notebook, but he also set a digital recorder on the sofa's middle cushion and switched it on.

"You're John Brook?" he asked.

"Yes."

"Are you in school?"

"Yes. I'm a senior at Horace Mann."

"College plans?"

"I've been accepted at Princeton, but I might go right to a hedge fund. Usually the funds take people out of college or business school, but I'm good with numbers and have connections and, well, money."

Buddy made a note. Then he said, "Were you at Camp Kateri over New Year's Eve?"

John's face darkened. "Yes."

"Did you hear anything when your aunt Brenda, your uncle Alton, and your cousin Ellen-Marie were killed?"

"No." John shook his head. "Not until the sirens, after Ben called the police."

"Where were you?"

"I was with everyone else until midnight. Afterward I visited my cousins, Lucy and William, at their parents' house. Then I went to our house."

"Do you know who'd want to kill Alton, Brenda, or Ellen-Marie Brook?"

"No."

"For the past week, you were with your parents and sister here in Manhattan?"

"Yes."

"What were you doing?"

"The usual. School, homework, friends."

"Anything strange or odd happen to you?"

"No."

"What about last night?"

John's eyelids flickered. "What about it?"

"Where were you?"

"I was, uh, with a friend."

"Who?"

"A friend from school."

Buddy waited a moment, and then said, "Name?"

"Ayla Cross."

Buddy wrote down the name and asked, "Where were you?"

"Her place—her parents' place—at 1095 Park Avenue."

Buddy made another note. "You were there all evening?"

"Yeah. I stayed over, went to school the next morning with her."

Buddy made another note. He said, "Do you know who'd want to kill Bruno, Natalie, Lucy, or William Brook?"

In an instant, John's face changed. Gone was the confidence, the buoyancy, the hint of defiance, which now were replaced by what appeared to be genuine pain. "Yes, I think so."

Buddy waited. He hadn't expected this answer.

John continued: "I mean, how do you tell if someone's angry or crazy enough to go ballistic? Is there a sign I should've noticed? It's just . . . just bizarre and I feel so badly. So . . ." He suddenly covered his face with his hands and began to sob.

Buddy didn't move. *This is a normal reaction,* he reminded himself. Even for an eighteen-year-old boy. Or young man. Buddy felt sympathy, but he was stuck on John's saying, *Yes, I think so.*

John wiped tears from his face, looked up, and met Buddy's eyes.

Buddy nodded once and said, "You have an idea who'd go after your uncle Bruno and his family?"

"Probably not, but . . ." John paused.

Buddy waited.

"I don't know. No, this probably isn't anything, but maybe it is."

Buddy waited.

John again met Buddy's eyes. "My cousin Lucy had just broken up with some guy she was seeing."

"His name?"

"She wouldn't tell me."

"Someone from her high school?" Buddy suggested. "A friend of her parents'?"

"I don't know," John repeated. "I guessed aloud—just like you're doing now—and she wouldn't tell me."

Buddy thought for a moment. He said, "Girls break up with boyfriends all the time. Feelings are hurt but nothing more. Why would this case be different?"

"Because," John said, "Lucy told me the guy turned crazy on her. Stalked her. Threatened her. Tried to break into their town house."

Buddy felt himself lean forward. He said, "Was Lucy's boyfriend violent?"

"Yes." John nodded. "He hit her in the chest"—John raised his hand and showed the area where a woman's breasts would be—"and bruised her and maybe broke a rib. She said he'd broken a rib, anyway."

Buddy made a note and asked, "How do you know this?"

"She showed me."

Buddy was quiet. He remembered the photographs hanging in the house at Camp Kateri, with the great-looking family wearing not much clothing. He said, "She *showed* you?"

John looked away, over at the blank television screen. Without meeting Buddy's eyes, he said, "I don't know anything else."

And then he stood and left the den.

Chapter Thirty-Three

Buddy's mobile vibrated. Alone in the den, he checked the phone's screen and saw it was Vidas calling.

He stood up and answered, "Yeah?"

"Boss, we've got ballistics on the gun fired through the painting in Bruno's foyer. Some weird shit."

As Buddy stared out through the large windows at the gray expanse of Central Park far below, he felt a twinge in his stomach. "How's that?"

"The bullet came from an unusual gun. Antique and expensive. They think it might be a French revolver that's a hundred fifty years old."

Buddy considered this information. The killer used hatchets, chemicals, and an ancient pistol. Was he some kind of connoisseur who avoided modern weapons? Some kind of virtuoso? Or were there two killers? He said, "Any way to track the antique gun?"

"The usual places," Vidas replied. "Gun registries, dealers, auction houses. But you know how touchy those guys have gotten."

"See if you can find anything," Buddy told him.

"Will do."

"And check on the whereabouts of Carl and his family last night. John says they were here in Manhattan, but I want to know if Carl or John could have done Bruno and family or Mei's apartment."

"On it."

Buddy thought more about the weapons used by the killer. He thought about Carl Brook and his brother Dietrich—and about John Brook's interest in joining a hedge fund.

Vidas said, "Anything else, boss?"

Buddy said, "Walter had a huge company. But maybe when Carl and Dietrich were younger they worked for someone else. Like a brokerage firm or an investment bank. Maybe something in finance. And if they did," Buddy explained, "they'd have been printed by the SEC."

Vidas took the next step. "We could compare those prints with whatever we found at the Carlyle."

Buddy said, "Call the SEC, and get back to me."

When they'd ended the call, Buddy paced the room for a few minutes. He listened to his shoes on the wood floors. Heard himself breathing. Sensed the momentum growing, the web of evidence being spun.

Chapter Thirty-Four

He brought Carl, Rebecca, and their daughter, Ariel, into the den, and pointedly closed the door on Robert Kahler. He sat down on the other end of the sofa from Carl Brook. Rebecca and Ariel each took one of the ottomans under the television screen. Ariel was slight, with very thin, glossy brown hair. Her fashionable eyeglasses had black frames not much different from her father's. She removed her glasses and held them in one hand.

He switched on the digital audio recorder and turned to Ariel. "Would you tell me your full name and your age?"

She sat up a little straighter, pleased to be asked the first question. She put on her eyeglasses and said, "My name is Ariel Mila Brook. I'm thirteen years old. Is Ben okay? Is he all right?"

"Yeah," Buddy told her. "He's all right."

"When will I get to see him?"

Rebecca put a hand on her daughter's leg. "Let the detective ask the questions, Ariel."

Ariel grew quiet.

Buddy said, "Would you tell me where you were on New Year's Eve?"

She nodded. "Mostly, I was in the lodge, playing with my cousins. Ping-Pong. Bowling. There's a bowling alley in the basement."

"When did you go to bed?"

"Twelve fifteen. I remember looking at my clock to be sure I was awake for the New Year."

"Do you remember anything unusual from that night?"

She nodded. "Yes." And then she waited.

Her father cleared his throat. "Tell the detective, Ariel."

Ariel said, "I smelled vetiver."

"Vetiver?" Buddy asked. He'd no idea what it was.

"Nobody in our family wears vetiver," Ariel explained.

Buddy turned to Rebecca with a questioning glance.

Rebecca said, "Vetiver is an ingredient used in perfumes. Ariel is always going into Bergdorf's with me and testing all the perfumes at the counter. She's destined to be a *perfumier*. I don't know how she can keep them straight, but she knows the difference between Hermès Hiris and Tom Ford's Costa Azzurra. She's already being tutored by Olivier Creed. She also goes with Carl to test the men's cologne."

Buddy tried to absorb this information. He didn't know about perfumes but jotted down the name Olivier Creed. He said, "Is vetiver in women's perfume, or in men's cologne as well?"

Rebecca said, "It can be in both. It's not uncommon in expensive versions of either."

"What is it?" Buddy asked.

Ariel said, "A blend of grass that flowers."

Buddy leaned forward and put his elbows on his knees. He watched Ariel carefully when he asked, "When did you smell the vetiver?"

"I don't remember."

"Where did you smell it?"

"I don't know."

Buddy asked, "Did you think it strange that you smelled vetiver when nobody in your family wears it?"

"Maybe." The girl nodded. "Or maybe someone got new perfume or cologne for Christmas. But I do remember walking around and smelling it and thinking, *Someone is wearing something with vetiver in it.*"

"Walking around in your family's house?"

Ariel shrugged. "I don't know where it was. It could have been the lodge."

Buddy said, "Do you know of anyone who might want to hurt your family?"

She thought for a moment and then slowly shook her head. "No."

Vetiver, he thought, making a note. Maybe that's what Ben smelled when he was hiding behind the pantry shelving. Maybe Ben could help with his investigation.

Chapter Thirty-Five

"Where were you at midnight on New Year's Eve?" he asked Carl and Rebecca when Ariel had left.

"In the lodge," Carl answered. "But first would you tell us when we can see Ben?"

Buddy considered this request, and Ben's preference not to see any of his family. "Ben's in police custody," he said. "We'll evaluate his needs during the course of our investigation."

Carl didn't respond.

Rebecca said, "The sooner we can see him, the better. Even if it's today. Tonight."

Buddy knew his face had reddened, his emotions rising against the idea of losing Ben. He couldn't give up the boy. Not yet. And maybe not to Carl and Rebecca, no matter how genuine their concern seemed, at least until he'd established their innocence in all the crimes. It was Ray Sawyer's decision, anyway. He said, "Ben will remain in police custody for the time being." Without pause, he continued, "On New Year's Eve, how long after midnight did you stay in the lodge?"

"Maybe five minutes."

"And then you returned to your cabin?"

"Our house, yes."

"Was everyone on good terms?"

"Good enough."

"No arguments? Disagreements?"

Rebecca stood and put her hands in the pockets of her wool trousers. She said, "There was an argument, earlier in the evening. Carl and his brothers. And I guess the wives, too."

"What about?"

Carl removed his eyeglasses, wiped off the lenses with his shirt, and put them on again. He said, "Selling our company to GE. And if we were to sell to GE, each family would receive about six billion dollars in GE stock, which we could sell and reinvest in various things. We'd no longer have most of our net worth tied up in one company. But under Brook Instruments' governing documents we can't sell unless all four brothers agree, and we don't. Or didn't until this week."

Buddy didn't follow the last part. "How do you mean?"

"Well," Carl said, and studied his hands. "My answer will throw suspicion on my brother Dietrich, and on me. But it's the truth. We're the only two brothers alive, and we're the two who wanted to take the company public."

"Alton and Bruno opposed the sale?" Buddy asked.

Carl nodded. "Exactly."

Buddy turned and looked up at Rebecca, who was pacing in front of the blank television screen. He said, "Do you know who'd want to kill any member of the Brook family?"

She stopped. Her expression was strained. "No, I don't. Of course not."

He turned toward her husband.

Carl slowly shook his head. "We have people suing us—any large business does—but nothing that would rise to this level."

Buddy threw in a changeup. "Do you work out a lot?"

Carl drew in his breath, making his chest larger. "Yes, I do CrossFit."

"What's CrossFit?"

"Serious fitness. Weight lifting, gymnastics, plyometrics, interval training. Pretty competitive stuff. You interested?"

Buddy didn't know what some of these things were. And he definitely wasn't interested, except to the extent it gave Carl the strength to commit murders with a hatchet. He turned the conversation to the past. "You know the history of your grandfather's money, correct?"

Carl showed no emotion. "Yes."

"His work for Hitler and the Third Reich. His use of slave labor from Auschwitz. His moving money by suitcase to banks in Zurich."

Carl's face remained impassive.

Buddy said, "You know about all of it?"

Carl nodded. "I do. So do my brothers and our wives. Those were the sins of somebody in the first part of the last century. It isn't logical or appropriate to punish us, or to make us feel guilty, for what my grandfather did."

"But he took the money."

"No," Carl said, his voice suddenly hard-edged. "My grandfather didn't *take* the money. He used it to create a legitimate business that now employs more than eight thousand people."

Buddy stood. He didn't like the way Rebecca was pacing and glaring down at him. When he stood, he was a foot taller than she was. He said, "Could others think the money is still dirty? Could the grandchildren of those who worked for your grandfather during the Holocaust want revenge? To ruin or destroy your family, as your family—or your ancestor, at least—destroyed theirs?"

Rebecca shook her head vigorously. "That's impossible."

Buddy said, "Maybe. Maybe not."

Carl said, "I agree with my wife. Your idea of a murderous Jew taking revenge for his ancestors working in the camps in the 1940s doesn't seem credible. I've never heard of a Jewish individual or group murdering a businessman's heirs for using their labor at one of the camps."

Instead of arguing the point, Buddy said, "Think carefully. Maybe the murders have nothing to do with Brook Instruments or your current business. Can you think of any other reason someone from the *distant* past—not now but in the 1930s and 1940s—might want to harm your family?"

Carl was quiet for a long while. Then he said, "Yes."

Buddy stopped moving. He didn't think he'd heard correctly. "You *can* think of a reason for murder?"

Carl raised his eyebrows. "Not a good reason, but a reason."

"Yeah?" Buddy asked. "What is it?"

"Art."

"What do you mean, *art*?"

"Paintings," Carl said. "Paintings worth more than two billion dollars."

Chapter Thirty-Six

Carl Brook led him from the den into a room that functioned as a picture gallery. Robert Kahler and Rebecca followed as Buddy looked at the paintings, the blinds drawn and an opaque louver softening the rays coming through the skylight above. Two oak benches sat in the center of the room, but there was no other furniture.

Buddy said nothing, just went from canvas to canvas. Each was unfamiliar to him. He could determine only that these paintings were old and beautiful and the kind of thing he'd seen on the rare occasions Mei had convinced him to visit the Metropolitan Museum of Art.

"This one"—Rebecca pointed to a medium-sized painting in an ornate frame of dark wood—"is a self-portrait by Rembrandt. It's worth fourteen to fifteen million dollars."

Buddy stared at the figure in the painting. A middle-aged man with skin the tone of whole milk, red-rimmed eyes, and a bulbous nose. He tried to understand its value, but he couldn't. He couldn't comprehend how any painting could be worth $10 million or more. The entire concept made no sense to him.

Rebecca took a couple of steps. "And this one is a portrait of Neptune by Michelangelo."

Buddy moved closer to a large disc-shaped canvas that was about three feet wide by five feet high. The painting's colors were vivid and the figure of the Roman god smoothly and perfectly made. "*The Michelangelo?*" he asked. "The guy who did the ceiling of the Sistine Chapel?"

For the first time Rebecca smiled. "Yes. That Michelangelo."

"What's it worth?"

"More than two hundred million."

Buddy stared at the painting. He was made uncomfortable by the art and its value, by the opulent condominium. He wanted to be back out on the street, a place he understood and that gave him confidence. But he had more to do before he left. He said, "Hang on a minute, my phone is vibrating." Stepping away from the Brooks and Kahler, he feigned receiving a call on his iPhone. Facing Carl Brook, he pressed the camera icon and tapped the big red button to record video as he raised the phone to his left ear and pretended to answer.

"Yeah."

He pretended to listen, at the same time turning to his right, slowly. He walked a few steps and turned farther. He said, "That's right, we'll have to postpone that investigation. Yeah, caught up in something." He moved in a tight arc and said, "It's politics, Andrew. Yeah, we'll deal with it. Later." Then, obscuring his phone screen, he smoothly hit the video "Stop" button and slid the phone back into the breast pocket of his suit coat.

He turned to Carl. "Your grandfather bought all these?"

Carl nodded. "Yes, these and others in our place. The balance of his collection is divided between my three brothers."

"And your brothers' art is as valuable as yours?"

"Roughly."

Buddy thought about this fact. He said, "Far as we can tell, nothing has been stolen from any of your family. But why would someone kill because of the art?"

Carl put his hands in the front pockets of his jeans. He said, "The people who sold the paintings to my grandfather *needed* to sell them.

We could argue about whether fair market value was paid—I think it was—but the sales might not have been as voluntary as when Rebecca and I buy over at Sotheby's. However, in a safe-deposit box we have a bill of sale for each painting, signed by the seller. My grandfather kept the documentation, in case there was any trouble."

Buddy thought about the bills of sale. He said, "Your grandfather bought from people who were forced to sell?"

"Forced to sell? Possibly. You'll recall that during the Third Reich, Hitler seized the bank accounts of the Jews, so they needed cash money. My grandfather had lots of it. And so he traded something they needed in return for paintings they couldn't use. In the concentration camps," Carl stated, "nobody cared about Rembrandt. A painting wouldn't buy you anything, especially not your life. It would be taken from you instantly. So before the Jews were rounded up, my grandfather offered money, something useful to them. With money, they might obtain visas or some way out of Germany. How many survived, I've no way of knowing. Perhaps some. Perhaps none."

Buddy said nothing. He didn't trust himself to speak in a professional manner. Carl's glib attitude toward the Holocaust repulsed him. His face must have betrayed his emotions, because Carl offered a further comment that he likely hoped would make his grandfather's behavior less odious but only made it more disgusting.

"I mean, even if Jews had smuggled these paintings, rolled up or not, into the camps," Carl said, "the guards or commandants would have confiscated every last one. At least my grandfather paid. What else could he do?"

"And," Rebecca interjected, "paid a market price. Nobody back then could have guessed what a Rembrandt would be worth today."

Buddy didn't know about art, but he knew bullshit when he heard it.

He also knew that if somebody had bought paintings by Rembrandt and Michelangelo from his family—while they were under duress and about to be murdered—he'd be furious with that buyer and his descendants. He didn't think he'd kill those descendants, but someone more desperate or more convinced of the righteousness of revenge might. Perhaps someone *had* killed, and Carl and his family were next on the murderer's list.

He looked Carl in the eye and said, "I think I understand. Would you send me copies of the bills of sale for the paintings your grandfather bought? I need to confirm that someone isn't taking revenge on your family."

Robert Kahler said, "We can't share that information."

But Carl nodded. "Robert has copies. He'll send them over tomorrow. They must remain confidential, okay?"

"Agreed," Buddy said.

As they walked out to the foyer and the elevator, Buddy asked, as casually as he could, "Do you own any firearms?"

Carl showed no expression, and gave no answer.

Kahler said, "What are you driving at, Detective?"

Carl held up a hand toward his lawyer. He kept his eyes on Buddy. "Yes, I have two. An old French .22-caliber called a Gaston, and a newer Walther PPK."

At the description of the Gaston, Buddy stopped and said, "May I take both guns into custody for testing?"

Carl stared at him a long moment, then shrugged. "Certainly, Detective. Whatever I can do to help. Did you want me to send them over to your office?"

Buddy said, "I'll take them now, thanks."

Carl inhaled loudly and his face flushed. He hesitated a few moments, then disappeared into the condo.

Buddy waited with Kahler, but neither spoke. Buddy pulled out his phone to be sure it had recorded the picture gallery, but he wouldn't watch the video in front of Kahler.

Carl brought out two small cases holding the handguns and handed them to Buddy.

Buddy said, "Two branches of the Brook family, with the exception of Ben Brook, have been lost. Two branches remain. We're recommending that we provide your family with security twenty-four seven. Is that acceptable to you?"

Carl shook his head, his eyes impassive behind the black-framed spectacles. His face showed sadness but no fear. He said, "We appreciate the offer, but we have one hundred percent trust in our building's security."

And none in the NYPD, Buddy thought. Maybe Carl was right: the force had failed to protect Mei and Ben. "You're sure?" he asked.

"We're concerned," Carl said, lines forming on his forehead. "But the security here is top-notch."

Buddy asked, "Where were you last night?"

"Here," Carl told him. "I was at home."

Chapter Thirty-Seven

Buddy didn't like glass houses. He didn't like how other people could see into them—how they could see the house's inhabitants walking around, making coffee, watching the Knicks. He admitted that the converse was also true. Houses like Ward's, with enormous windows, provided expansive views of snow-covered lawns and woods. He liked the scenery and the light but wished for more privacy, especially now, when Mei and Ben were staying with Ward and he was so far away, in the city.

Rose Gallatin had opened the tall mahogany door to Ward's house. A moment later he was standing in the sunlight-filled living room with its large marble fireplace and its nine-foot Steinway concert grand with the lid fully open, as if it were on stage. Not a great memory for him. He listened for Ben's voice but heard nothing.

The late afternoon sunlight fell upon him and the piano. He realized that he was visible to anyone watching him from the woods. Not that anyone was watching him, other than the two security guards, each with a Rottweiler. He told himself that he was—and more importantly, Mei and Ben were—safe here. His imagination was creating phantoms where there weren't any.

"Ms. Gallatin," he said, "is there a way to . . . block the sunlight?"

She began walking toward the hearth. "Yes, there are blinds."

"I don't see any."

"They're recessed, until they come down."

She pressed a button on the wall, and a set of white blinds began extending down over the great glass windows. The hum of a hidden electric motor sounded. As the blinds reached to an inch above the maple floor, he noticed they didn't obscure all visibility from outside. He could see faint outlines of leafless trees in the wood bordering the yard. Which meant that someone in the trees might be able to see his shape—his height and weight and location in the room—if not particular details. This observation worried him but he concluded there was nothing he could do.

Chapter Thirty-Eight

In the trees at the edge of the lawn, a solitary figure stood downwind of the security patrols and the Rottweilers. He watched through high-resolution surveillance binoculars made by Brook Instruments as the police detective followed the older woman out of the mansion's living room.

The detective had stared directly into the thicket of wild raspberry stalks where the lone figure was hiding, but the detective's vision hadn't been sharp enough to see who was hidden in the wood.

The figure waited for nightfall.

Chapter Thirty-Nine

When Ms. Gallatin led Buddy into the pool room, Ben stopped playing. Ben pushed his wet hair out of his eyes and watched Buddy carefully.

Buddy took in the large lap pool—not the full-sized Olympic version he'd expected. He walked over to the side of the pool, rested one knee on the beige travertine, and smiled. "How are you, Ben?"

"I'm okay." He paused a moment, before saying, "The water moves. It pushes you to one end."

"You like that?"

"Yeah."

"I'm sure you're a better swimmer than I was at your age."

Buddy looked over at Ward, who was standing in the deep end, submerged in water up to his navel. Buddy saw the puffed-up deltoids and pectorals and knew that Ward had begun to work out and lift weights once again, as obsessively as he had before he'd been voluntarily committed for psychiatric care a couple of years earlier. He was handsome, in great shape, and a billionaire. Instinctively Buddy turned to Mei.

She'd been sitting on a teak chaise lounge. She wore a pair of Ward's blue jeans and a white button-down shirt with the sleeves rolled up to her elbows. He thought she looked beautiful and that she fit seamlessly into this kind of life. He didn't want to lose her, yet how could he compete with Ward, who had so much?

He stifled his jealousy and realized he shouldn't insult his brother. Mei and Ben's security depended on their remaining in this fortress.

But those insecurities remained as he stood in the large cedar-paneled room. When he saw Ward, he saw his father who'd abandoned him and his mother. Like the architect Louis Kahn, his father had two families. One day when Buddy was a boy, his father had divorced his mother and married Barbara Mills, heir to a manufacturing fortune. A year younger than Buddy, Ward was their secret son and, so, Buddy's half brother. Who soon received all his father's attention. His father became rich while Buddy and his mother were poor. Buddy's anger hadn't cooled when his father died.

Mei stood, smiled, and walked over to him as Ben returned to the pool. Buddy bent down and embraced her. Her arms went around his back and she squeezed much harder than usual. And she didn't let go. Not right away. Her obvious affection reassured him.

She said, "It's good to see you."

"Are things all right up here?"

"Yes. Last night just frightened me. And I'm tired. I sleep better when you're next to me."

"I do, too."

"Can you stay here tonight?" she asked as they parted.

"For dinner, but then I need to get back."

"You can't take a day off?"

His face showed disappointment. "I wish I could, but I'm running this case."

She said, "Vidas couldn't do it? Not even for a day?"

He shook his head. "He wasn't at my interview today with Carl Brook's family, and he hasn't seen Camp Kateri in the Adirondacks. I still have to give him direction, but in time he'll do more."

"I trust you," she said. "You'll solve the case."

He was relieved she didn't push him to stay, for he couldn't leave a serial killer to wander freely around New York. He was a hunter, and that's what he'd always be. He said, "I'll come up tomorrow or the day after, and I'll stay overnight. I promise."

She gave a wan smile. "I miss you when you're away," she told him. "That's all."

They sat side by side on the chaise lounge. From this perch they watched how Ben swam against the current and how, when he veered off to one side or the other, Ward held him at the waist and gently guided him back to the center of the pool.

Buddy said, "He needs practice."

"Yes," Mei agreed, "but give him time."

They were quiet. Buddy heard the Rottweilers outside bark loudly, but only for a moment. And then everything was still except for the sound of Ben's splashing and the hum of the lap pool's motor.

Chapter Forty

Buddy asked, "When you were staying with Mr. and Mrs. Sawyer, did they talk to you about where you might live?"

They were finishing the baked salmon that Ms. Gallatin had made for them, together with green beans and baked potatoes. Ward circled the table with the remnants of a second bottle of Cakebread Chardonnay—he'd drunk most of the first bottle by himself.

Ben glanced at Buddy, then lowered his eyes to his plate.

A shadow crossed Mei's face. She said to Ben, "We don't need to decide tonight, and your aunts and uncles will talk with you about it."

"No!" Ben said loudly, dropping his knife and fork on his plate, raising his face and looking at each of them in turn. "Not with *anyone* in my family."

"Would you tell us why not?" Buddy asked. "I thought you liked your aunts and uncles and your cousins."

His light-brown eyes opened wide. "I don't want to live with them, and I don't want them to adopt me."

"Would you tell us why?"

"Because I don't want to. And because when they're killed, I'll be killed, too."

Buddy realized that nobody had told Ben—or Mei—about the fate of his uncle Bruno and family. Ben lived in a ten-year-old's world of movies and video games, not the world of crime. He hadn't seen the *Gazette*'s three-inch headlines, hadn't read Sophie Bardon's innuendo-laced articles. He'd been out of school and remained innocent. This wasn't the right time or place, yet Buddy thought this news should come from him rather than someone else.

He got up, went around the table, and knelt beside Ben's chair.

The boy looked down at Buddy, whose dark eyes were alert and friendly.

Buddy put a hand on Ben's shoulder and said, "I understand your fear. Because last night your uncle Bruno, your aunt Natalie, and their family . . . they, uh . . . they didn't make it."

Ben stared at him, his eyes wide.

Buddy said, "I'm sorry, Ben." He pulled Ben toward him and kissed the top of his head.

Ben pushed him away, and as he did, Buddy could see the boy's eyes filling with tears, his face distorted with confusion and grief. Ben began to cry loudly and said, nearly screamed, "What *happened* to them? Was it like my mom and dad and Ellen-Marie?"

"No," Buddy said quickly. "No. They were"—he didn't want to use the word *gassed*—"they were poisoned. They didn't suffer."

"But they're dead?"

"I'm sorry." Buddy didn't take his eyes off Ben, but he knew Mei was as shocked as the boy. He added, "I'm going to catch the person who hurt your family, so you're safe for the rest of your life."

"No," Ben said. "No! I'll never be safe. Don't you see? Don't you see they'll get everyone in my family? No. No!" Ben shook his head frantically, and then he stopped. He held himself very still and said, "Don't you see? If I live with anyone but you, I'll die. You even have a bedroom for me. I want to stay with you and Mei. I want to live with you. If you won't let me, I'll *die*!"

Buddy didn't know how to respond. He'd known Ben for fewer than two days. This was too much, too fast. Despite what Ray Sawyer had said about the trust set up by Ben's parents, didn't his aunts and uncles have legal claims on him? Weren't they his godparents or something? And wasn't it Ray Sawyer's decision?

Chapter Forty-One

Buddy's mobile phone rang, ending his time at the dinner table. He was grateful for the distraction. He could see Mei struggling with Ben, trying to deflect Ben's wish to live with them. He didn't know what he'd have said. He supposed his phone had saved him from having to find a way to say no. He stepped away from the table and walked into the living room. He was glad the blinds were drawn, but guessed that the security guards outside could see his shape. Taking a few paces back from the windows, he placed a hand on the lid of the Steinway.

"It's Vidas," came his partner's voice.

Buddy turned back and saw Mei and Ben getting up from the table. They then followed Ward, carrying their dishes into the kitchen. Ms. Gallatin came for the serving dishes on the table, and for the water and wine glasses. He spoke into the phone. "What do you have?"

"No prints for Carl. But the SEC has prints for Dietrich Brook. At age twenty-two he worked for a few months at J. P. Morgan."

Buddy felt a rush of anticipation, mixed with the satisfaction that he'd been right about Dietrich. In the modern world you left prints and other trails he could track.

Vidas added, "They're sending over a copy of the prints tomorrow morning. We can compare them to what we found from the Carlyle evacuation."

"Found?" Buddy said. "What did you find?"

"SWAT was about to call you, but I wanted to give you the 411 and see what you're thinking."

Buddy felt his spirits sink. He guessed that taking identification from each person visiting, residing, or working in that building would yield nothing. And now, after a difficult day with new leads but few of them immediately promising, Vidas was calling to give him bad news to ponder on his drive back to the city.

"Buddy?" Vidas said.

"Yeah?"

"Thought you'd hung up."

"I'm just thinking."

"There's more to think about," Vidas told him, having already heard Buddy's theory of the descendants of Holocaust victims killing the Brooks. "There were fifteen people with German passports and three with Polish."

Buddy knew that if these people were visiting rather than residing in the country, they'd have come in through a border and would show up in the Automated Targeting System run by the Department of Homeland Security. He said, "Did you run them through the ATS?"

"Working on it."

"Any other foreigners?"

"We've got four Brits, one Saudi, a Russian, an Egyptian, two Indians, one from Sri Lanka, two Canadians."

"Any unknowns?"

"Three without ID."

"American?"

"Spoke English, but not necessarily American. But here's the thing," Vidas said. "These three—two men and one woman—gave names and addresses, but I followed up, and all their info was bogus."

Buddy tensed. "Made-up names?"

"Or made-up addresses, or both. The addresses they gave didn't exist. Except for the woman's. Turned out to be Pike Place Market in Seattle."

"So we have to print a suspect and then compare those prints to what we took last night inside the Carlyle. Without the prints, we have nothing."

"That's right. We need a suspect—and maybe Dietrich Brook is our man. I'm still checking the alibis you gave me for Carl and his son, John. But I've confirmed that Dietrich was in town."

Buddy thought that if the killer weren't Carl or Dietrich Brook, finding a matching print would be a needle in a haystack. He glanced toward the empty dining room. He needed to find Mei and Ben, before getting on the road back to Manhattan. It had already been a long day. But there was one thing he needed to confirm. Into the phone he said, "Would you call the medical examiner? See if Lucy Brook had a bruise on her chest, or a broken rib."

Vidas said, "Will do. Anything else?"

"See you at the shop," Buddy said. "Eight a.m."

He ended the call and saw Ms. Gallatin wiping off the dining room table. He asked, "Where are Mei and Ben?"

"She's reading to him in his bedroom."

"Which is where?"

"Follow the hallway behind the kitchen," she said, pointing.

Buddy thanked her. He went through the kitchen and along a wide hallway with its maple floor covered here and there with rectangular Oriental rugs in black and emerald. He looked ahead and saw that the hallway ended at a large glass window that looked out at the woods. There was one door on the right, which he saw was a bathroom, and two doors on the left. He came to the first door and looked into the room. He saw the glow of a reading lamp on the bedside table and closed blinds, but it was empty. He went farther, to the second door on the left, and looked into that room.

Sitting on a white duvet, Mei was reading to Ben. The boy was under the duvet and staring at the pages of the book, silently following along. Both leaned against the pillows in the queen-sized bed. Mei, despite her exhaustion, glowed in the light from the bedside table. Ben appeared small and vulnerable, but he was mesmerized by her soothing voice.

Buddy noted the vertical blinds were closed, just as in Mei's bedroom. He said, "Good night to both of you. I'm headed back to the city."

Mei stopped reading and looked up. Her expression warmed.

Ben sat up. "But you're coming tomorrow night, aren't you?"

"Yes. And I'll stay over then or the following night."

Ben seemed satisfied.

Mei said, "Come give me a kiss."

He went around to her side of the bed, leaned down, and gently kissed her lips. Then he kissed the side of her head.

As he did, she turned her face and murmured, "We have a lot to talk about."

Chapter Forty-Two

A few minutes later Ward stood with Buddy by the front door. When Ward put his hand up to the luminous green surface of the security system's fingerprint reader, the reader turned gray, and he unlocked the door.

They stood on the bluestone patio, their breath making clouds in the landscape lighting.

Ward said, "If the legal system will allow it, you're going to adopt Ben, aren't you?"

Buddy stuck his hands in his coat pockets and shook his head. "I can't imagine having a child. I mean, not really."

Ward turned toward him. "He's a great kid. Why not?"

Buddy said, "Easy for you to say. You have everything. All the resources you'd need for a kid."

Ward's eyes narrowed. "*I* have everything?"

"Yeah," Buddy said, waving a hand at the extensive grounds, the mansion. "Look around."

Ward kept his eyes on Buddy's. "Your perspective is off. It's *I* who envy *you*. From where I'm standing, you have everything. Purpose, for one thing. Yes, your job. It matters. Another thing you have? The love of a smart, very beautiful woman. And the possibility of adopting a boy like Ben. My wife"—here Ward pointed at Buddy's chest—"was murdered. And before that, before you and I had reconnected, she had three miscarriages. So we decided to adopt. But Anna was murdered in Rome. She's buried somewhere in the Tiber or out in the Tyrrhenian Sea. Her life ended and so did mine. Now the agencies would have nothing to do with me—I'm single and had a holiday in a psych ward. Now you're all I have."

Buddy shook his head, not understanding.

Ward said, "You, Mei, and Ben—if he joins your family. Our family."

Our family. Buddy stood in the cold, thinking about this. He hadn't known about Anna's miscarriages or her and Ward's decision to adopt. And he'd never have guessed that Ward might envy him. It seemed impossible. He'd always believed that Ward had been the one with everything.

He heard Ward go back inside and lock the door behind him. Buddy imagined him setting the alarm system. Although he looked around and didn't see or hear Ward's security service and the Rottweilers patrolling the grounds, he knew they were out in the darkness, just beyond the illuminated landscaping nearer the mansion. He noted the stillness and peacefulness of the big lawn bordered by woods.

It's safe here, he thought as he walked along the crushed-rock drive, climbed into the Charger, and began his drive back to Manhattan.

Chapter Forty-Three

Ben lay awake, listening to the sounds of the unfamiliar house. It was very quiet—much different than his family's town house in the city. He decided that he liked the quiet, but wished Buddy had been able to stay.

In the darkness he sighed and turned over.

He thought of Buddy's arrival that evening, the way Buddy had smiled and given him a big hug when he climbed out of the pool. Buddy had gone to the city for *him*, so that once again he'd be safe. It was just . . . it was just that he wanted Buddy to stay near him. He felt safe when Buddy was around. Almost happy. Not that he didn't miss his mother and father and Ellen-Marie. He missed them so much that if he *really* thought about them, he wouldn't be able to survive each hour of the day. Although he tried to suppress his memories, they were always hovering at the edge of his thinking.

He heard himself sob. Tried not to cry. But he couldn't stop himself. Couldn't halt the sense of utter loneliness. And yet he wasn't quite alone. He began to feel something like hope, or at least the possibility of hope, since he'd met Buddy and Mei. *They care for me,* he told himself as he imagined Buddy's comforting bulk and Mei's gentleness. *They care about me.* When he imagined going to live with his aunts and uncles, he felt sick with fear. He couldn't live with them. He had the premonition that if Buddy and Mei gave him up and forced him to live with Uncle Carl or Uncle Dietrich, he'd be killed in a way that was even worse than how his family had died.

He forced himself to inhale and exhale, slowly.

But then the familiar sensation of alarm overtook him. *What if,* he thought, *Buddy and Mei don't want me?*

What will I do?

Where will I go?

Who will love me?

Anyone?

Chapter Forty-Four

Mei removed the panic bracelet, set it on the bathroom vanity, and stepped into the shower.

The water fell onto her back, its heat soothing her neck and shoulder muscles. Her neck was sore from lying on Ben's bed and tilting down her head to read from *Charlie and the Chocolate Factory*. She'd no idea why Ward had the book in his library. Probably something from his own childhood. Ben had followed the story carefully for about twenty minutes and then turned aside to sleep. She'd slipped from the bed, set the book on the night table, and switched off the light. She'd wanted to read more, to feel his boy's form curled up against her, to hear his clear, inquisitive voice ask questions just a while longer. She thought his light-brown eyes so expressive, his long hair so handsome, his dependence endearing. She couldn't understand how anyone could wish to hurt him. Instinctively, she wanted to protect and help him.

And then she closed her eyes as she recalled his statement at dinner. *You even have a bedroom for me.*

When she'd told Buddy that tomorrow they needed to talk, she meant that they needed to talk about how he felt about Ben. She didn't know if she could love Ben, but she thought perhaps she could. But how would he—how *could* he—fit into their busy lives? How much did it matter that they weren't related to him? That she and Buddy had never met his parents and didn't know what they'd have wanted for him?

After her shower she dried off and opened the large tote that Buddy had packed for her. She found a sleeveless T-shirt and short pajama bottoms, and put them on. Having Ward see her once in almost nothing was one too many times. She withdrew her cosmetic bag, put moisturizer on her face, and then brushed her teeth. After switching off the light, crossing the hallway to her bedroom, and closing and locking the door, she climbed into bed and pulled the thick duvet over herself. She soon felt warm and comfortable. Tomorrow night, Buddy would join her here, and it would be hot under the duvet.

As she entered a deep sleep, she didn't remember that for the second consecutive night she'd left the panic bracelet on the bathroom vanity. She also didn't notice that the room was perfectly still. That the warm air coming through the registers had ceased. That the furnace had stopped. That the house had lost power.

Chapter Forty-Five

The lone figure outside the house moved forward.

The two men patrolling with Rottweilers had separated. They walked the property in clockwise circles.

After the lone figure had broken into the garage and switched off the power, he cut the line for the backup generator, cut the landline for the alarm system, and then slipped back into the woods bordering the house, always careful to remain downwind of the dogs.

The two men on patrol had seen the exterior lights go out, but instead of panicking, they'd kept their watch of the estate. Ward or Ms. Gallatin had shut off the lights, they assumed. They kept a buffer between them: one man and dog on one side of the house, one man and the second dog on the other. They believed this to be a comprehensive method, yet it was a mistake.

From downwind the figure crept up on one of the patrols behind the house. With stealth and grace he swung the hatchet at the guard's neck. No sound as the man fell. The Rottweiler turned in surprise and bewilderment. He stepped on the leash and with his fist hit the dog in the head, knocking it out. It lay there, panting softly.

He ran clockwise, around to the front of the house, gaining speed. Ahead were the second guard and Rottweiler turning the far corner of the house, where they'd pass by the garage and then move along the darkly lit rear. Faster. Faster. He was a blur of black in the black night, his face indistinct under a black mask.

He felt the anticipation of what would come. Of the young boy's death, which couldn't be helped. Tonight was simply another piece of the plan set in motion at Camp Kateri. For what the family had done. The figure inhaled the crisp night air. He was fully alive, agile, a powerful athlete. He charged toward the garage.

The second guard and Rottweiler marched through the darkness. As they rounded the garage and headed along the back of the house, the dog smelled blood and death ahead. It strained at the leash, pulling hard and growling. Its ears lay flat against its large head. The guard jogged forward, his attention in front of him. He didn't watch his six. He had no warning and likely felt a sharp pain, and then nothing, as the hatchet blade nearly decapitated him. The hatchet was swung with practiced ease. A wide arc that gathered speed as it traveled, barely slowing as it cut through skin, muscle, arteries, and the spinal column just below the brain stem. The guard crumpled to the ground, his heart pumping blood up through his carotids, throwing a foul mist into the air.

The dog turned and leaped at the lone figure, but the figure was ready. He kicked the dog backward, stood over it, and twice punched it in the head. Now it lay quietly, breathing but with its eyes closed.

Everything was still.

He approached the house and set the hatchet on the ground. This was a new tool, bought that very morning. Beginning New Year's Eve, this hatchet's predecessor had proved to be a very effective weapon. Tonight, this one had proved the same.

He removed the small mountaineering backpack that contained two items: a portable glass cutter and a Beretta 9 mm with a modified suppressor attached to the barrel. Wearing form-fitting rubber gloves, he stuck the gun between waistband and skin, and returned the hatchet, dripping with blood and tissue and cartilage, to the backpack. After withdrawing the glass cutter and fastening the backpack and putting it on, he approached the ground floor windows at the back of the house.

There appeared to be two adjacent bedrooms, each with a wide pane of glass set in a casement. Each windowsill measured about three feet off the ground. This made for great views but poor security. He approached one window and then the other, trying to see through the blinds to determine where the boy was sleeping. In the left bedroom, he could make out nothing. The blind fitted almost flush against the window jamb. A few paces to the right, he attempted to look between the other bedroom window's blind and the window jamb. He squinted. A muted night-light cast a weak glow over the room. The bed was a Japanese platform, very low. From the cold outside he could see what appeared to be a small person asleep. A small person with dark hair. The woman or the boy, he determined, it didn't matter which.

He held the glass cutter up toward the window. The base of the cutter had a black suction device on one side that would anchor it to the window. Extending out from it, connected to the base, was a stainless steel arm ending in a steel claw that held a diamond-tipped blade. Quietly but confidently he pushed the base and its suction cup against the window. After a moment he stopped supporting the cutter. Its seal was tight against the window. He put one hand on the cutter's base, and the other on the claw that held the blade. The steel arm was thirty-six inches long, and its diamond tip moved slowly in a large arc around the base as he pulled it in a circle. The blade made almost no sound as it cut the glass. He didn't stop halfway, to see if the figure in the bedroom had stirred. He simply continued. His pulse jumped.

When the blade had moved three hundred sixty degrees, he lifted the steel arm and blade away from the glass, and then in a swift, powerful motion, pulled on the base and suction cup.

The disc of cut glass popped out, almost silently, invisible in the darkness.

He waited ten seconds. No alarm. No sirens. But he knew the alarm system likely had a cellular backup. In five minutes the police would be here.

He peered through the round hole in the window and parted the blinds. No visible movement within the bedroom. He set the glass on the snow and peeled the rubberlike suction cup from the glass. After stowing the glass cutter in the backpack and again strapping on the pack, he approached the window. Put both hands through the hole and spread them wide on the wood floor. Then he pulled up through the hole and into the bedroom.

Chapter Forty-Six

Mei woke to an odd sound. Was it a piece of china set on a table?

Strange. And though she was under the heavy duvet, she felt the cold upon her face. A draft. But in Ward's house?

She heard the rustling of the blinds, sat up, and looked around. A dark figure vaulted into her room.

But she didn't freeze—she moved. Instinctively she knew that if she didn't get out of the room, she'd have no chance. No chance at all.

Slipping out of bed, she reached for the panic bracelet on her left wrist but found nothing but smooth skin. Then she remembered: she'd left it on the bathroom vanity across the hall. And then she remembered Ben.

She darted to the door, quietly unlocked and opened it. As she went into the hallway, she looked back and saw the black figure stand up in the bedroom, see her, and lunge forward.

She screamed and slammed the door behind her, turned left along the hallway, and ran to Ben's door. *Thank God,* she thought, when she found it unlocked.

She leaped into his room, slammed and bolted the door, and ran toward the bed. Her eyes swept the room. No figure dressed in black. No hole where the window was supposed to be. She went to the bed, grabbed the duvet and the blanket and sheet beneath it, and yanked them down. Ben stirred. Even in darkness she could see the panic brace-let on his right wrist. She took hold of his wrist, roughly, and began pressing at the bracelet, unable to make out the red panic button.

Crash!

The sound came from the door. Not a fist pounding but more likely a kick. And then another, louder. Bash! Bash!

But the door held. It was solid, and Mei had noticed the handle and lock were stainless steel, large and heavy.

Crack! Crack!

Mei heard the door shudder from the impact of bullets.

The shots were like clangs of metal on metal, loud in the silent house. Mei grasped Ben's arms and pulled him up.

He woke and said, "Mei. What? What are you *doing*?"

"Get down," she told him, pushing him onto the floor and lying on top of him. "We're being attacked!"

"No!" he cried. "We can't be!"

"Shhh," she said, holding him tightly. "Shhh."

Crack! Crack!

More pounding on the door. The room seemed to vibrate. Mei tensed and began to sob. Thirty seconds, she guessed. If she were lucky, she'd live thirty seconds. Ben might live five or ten seconds longer. Gripping his shoulders, telling him over and over that it would be all right, she wished Buddy were here. How sad it was to die like this, with so much life remaining, with so much love in her heart.

"It's all right," she told Ben. "We won't suffer. It's all right."

"No!" he shouted. "No, it isn't all right!"

CRASH!!!

The door opened. Mei tensed, ready for the bullet or the blade. Ben screamed, "*Buddy!* Help! Help!"

Chapter Forty-Seven

Ward heard the sound as he woke. At first he didn't recognize it. But three seconds later he knew the loud beeping came from the phone on his night table. The master bedroom was on the second floor of the house, in a different wing from the guest bedrooms where Mei and Ben were sleeping. *Had been* sleeping, he corrected himself. At least one of them was awake, unless in sleep they'd somehow set off a bracelet alarm by accident.

He'd take no chances. He jumped out of bed in his boxer shorts and pulled open the drawer of the night table. He took out a black .44 Magnum Research Desert Eagle and flicked off the safety. He didn't check to confirm that it had one round in the chamber, seven in the magazine, for he'd loaded it himself.

He stood to the side of the master bedroom door and listened.

Nothing.

With his left hand, he pulled open the door. He saw no one in the hallway. Crouching along the right wall, he stepped quickly but carefully, his bare feet making almost no sound on the maple floor. Easing around the corner to the staircase, he bobbed his head forward and saw nobody.

False alarm, he thought as he went down the staircase. He lowered his gun a few inches.

On the main level he headed through the living room toward the kitchen and the back hallway that led to the guest bedrooms. He heard and saw nothing unusual. And then he did. Complete darkness. Utter silence. The digital clocks on the oven and microwave were dark. There was no sound of the furnace. No air being pushed through the house. It was cold, nowhere near sixty-eight degrees. Either the backup generator had failed, or someone had disabled it.

Now he heard banging sounds, as if someone were trying to bash in one of the doors or the walls back in the bedroom area. Increasingly careful, he moved soundlessly into the kitchen, checking both sides of the center island for someone lying in wait.

Crash! CRASH!

The noise in front of him echoed through the house as he sensed someone approaching him from behind. He spun in a circle and found himself aiming his gun directly at Ms. Gallatin.

"Mr. Mills?" she said, ceasing all movement. "It's me—Rose."

"Stay behind me!" he ordered.

They heard new sounds from the hallway to the bedrooms. Ms. Gallatin might not have recognized them, but he did. Gunshots fired through a suppressor, what many referred to as a silencer. But in the quiet house after midnight, the sound of the shots was shocking, jolting him into a state of intense awareness.

Raising his gun, gripping it with both hands, he charged out of the kitchen and around the corner into the back hallway. He saw an indistinct figure in the faint green light of the battery-powered smoke detector attached to the ceiling. It wasn't Mei or Ben but larger than both. Dressed all in black with a black mask. Kicking at the door to Ben's room.

Ward heard the door lock give way.

He stopped, breathed in and then slowly out, to steady himself. Then he fired two shots. A double tap at the torso.

The figure spun backward, away from Ben's door, into the center of the hallway. Ward heard an expulsion of air, as if the bullet had hit the lungs or chest. The figure raised an arm, pointed at him. He heard a shot and jerked to the side. Then he fired again at center mass.

Another expulsion of air, but no grunt or groan or cry. The figure turned away from Ward and ran toward the window at the end of the hallway, not slowing or stopping but diving headfirst through the glass and out into the yard.

Even as the glass shattered, Ward fired another two rounds at the figure, and then rushed along the hallway to Ben's door. He stood outside and called, "Ben? Are you there? Are you all right?"

No sound came from inside the bedroom.

He felt a great weight on his shoulders. Ben was gone. The bullets from the intruder's gun had penetrated the door and struck the boy. But where was Mei? Had he lost her too?

"Mei?" he called from outside the door. "Are you all right?"

He listened carefully, thinking he heard the rustling of bed linens or clothing. "Mei?" he called again. "We're alone again. The attacker's gone." He turned and motioned for Ms. Gallatin, who'd followed him into the hallway, to come to the door. He didn't need to explain. She knew Mei was more likely to trust her than anyone else in the house.

She put her face near the doorjamb. "Mei? Ben? This is Rose Gallatin. It's over. The person who broke into the house is gone. We're standing out here. Are you and Ben all right? Would you please say something?"

A rustling noise from inside the room. Faint sounds of feet on the wood floor.

"Ward?" came Mei's voice.

"Yes. Are you and Ben hurt?"

"We're okay."

Sobs and then crying. Ward knew it was Ben, terrified by the attack, the third attempt on his life in recent days. He wondered how much longer Ben could survive, physically and mentally. How often someone could save him. Ward believed this was the last time. Fate couldn't be pushed too far. During the next attempt on the boy's life, he or Buddy might not be present. There might not be an escape down the fire stairs of the Carlyle Residences.

And there were no more secret tunnels hidden behind pantry shelves.

Chapter Forty-Eight

Buddy woke. Tensed at the sound of the burglar alarm. His arm shot out to the nightstand as he grabbed for the Glock.

But then he realized the loud noise wasn't the alarm system but the ringer on his phone. After letting go of the Glock, he picked up the phone and saw that it was Ward calling at one thirty. He swiped the screen and said, "What happened?"

Ward said, "Everyone's all right. But someone cut the power and disabled the generator and thus, the security system. The person then cut a hole in the window of Mei's bedroom."

Buddy felt his stomach tighten.

Ward said, "Mei got out in time, went to Ben's room, and locked the door. Someone tried to bash and shoot his way into Ben's room, but by that time I'd run downstairs and shot him. At least twice."

Thank God, Buddy thought. The case was solved. At last, Mei and Ben were safe. He said, "Describe the killer."

"I can't," Ward said, disappointment in his voice. "He had a Kevlar vest. There's no blood on the floor and he's gone."

Buddy felt like he was going to vomit. He slid out of bed, stood up, and began pacing the room. He breathed deeply and tried to relax his shoulders. His skin went hot and then so cold he began to shiver. "Fuck," he said. "You didn't go after him?"

"Couldn't. I had to make sure Mei and Ben were safe."

Buddy imagined them safe but with broken bones and smashed faces. "Injuries?"

"None. But they're shaken up."

Buddy stood straight. "I'm driving to your house. Now."

"That would be a waste of your time."

Buddy pounded his left heel into the Persian rug. "I'm coming up!"

"Look, Buddy. The entire Greenwich police department is here. The coroner's here, too. The attacker took down my two security guards *and* the Rottweilers. There's no way in hell anyone's coming back here tonight to do more damage. And I'm armed to the teeth."

Buddy reluctantly saw his brother's logic. He also considered who'd known Mei and Ben had gone to Greenwich. He hadn't told Chief Malone, Vidas, Ray Sawyer, or anyone else. How had the killer discovered their location? Someone, he concluded, must have guessed or followed them.

He said, "You've got to stay with Mei and Ben at all times."

"I will," Ward confirmed. "They're taking over the master bedroom. They'll try to rest, but I won't sleep at all. I'll be sitting in a chair, awake the entire night. You have my word. And then tomorrow I'll personally drive them back to Mei's place at the Carlyle. Tonight has shown us the killer knows everything. He's omniscient."

Chapter Forty-Nine

Several hours later, at dawn, a solitary figure stood at the southwest corner of Central Park. He looked past the cars going around Columbus Circle to the dark towers of Time Warner Center. The frigid wind had no effect on him. He was hot inside. He was ready.

But last night he'd dived through a window at the estate of Ward Mills. His forearms were sore where he'd gone through the glass. Body armor had protected him from the bullets, leaving only bruises. Yet he'd shrug off his failure to kill the boy last night. He'd use the soreness and pain as motivation. He knew he couldn't be stopped. He was free and he was right.

In the two years he'd spent planning the events that began on New Year's Eve at Camp Kateri, he'd studied the security protocols at Time Warner Center. He'd been in the buildings two dozen times. He'd observed the doormen, the guards behind the desk, the numerous cameras mounted to the high ceilings that observed and recorded everyone who arrived and departed.

He smiled to himself, knowing he'd learned how to gain entrance to the condominium unobserved and anonymously. The method he'd devised wasn't to walk in the front door. No, he wouldn't walk at all. He'd be brought in by someone else.

When darkness covered the city, he'd execute his plan. *Execute,* he thought. A fitting word.

He took a last yearning glance at the top floor of the tower, and then turned away and melted into the throngs of pedestrians going to work.

Chapter Fifty

That morning Buddy drove down to SoHo for an interview with Dietrich Brook. He sipped from a large black Dunkin' Donuts coffee. He ran the heater hot. After he'd pulled the Charger in front of a former warehouse on Greene Street, he looked up at the building's high walls—walls that seemed forbidding and insurmountable.

After climbing out, he stood for a moment at the corner and watched bundled-up people push forward to the curb. Many had wrapped their faces in scarves. Most wore stocking caps or other hats. Some wore sunglasses despite the grayness of the day. All had turned up their collars against the needlelike wind. He saw a homeless man shuffle up beside him. The man wore a stained red parka much too large for him, a Mariners baseball hat, and mismatched black leather gloves. He pushed a metal Whole Foods shopping cart filled with a sleeping bag and clothes that were old, greasy, dirty. Buddy looked at the man's face. He had a bulbous nose and bright blue eyes that were intensely focused on the stoplight.

Where was the man going? Buddy wondered. A shelter? A place to buy coffee and something warm to eat? A liquor store?

Buddy said, "You need anything?"

The man looked up at him and shook his head. "No, sir. I'm good. Gotta hoof it."

The light turned and the man shoved his cart into the intersection. He moved with purpose. Buddy wondered what kept him going, day after day in the cold. The basic animal desire to survive? Perhaps in the end this was all that mattered. Buddy knew he didn't have the inner strength of this man. He knew that if he didn't have Mei and his work, there wouldn't be a reason to keep going. Everything, including himself, would just stop.

He thought he should have offered the man five dollars. Or ten. For coffee or a sandwich or even for whiskey. But he was already turning toward the large building to his right.

After buzzing through the street-level security door, Buddy rode up in the elevator to an upper floor. Dietrich Brook opened the heavy stainless steel sliding door and offered his hand to Buddy. "Detective," he said.

Dietrich Brook was handsome, with graying brown hair over a patrician high forehead and a sculpted jawline. He wore black trousers of fine wool, a gray zip-up turtleneck sweater, and loafers with silver horse bits. Lean and almost gaunt, as if he ran marathons, and forty-eight years old, he was a strong and sleek animal with none of the puffed-up muscles exhibited by his brother Carl. His eyes were blue and abnormal. They weren't only cold and lacking expression, they seemed lifeless.

Buddy shook Dietrich's hand. It was as firm as Carl Brook's grip. *Strong enough to wield a hatchet with ease,* Buddy thought. He said, "Thanks for agreeing to an interview. I'm looking for any information that might help identify the person who . . . who has caused such damage to your family."

Brook's eyes remained expressionless, but his brow furrowed. "Thank you, Detective." His voice was in the middle range, calm but authoritative. "We don't know who's done these things or why."

"I understand," Buddy said. "But sometimes people have information they don't realize is important to the case."

Brook said, "We can spare a few minutes, but not long. Talking about it is painful."

"I understand," Buddy said again.

Brook watched him warily. "We grieve in our own ways."

Buddy nodded slowly.

Dietrich Brook led him into the condo. Long ago the high-ceilinged room with concrete columns and concrete floors and brick walls had been cheap. But no more. This much space in SoHo, with its twenty-foot ceilings and huge windows, was worth a fortune. The Brooks had decorated the living room with industrial-type furniture mixed with an enormous but low sectional the color of tobacco. There was modern sculpture of metal and plastic and fur, all of it ugly, to Buddy's eyes. And on a brick wall facing this hodgepodge hung an enormous painting that was everything its surroundings were not: beautiful, elegant, filled with light and placid water reflecting a shimmering sun above sepia-colored buildings.

Buddy stopped. He couldn't help it.

Dietrich Brook stood beside him and said, "Canaletto."

"What?"

"A who not a what. This is by Canaletto, the Venetian painter from the Renaissance. This shows a view of the Grand Canal, and here"—Dietrich Brook pointed—"is the Doge's Palace."

Buddy followed Brook's index finger, but every building on the Grand Canal looked like a palace to him. And what was a *doge*? He just nodded and wondered if the painting had once belonged to someone who'd been sent to the gas chambers at Auschwitz.

He wondered the same thing about another piece on the next wall, this one of a statuesque man with wings looking down upon a young woman who cowered in his presence. Buddy assumed it was the angel Gabriel—or was it Michael?—appearing to the Virgin Mary.

Dietrich Brook extended a hand toward the open kitchen adjacent to the living room and said, "Detective Lock, this is my wife, Lydia, and my daughter, Hayley."

Buddy looked over at them. Lydia Brook was tall and attractive, with chestnut-colored hair. She wore blue jeans and a cable-knit ivory-colored fisherman's sweater that fit her elegant frame perfectly. Except for her ashen skin, she was a classically beautiful woman fit for a billionaire. The daughter, Hayley, had fair skin, full lips, and blonde hair pulled into a braided ponytail. Around eighteen years of age, she wore tight Lululemon yoga pants, a blue chambray shirt with its top three buttons undone, and brown knee-high boots.

"Good morning," he said.

Lydia Brook stepped forward. "How is my nephew?"

Buddy's stomach tightened, but he said, very calmly, "He's well."

"Can he come to live here?"

Hayley added, "We miss him."

Buddy knew he was in danger of losing control of his emotions. "Ben's in police custody pending completion of this investigation," he told them. Relieved that nobody challenged him, he said, "I won't interview you together because I want your recollections, one at a time, rather than everyone's recollections jumbled together."

Dietrich Brook shook his head. "No, Detective. This morning you'll interview me. Nobody else."

Buddy showed no reaction, and when Dietrich Brook left the kitchen, walked past him, and headed through the cavernous living room to a back hallway, Buddy followed. A few yards into the hallway, they came to a door on the left. He entered an office complete with a modern desk with stainless steel legs and a glass top, and a futuristic black chair. His feet made a scratching noise as he trod across a rug made of dried grasses.

Dietrich Brook sat in the chair behind the desk but said nothing.

Buddy sat in an armchair on the other side of the desk. He switched on his digital audio recorder, set it on the desk, and faced Dietrich Brook.

"Dietrich Brook," he began, "did you hear or see anything unusual on New Year's Eve?"

"No," Dietrich said, without hesitation.

"Think about it for a while," Buddy suggested.

"I have, but there's nothing."

He watched Dietrich's eyes. They were opaque, an unreadable mask.

Buddy said, "No guests present? No unusual staff?"

"No."

"Did any member of the family argue with any other member of the family?"

"Not that I recall."

"No disagreement with any of your brothers?"

"No."

"You didn't argue about whether to sell Brook Instruments?"

Dietrich Brook smiled. "I wouldn't say we argued. Our positions were nothing new." Dietrich Brook pushed out his chin, perhaps to show that he'd accept no guff from Buddy. He continued, "For the past several years, Carl and I have wanted to sell the company, and Alton and Bruno have not."

Buddy nodded once and changed direction. "Has anyone filed a claim or made noises about filing a claim against your art collection?"

"No one."

"Do you know of any claims against any of your brothers' art collections?"

"No, I do not. And the deaths of my brothers have nothing to do with art."

Buddy raised an eyebrow. "How can you be sure?"

Dietrich opened his hands. "Because the collections are worth more than two billion dollars. Most of the paintings are hung with French cleats, so you can lift them off the walls fairly easily. Yet not one of them is missing."

"What about the work that Jewish prisoners were forced to perform for your grandfather's company during the Third Reich? Could any of their descendants be after your family?"

"No."

"You haven't been contacted or threatened by any Holocaust survivors or their descendants, either in written or oral communications?"

Brook's face showed irritation. "Oh, I suppose people might contact us, asking for money—*reparations*, they call it. But we pass those letters on to our lawyers, who handle it. I give it no attention."

Buddy stared into the dead blue eyes. He said, "Are you sorry for what your grandfather did?"

"Not at all," Dietrich Brook replied, shaking his head. "The work he gave those people kept them alive as long as possible. Who knows, maybe they survived because of my grandfather."

Buddy wasn't sure if Dietrich really believed his grandfather bore no responsibility for using Jewish slave labor during the Holocaust, but he knew he'd get nothing more on the subject. So he took the gloves off. It was part of the job. He said, "Now that your brothers Alton and Bruno are gone, you and Carl can sell Brook Instruments, can't you?"

"No."

"Won't you and Carl cash in?"

Dietrich's face turned dark red. "Detective, you're implying I killed my brothers and their families for money. What kind of idiot are you?"

Buddy ignored the insult. "Don't Alton's and Bruno's shares come to you and Carl?"

Dietrich Brook's eyes didn't show anger but instead became cold blue discs. With strange calm he said, "Detective, you're out of your depth."

Buddy kept up the barrage. "Since you and Carl control the majority of the voting shares of Brook Instruments, why can't you vote to sell it?"

"Because all four blocks of shares must agree."

"So who has control of the shares that belonged to Alton?"

Dietrich Brook said nothing.

Buddy was stunned. He'd figured it out. *Of course.* A $24 billion transaction was being held up by a ten-year-old boy—or by his trustee, Ray Sawyer. And if that ten-year-old boy were to die, then the shares he owned would be divided evenly between Carl and Dietrich, and they'd have total control of Brook Instruments and its $24 billion sale price. They could sell Brook Instruments to GE, and they could turn around and sell as much of their GE stock as they wanted. The money would make their families important and famous for generations.

He stared across the small room at Dietrich Brook, who again thrust his chin forward in a gesture of invincibility. The assertion of privilege made Buddy's chest burn.

Their silence lasted a minute, perhaps longer.

Dietrich got up from the chair. "You're finished, Detective."

Buddy kept the digital audio recorder running. "Mr. Brook, would you give me copies of the bills of sale for the paintings you inherited from your grandfather?"

Brook's eyes narrowed. "Fuck off."

Buddy stood, picked up his audio recorder, and left the room. With Dietrich two paces behind him, his walk to the foyer was without incident. As he pushed the button for the elevator, the heavy metal door behind him slammed into its frame with such force that it clanged in the small lobby.

Chapter Fifty-One

Mei saw the office towers of Manhattan come into view above the horizon. She turned around in the front seat of Ward's Range Rover to look back at Ben. His expression was anxious. He was sitting quietly in the plush black leather, well dressed but small and fragile. He was only ten, but he wasn't stupid. He was aware of the risk they were taking by returning to Manhattan. But the events of last night had shown that nowhere was safe. Danger made Mei yearn to be in the same city as Buddy, even if he spent all day and even into the night at work. Ben, she knew, wanted the same.

"You okay?" she asked Ben, though his face gave her the answer.

For a moment he was quiet. Then his eyes brightened as he said, "Do you have a gun?"

She shook her head. "No."

Ward said, "You will."

She turned to him—he was in the back seat, behind the driver—and studied his face to see if he was joking, but his expression was grim, determined. She said, "I don't know how to use a gun."

"Yes, you do."

"I've never even *held* one," she told him. "I can't be like you, rushing down a hallway in the dark and firing at someone."

"You don't have to be like me," he said. "But you need to be able to defend yourself. I've brought a gun for you, a small .38 caliber."

She looked at him. "Where is it?"

He patted the messenger bag between his feet. "Here. I'll give it to you when we're at your place."

"I won't accept a gun," she said. "And that's final."

Ben's voice filled the SUV. "But Ward *saved* us with a gun."

Mei hesitated.

Ward glanced at her, saw her expression, changed the subject. "Ben," he said calmly, "would you like to go back to school this week?"

Ben nodded. "I want to be in school, but not *my* school. Everyone will ask me about what happened, and I won't know what to say. And how can you and Buddy protect me?"

Ward reached over and put a hand on his arm. "I know of a great school for kids like you. Top notch security. I'll call and see if we can visit later today. I'll hire two bodyguards to take you there and back. And they'll guard Mei's apartment, one in the lobby, one in her foyer."

Mei didn't like how Ward offered something or made a decision and expected everyone to agree and accept it. She felt herself stiffen. She said, "Bodyguards are appreciated, but I won't have one inside my apartment. I don't have room for them, and I want some privacy."

"No," Ward said, all the fingers with his raised hand extending outward. "You'll be much safer with one guard in the building lobby and one in your foyer. It's absolutely necessary to have a guard with you, Mei."

Mei saw the logic, but she wouldn't live in a prison. She didn't like Ward's hand so near her face. And she didn't care for his controlling tone. Thank God Buddy managed to be both strong and respectful. She said, "Guards anywhere but in the apartment. That decision is final. You can put one in the building lobby and one in the exit stairs and even a third in the elevator, but nobody in the apartment."

Ward lowered his hand and sighed. "All right. But would you let me give you the small revolver? Just until Buddy arrests the killer? Just in case someone gets past the bodyguards?"

Mei began to refuse, but Ben interrupted.

"Ward's gun is the only reason we're alive," he told her. "We must have a gun with *us*."

Mei didn't respond. Not right away. She didn't want to shout at Ben or Ward. Instead she considered Ben's logic and decided it was correct. She hated guns, yet she wanted no guards in her house, and she wanted Ben to be calm. "I'll agree to the handgun," she said evenly, while silently promising herself that she'd never use it.

◆ ◆ ◆

Once they'd settled into her apartment, she left Ben in the kitchen, where he snacked on an apple she'd cut for him. She led Ward into the master bedroom and closed the door.

Ward carried the messenger bag. Black ballistic nylon. He unzipped it and withdrew a nylon case in the shape of a gun. He unzipped the case and pulled out a small black revolver. It had a snub nose and a stock with a nubby surface to enhance the grip. He opened the gun's cylinder, held it up to the light, and confirmed that all six chambers were empty. He handed it to her.

She took it in her right hand. It was cool. Heavier than she expected. She looked up at him.

He said, "There's no safety. Just point and shoot. Like a camera."

"How far away do I have to be?"

"Any distance. But this one's for a relatively close target. If you shoot at someone a football field away, you'll miss. If you're shooting someone in this bedroom, you'll hit him. Just aim for the center mass. Nothing fancy like aiming for arms or legs or shoulders or head. Chest only. Got it?"

"I think so."

He reached into the bag and took out a box of fifty rounds. He handed it to her.

She took it quietly.

He said, "Normally I'd tell you to keep the gun loaded. But with Ben in the house, I'd keep the gun in the top drawer of your night table and the ammunition on an upper shelf of your closet. Somewhere Ben can't reach. Ideally you'd lock everything. Do you have a safe?"

She shook her head.

"Then keep the box on the top shelf of your closet. You see how to do this? You press this small button—it's an ejector release—and the cylinder rotates out. You put in the rounds and push the cylinder closed. Then you aim and fire. Okay?"

She nodded, just staring at the gun and considering what it could do. She said, "Would you give me a moment?"

He set the gun case on the bed, closed the flap of the messenger bag and put it over his shoulder, and then left the room, closing the door behind him.

Wishing away the revolver, she set the box of ammunition on the bed and took up the gun case. She zipped the revolver into the case, went into her closet, used her elbow to flick on the light switch, kicked the stool to the far corner, and stepped up on it. She pushed the gun case under a stack of sweaters, far back on the top shelf, against the wall. Then she climbed down, went out to the bedroom, picked up the ammunition, and took it into the closet. Again standing on the stool, she pushed the box under the pile of sweaters to the right of the sweaters under which she'd hidden the revolver. Then she climbed down, kicked the stool to the other side of the closet, and walked out into the bedroom. She stood there and realized she was breathing rapidly and perspiring. She noticed the faintest indentation on the bed where she'd set the box of fifty rounds.

She reached out with both hands and smoothed it away.

Chapter Fifty-Two

Tourists out on the streets braved the bitterly cold air that went right through Buddy's overcoat. He raised the coat's collar and pulled his leather gloves on more tightly. *At least the sidewalks aren't as crowded as usual,* he thought, as he made his way over to West Forty-Seventh Street. He had a private matter to deal with over his lunch hour. Something that had to remain secret from everyone on earth except himself and one man.

Steam rose, white and ghostlike, through the sidewalk grates, proof of a massive subterranean world that powered the one Buddy could see. Above him soared residential buildings and office towers of granite, limestone, steel, and glass. Hundreds of feet below him ran the sewers, power lines, and subway trains that burrowed through a maze of tunnels. Connected worlds, he thought, but the connections were often invisible. He looked into a store window and caught his reflection, his expression. His face was blank, his eyes tired.

Forty-Seventh Street between Fifth and Sixth Avenues, a small doorway with a smaller rectangular window. Mid-block, and you wouldn't notice it unless you knew what to look for. He pressed the buzzer to the right of the door and looked up at the camera mounted on the lintel. A moment later he heard the buzzer. The lock pulled back. He pushed on the door and stepped inside.

From the breast pocket of his overcoat, he pulled a stack of hundred-dollar bills. They were bound neatly with a paper band, as if they'd just been printed or put into circulation by a bank. Or they'd been turned into NYPD's property clerk after a drug bust, although they hadn't. He set the stack of bills on the glass counter.

The old man took the money quickly, nodded once at Buddy, and then pushed a small package across the counter. Buddy picked it up and put it in the same breast pocket of the overcoat where the money had been.

The man said, "You not check it?"

Buddy shook his head. "I trust you. Why don't you count the money?"

The old man shrugged. "I trust you."

They nodded once to each other, and then Buddy backed slowly away from the counter and went out the door and onto the sidewalk along Forty-Seventh Street. He pulled the door closed and confirmed the lock was set. He glanced once more through the rectangular window, but suddenly the entire shop was dark. He couldn't see the old man.

Chapter Fifty-Three

Early afternoon, Buddy stood on the sidewalk, looked up, and saw the security camera.

Vista was a private school, kindergarten through eighth grade, for the children of the rich and famous. It was located at the intersection of Tenth Avenue and West Twenty-Eighth Street in Chelsea, and tuition, at $45,000 per student per year, didn't include books, music lessons, field trips to Los Angeles and London and Paris, or donations to frequent capital campaigns.

He brought his eyes down and followed Mei and Ben inside. They stood at the security desk and showed their driver's licenses to an armed guard. The guard typed their information into his computer and issued them visitor badges, and a third badge to Ben, though he had no identification. All three of them held up their badges to a scanner embedded in the flat surface of a three-foot-high electronic turnstile. The scanner flashed green. They walked into the school lobby.

Buddy thought that someone with a glass cutter—someone like the person who'd tried to kill Mei and Ben at Ward's house—could get in through a perimeter window, but not silently or without being noticed by the many students and teachers. Vista was probably the most secure elementary and middle school in the United States. Buddy knew why. He turned around and saw a movie star picking up her daughter, and a news anchor picking up his daughter and son. He tried not to stare. He was from New York and was supposed to be jaded.

He felt a hand on his shoulder and tensed.

"Relax, Buddy." Ward's voice.

Buddy turned to see Ward standing beside him in a navy-blue windowpane suit with a white shirt and a light-blue tie with a pattern of little white Ferraris across it. His sandy-colored hair was pomaded back. He'd draped a camel-hair overcoat over one arm. Stylish and clean-shaven, Ward seemed at ease at the school for the wealthy.

The headmaster met them. Or met Ward. He was about fifty years old with salt-and-pepper gray hair, a fair complexion, eyeglasses with faux tortoiseshell rims, and a blue suit that wasn't as nice as Ward's. He extended a hand. "Good afternoon, Mr. Mills. I'm Ty McConnell. Mr. Bloomberg has great praise for you."

Ward shook his hand and said, "You're very kind, Mr. McConnell. Mike's an old friend. May I present Buddy Lock, Mei Adams, and Ben Brook?"

"How do you do?" McConnell said, taking Buddy's proffered hand and then bowing slightly to Mei and Ben. "I'm happy to give you a tour of our school. Normally there is a long wait-list, especially at Ben's grade level. But in Ben's case we'd make an exception. If we can't help a friend in need, what good are we?"

Mei said, "Thank you, Mr. McConnell."

"Come along, then," he told them, and ushered them to the right and along the main-floor hallway.

Halfway down the hallway they came to a set of doors on the left. McConnell led them through the doors into an auditorium complete with rows of cushioned seats on a floor slanting down toward a large stage. Buddy thought it was better than some of the professional theaters at Lincoln Center. Then he remembered that many of the Vista students had parents who performed at Lincoln Center and on Broadway. Maybe not the most normal environment for a boy, Buddy thought, yet safety was key.

When they'd left the auditorium, Mr. McConnell led them into a classroom.

Ben smiled as he saw a full-sized velociraptor on display. "Hey, look at this!" he said, turning to look back at Buddy and Mei with an expression of joy. An expression they'd never seen.

Responding to Ben's enthusiasm, Mr. McConnell described the dinosaur and how it had been extinct for millions of years. Buddy listened carefully, relieved Ben seemed comfortable here. He observed the skeleton's chocolate-colored bones. Its eye sockets were large and its teeth sharp. The claws on its hind feet curved like sickles. It had been a vicious predator, McConnell explained, expert at taking down weaker animals.

Buddy considered asking McConnell to move on, away from any subject related to death. Yet Ben's face was alert, hanging on the headmaster's every word. He crouched down to be nearer the feet. His right hand touched one of the dinosaur's claws. He tilted his head as he studied the ancient animal. Buddy realized that instead of being frightened, Ben was intrigued and possibly inspired. It seemed Ben wanted to be predator rather than prey. Buddy thought that wish might save him.

Chapter Fifty-Four

Midafternoon in the bull pen at the Nineteenth Precinct, Vidas rolled back his chair and looked into Buddy's cube. He said, "No surprise, but you can't go to your local hardware store and buy enough cyanide to kill a family. So that leaves us with national suppliers. But even that's mostly limited to educational and industrial research facilities."

Buddy turned to his partner and listened carefully. He saw Vidas's loosened tie and tired eyes, but his partner's face showed eagerness and the excitement of the hunt. Buddy said, "A high school or university student couldn't get his hands on it?"

Vidas moved his head right and left as he thought. "Yeah, a student could get enough to poison someone by putting it in a soda, but he couldn't get the quantity needed to gas four people."

Buddy nodded, thinking Lucy Brook's mystery boyfriend was looking less and less likely as a killer. "So we go up the food chain. Who can get bigger quantities?"

"Distributors. Manufacturers."

"Any in the New York area?"

"Only one. A place in College Point, by La Guardia."

Buddy stood. "Come on. Let's knock on the door."

◆　◆　◆

A bulb of land in northwest Queens that jutted into the East River, College Point was packed with retail, residential, and industrial buildings.

Vidas pulled his unmarked Ford Fusion into a small parking lot and truck dock by a low-slung gray-painted warehouse building on Fifteenth Avenue. A sign on the service door read "Employees Only."

Buddy climbed out of the car, walked up to the door, and tried the knob. It was icy cold and wouldn't turn. He pounded twice on the metal door, took a step back, and held up his badge wallet.

A man opened the door. He was tall, very thin, disheveled, with graying blond hair and large glasses atop a long nose. He wore jeans, hiking boots, and a fleece pullover with "Blu Chemicals" stitched onto the breast pocket.

Buddy said, "Detective Lock, NYPD. This is my partner, Detective Vidas."

The man didn't respond, only pushed open the door and ushered them inside.

A moment later Buddy and Vidas were standing in an office. Behind them a metal lattice separated them from dimly lit shelves weighed down with containers of different colors, sizes, and materials. The tall, thin guy had a metal desk and an old metal chair with a seat of olive-green vinyl. He pointed at Vidas and said, "You called for an appointment half an hour ago?"

Vidas smiled. "Yes, sir. We're investigating a crime involving industrial amounts of cyanide. As you're the primary distributor in the New York area, we thought we should start with you."

The thin man watched Vidas carefully but gave no response.

Vidas continued, "Have you sold large quantities in the past twelve months?"

The man stared at Vidas through his large eyeglasses. He didn't move or say anything.

Knowing Vidas was about to keep talking, Buddy touched his elbow. *Give the guy room,* Buddy thought. *Let him answer.*

The thin man observed the gesture but still didn't reply. After a long moment he dropped onto the green vinyl chair and touched his computer mouse with an index finger.

Buddy couldn't see the computer screen, but he waited patiently. He saw the thin man click the mouse a few more times, and then the printer on the desk whirred and spit out two pages. The man stood and handed them across the desk to Buddy.

Vidas moved next to Buddy as they looked at the information on the sheets. Date of purchase, names of institutions, quantity purchased, and dollar amount of sale were displayed in neat columns.

Buddy scanned down the list of names until one name, in particular, struck him. In October of the previous year, Blu Chemicals had sold a large quantity of cyanide to someone having an address that Buddy recognized.

He stared at the name: C. Brook Inc.

Vidas drove them by One Police Plaza just north of the exit off the Brooklyn Bridge in Manhattan, on their way back to the Nineteenth Precinct farther uptown. They'd been summoned, without explanation, by Chief Malone. When they were waiting outside his office, a technician in a white lab coat took a chair opposite them. He kept his eyes from theirs, focusing instead on his mobile phone. Under the phone he held a slim brown folder.

Buddy thought he was about to be ambushed. He turned to Vidas and raised an eyebrow. Vidas only shrugged.

Chief Malone opened his office door and waved them in, making no apology for keeping them waiting. The technician followed, having dropped his phone into one of his lab coat's pockets.

Malone went around his desk but remained standing. None of them sat down.

Malone said, "This is Chris Donohue from ballistics. Tell the detectives what you found, Chris."

Chris Donohue turned to them. He said, "Carl Brook's Walther PPK doesn't match the bullet you found in the wall behind the painting in Bruno Brook's foyer. But Carl Brook's other gun, the .22-caliber Gaston, is an exact match to the bullet and shell casing. The pin in the antique gun leaves a star-shaped groove on the bottom of the casing. Which CSU found, by the way, under a chair in the living room off the foyer. The gun was fired recently and not cleaned. Plenty of GSR—gunshot residue—on the grip, stock, and trigger. And a clear set of prints."

Malone looked at Buddy.

Buddy kept his expression calm.

Vidas said, "We just got back from College Point." He held up the computer printout from Blu Chemicals. "Back in October, Carl Brook bought a shitload of cyanide, the main ingredient in Zyklon B."

Buddy sensed he was about to be railroaded into doing something he wasn't ready to do. Not yet, anyway. He prepared to dig in his heels as he said, "So the idea is that on New Year's Eve, Carl kills Alton and family—except for Ben—and then Bruno and family here in Manhattan, all so he and Dietrich can sell Brook Instruments to GE?"

Malone put his giant hands on his hips and nodded. "Smells like motive, doesn't it?"

Vidas said, "Yeah, Chief."

Buddy said, "Carl is already rich. Why would he do it? Especially when he knows he'd be our prime suspect, along with his brother Dietrich?"

Malone widened his eyes. "We're dealing with a serial killer. He wants more money and he's a fucking psychopath. He thinks he can outsmart us and get away with it."

"He *has* money," Buddy repeated, aware that his reasoning sounded weak. Yet when he recalled Carl Brook, a privileged billionaire who flew on private jets and had a huge condo in Time Warner Center, he didn't see him taking the extreme risks inherent in wiping out much of his extended family. Or even having the stomach for murdering with a hatchet. But he'd been wrong before and might be wrong now. He said, "What are you suggesting, Chief?"

Malone's skin reddened. "Today I'm suggesting you focus on this guy and move toward an arrest. We've got motive and we can tie him physically to the crime scene."

"His *gun* to the crime scene," Buddy said. "We don't know who fired it."

Malone's face tightened. He stared at Buddy for a moment, then growled, "Today it's a suggestion. Soon it will be an order. So get out of here and go to work."

Buddy didn't move. He kept his eyes on Malone's. He said, "It feels too easy, Chief. The gun, the cyanide, all of it."

Malone shook his head angrily but didn't respond. Just pointed at the door.

Taking his time, Buddy turned and walked out.

Chapter Fifty-Five

Two hours later, Buddy stood with Mei and Ben at the cologne counter at the Bergdorf Goodman men's store, Fifth Avenue and East Fifty-Eighth Street.

Buddy looked down at Ben and said, "You told Ray Sawyer you noticed an unusual scent at Camp Kateri. I'm sorry for asking you to remember that night, but I need your help."

Ben said, "I want to help. But I don't know what I smelled."

"That's why we're here," Buddy explained. "And you weren't imagining things. Your cousin Ariel told me she smelled vetiver on New Year's Eve."

Ben asked, "What's vetiver?"

Mei said, "It's an ingredient in perfumes and colognes."

"This is a long shot," Buddy admitted, "finding a particular cologne or perfume and tying it to the killer, but I'd like to try. Ben, will you help me?"

Ben nodded. "Yes."

Buddy took his hand as they faced the display case. Bottles of cologne stood on a silver tray atop the glass counter. Behind the counter stood a well-dressed sales clerk with perfectly cut brown hair, a dark suit, white shirt, and solid navy-blue tie.

Buddy badged the clerk and said, "As part of an NYPD investigation, I need this young man to sample all of your colognes. Okay?"

"Yes," said the clerk, then pressed his lips together to show he wasn't happy but would do it. "Some are here on this tray," he explained, waving his hand over the tray, "and some are under the counter. I'll set all of them on the counter so that you can go through them quickly and efficiently."

And be on your way, Buddy thought.

Ben said, "Do I have to put all the cologne on me?"

The clerk smiled and looked across the counter and down at Ben. "Not at all. I'll spray or dab one of these cards"—he picked up a small white card printed with the words Bergdorf Goodman—"and then hand it to you. Will that be all right?"

"Yes."

"Good. Allow me to set out the bottles."

They watched as the clerk bent down and pulled bottles from shelves in the glass case and lined them up in a neat row on the counter. When he'd finished, he pointed to each bottle and counted aloud. "Seventeen," he said, looked up, and smiled at Ben and then at Buddy. "All right? Let's begin on your left, my right, okay?" Without waiting for an answer, he took up one of the cards, held the test bottle a few inches from the card, and sprayed. Then he waved the card in the air, back and forth, to reduce the concentration of the scent, and offered it to Ben.

Ben took it and smelled. He shook his head. "That isn't it." He handed the card to the clerk, who dropped it in a wastepaper bin they couldn't see. The clerk bent to return the corresponding bottle to one of the glass shelves below the counter.

"Scent number two," said the clerk, holding up another card and spraying atomized liquid on it. He waved the card back and forth and handed it to Ben.

Ben held it up to his nose and inhaled. He moved the card away and held it up again.

Buddy leaned toward him but said nothing.

Ben inhaled a second time. Slowly he shook his head. "No."

The clerk removed the bottle, set it on one of the glass shelves below the counter, picked up another card, and sprayed it with the third bottle in the row. He handed it over to Ben.

After inhaling, Ben thought for a moment and then shook his head.

This is hopeless, Buddy thought. *He won't remember. He could get it wrong. Or he could make it up to please me, so I won't send him to live with another family when this is all over.*

The clerk and Ben repeated the process, over and over and over again. Mei put an arm around Ben's shoulder and kissed the top of his head.

He looked up at her, his eyes fearful and sad.

Mei smiled. "Don't worry. If the scent you remember isn't one of these, Buddy has other ways of getting the killer."

"That's right," Buddy said. "This won't make or break my investigation. And when we're done here, we'll go to Starbucks and get you a hot chocolate. But you might as well finish."

Ben nodded and turned to face the counter. The clerk handed Ben another card.

He sniffed and shook his head.

Again.

And again.

Ben's shoulders dropped. Buddy's spirits dropped.

Ben took another card and inhaled. He hesitated a moment, then shook his head and returned the card to the clerk.

Buddy clenched his fists. Why had he subjected Ben to this wild goose chase? This exercise was traumatizing the boy, forcing him to recall the most awful moment of his life.

Ben inhaled while holding up another card. He waited a moment. He inhaled again. He brought the card down and set it on the counter.

The clerk made to reach for the card.

Ben shook his head. "No."

"I'll throw it away for you," the clerk said.

"*No!*" Ben raised his voice and took up the card. A third time he brought it up to his nose and sniffed.

Mei looked at Buddy.

Buddy held his breath.

Ben turned around. He was smiling. And then he started to cry. He held the card out to Buddy.

Buddy took the card and smelled it. He recognized lime and some other things, maybe leather. He looked at the clerk. "What's in this stuff?"

The clerk nearly blanched at "stuff," an inelegant word. He said, "It's a masculine scent, sir, with lemon and lime and bergamot at the top, but it's anchored by vetiver."

"Vetiver?"

"That's right, Detective. More in this cologne than most of the others. Vetiver gives it the earthy undertone that forms a nice contrast with the lemon and lime."

Mei stood behind Ben and put her arms around him, her hands on his chest.

The clerk said, "Is everything all right?"

Buddy ignored the question and asked, "What is this?"

The clerk picked up the bottle and held it out to Buddy. "It's called Zizan and made by Ormonde Jayne of London. A wonderful scent, don't you agree?"

Buddy studied the bottle. The cologne's color was similar to bourbon. "Can I buy this anywhere?"

The clerk knit his brow. "Not just anywhere, but other places besides Bergdorf's."

Buddy asked, "How much for this small bottle?"

"One hundred fifty dollars."

Mei touched Buddy's arm. "Do you need it for your investigation?"

He knew she was offering to buy it for him, yet he shook his head. He took out his notebook and wrote down the brand of cologne. He set the card on the counter. "Thanks, man."

The clerk shrugged. "Sure, Detective. Can I interest you in a scent?"

"Not today."

Buddy crouched down until his face was near Ben's. He looked carefully into Ben's light-brown eyes. For the first time he noticed hazel flecks in the irises. He said, "Thank you for going through that. I know it was hard, and I'm sorry for asking you to do it. Now I've got to get back to work, but I'll see you in a couple of hours."

Ben didn't move. "But did I help?" he asked. "Did I help you?"

Buddy touched the boy's shoulder. "You damned . . . you sure did. You helped me a heck of a lot."

"Will you be able to get the person now?"

"I'll get him soon. I swear to you, I'll get him soon."

Chapter Fifty-Six

Early evening as Buddy walked into the Nineteenth Precinct's bull pen, Vidas rolled back his chair and said, "I found Carl Brook and his family."

Buddy stood between their cubes and remembered the alibis claimed by Carl and John. "The night of the Bruno and family killings and the attack at the Carlyle?" he asked.

Not answering directly, Vidas stood as well, and pointed at his computer screen. "You want to see the video?"

Buddy moved closer to the screen. "Show me."

Vidas sat down and rolled his chair near his computer. Using the mouse, he moved the images on the screen forward and backward. They seemed to show a street corner, with a section of Park Avenue's mall in the background.

Buddy said, "What am I looking at?"

"The intersection of Park and Eighty-Ninth, from the DOT's camera on the traffic light. The date and time are running on the lower right." Vidas pointed. "So this is the night Bruno and his family were killed, about an hour before their deaths. Here's the canvas canopy for 1095 Park. See this guy about to go into the building?"

Buddy leaned forward and squinted. He knew the city's Department of Transportation had installed cameras at many busy intersections around the city. They monitored traffic flow and accidents, but the cameras also had become an important tool used by the NYPD, if the crime occurred within camera range. Recognizing the handsome figure with the square jaw, he said, "John Brook."

Vidas nodded. "Right. He's carrying an oversized backpack, probably a change of clothes. I've scanned the tape, and he doesn't leave the building until about twelve hours later."

Here, Vidas forwarded the tape until it was seven the next morning, then slowed the tape to regular speed. A few minutes later Buddy watched John Brook walk out from under the canopy, accompanied by a girl with long dark hair. John kissed the girl on the side of the head, and they held hands as they walked north.

Vidas added, "I looked at other cameras around the building, in case John sneaked out through a fire exit or something, but he didn't. He was in the building all night, probably having a good time."

Buddy ignored the comment and said, "What about Carl? Was he home like he told me?"

Vidas chuckled. "Not exactly."

Buddy looked at his partner. "What was he doing?"

Vidas clicked a few icons, and then more video ran. "This is another DOT camera, the intersection of Riverside and Ninety-Fifth on the Upper West Side. I used a different camera to watch the entrance of Time Warner Center that night from four p.m. until the next day. A few minutes after six p.m., Carl Brook leaves. He walks up Columbus. I followed him on the various cameras all the way to here. The time stamp says 7:04. And . . . you see him?"

Buddy recognized Carl Brook walking east through the intersection. "Yeah."

"Okay," Vidas said. "He goes up Riverside about thirty yards and stands for a second outside this building. See?"

Buddy watched the tape of Carl Brook traveling up the West Side as Vidas had described. Saw Carl's hand go up and ring a buzzer to the side of a door. Saw the door open and Carl disappear inside.

"He's there until one thirty a.m. Then he takes a cab down to his condo at Time Warner Center."

Buddy said, "You're sure he didn't leave?"

Vidas turned and looked at him. "There's a dead spot, without a camera view of the side of the building, where there's another door. So I checked the streets around the building for Carl Brook walking. I didn't think he left, but I couldn't be sure. He could have gone out the side entrance and jumped in a cab. So I thought he was with his mistress or something. But when I searched for the ownership of the units in the building, I got stuck with a bunch of companies with bullshit names. So I called up a guy I know in Vice, and asked him about the address. Does he know of anything happening there? Turns out he does. It's a brothel, run by a friend of the governor's. And off-limits, at least for now. I asked if he could verify that Carl Brook was there from seven p.m. until one a.m. He hung up on me, and I thought he'd blown me off. But he called back an hour later and confirmed. Didn't tell me how, but he confirmed."

Buddy said, "You trust the guy?"

"Yeah."

"What about the hooker—or the madam—who confirmed? Trust her, too?"

Vidas waited a moment, and frowned. "Not really."

Buddy said, "Exactly. 'Not really' means not at all." Buddy straightened. "Maybe Carl is innocent. I have a hunch he is, but we can't alibi him to my satisfaction. But let's say he was at the brothel. So he didn't shoot the antique French Gaston at the painting in Bruno's foyer. Didn't kill Bruno and family. Couldn't have attacked Mei's place at the Carlyle. He's innocent, and Malone should stop busting our balls."

Vidas shook his head. "Not for New Year's Eve he's not innocent. Not necessarily. Carl has no alibi other than his wife. And not for the attack at Ward's house in Greenwich. On that night they say they were at home, but once again Carl's alibi is his wife. There's no video of Carl leaving his place at Time Warner Center, but he might not have been home at all that night."

Buddy recalled Carl's movie-star looks and strong physique, and the way Carl had benefited from the deaths of his brothers. Buddy thought Carl might have been involved behind the scenes in those deaths, might have coordinated with someone else. Maybe with Dietrich Brook, who'd given no alibi for any of the murders.

Buddy checked his watch. It was already half an hour later than when he'd promised to be home. He wanted to stay and think about Dietrich Brook, but he needed to go.

He patted Vidas on the shoulder. "Nice work. But don't stay too late."

"No worries, boss."

As Buddy left the bull pen and passed the desk by the entrance, the receptionist held up a manila envelope for him. "Package for you, Detective."

Buddy took it and looked for a return address, but there wasn't one. He stopped, ripped open the flap, and pulled out a short stack of letter-sized paper.

They were photocopies of documents of differing sizes, all written in a language he couldn't read but guessed was German.

He knew what they were. Bills of sale for the paintings Carl's grandfather had bought from desperate Jews who were sent to Auschwitz. He held the papers carefully, as if they were a sacred trust he had to find a way to honor. They were from another world, but he knew that world had turned into this one and left all kinds of monuments and ruins. And signposts.

Carefully he slid the copies back into the envelope. Later tonight, after everything else he needed and wanted to do, he'd study them. He'd try to discover if they held any secrets. He believed they might, if he could use them to reach back to Nazi Germany.

Chapter Fifty-Seven

Buddy walked through the lobby of the Carlyle Residences and pressed the button for the elevator. He had butterflies in his stomach, just as he had when he met Mei for the first time. He'd come up this elevator to interview her during his investigation of the Death Clock Murders. One of her close friends, Mayor Blenheim's sister, had been a victim. Not an auspicious beginning.

But a few days later she'd agreed to meet him at a jazz club in the Village, the one with no sign above the door. It was near the Vanguard but not famous—and that was the point. The walls and floors, even the tables, were dirty, and the lighting was dim but the music was good. To Buddy, that was all that mattered.

They'd heard a quartet play Miles Davis and Coltrane, and then mix in some new stuff. Buddy didn't care much for the new but liked the old. Davis's "Flamenco Sketches." Soulful, lonely music that often eased the pain of too many late nights working and no woman to come home to. The white-haired guy at the piano got the opening piano chords just right—almost tentative, not too loud. Then the stronger but more melancholy trumpet had cleared away the voices of the club, bringing focus to the music. He'd watched the trumpet player, a thin Hispanic man in his fifties, who closed his eyes and swayed slightly to the music. It had felt good, hearing the sound. And hearing it with Mei.

He'd thought she was too beautiful to be there with him. That maybe he'd made a mistake asking her anywhere at all. Yet between numbers they'd talked easily. Twice she'd put a hand on his forearm. And after the first set she'd asked about his interest in music, not to be polite but because she was interested.

He'd paused for moment to look at the blue light over the now-empty stage, at the other patrons talking and drinking and getting up or sitting down. Then he'd told her of his childhood and teenage years as a concert pianist. He'd confessed to his failure at Carnegie Hall, to giving up. This wasn't a story of victory that a man would usually tell on a first date, yet he'd told it anyway. Instead of seeming put off, she'd grown more interested.

"Does it help you?" she'd asked. "Your background as a pianist?"

He wasn't sure he'd heard right. This wasn't a question he'd ever gotten before, but it was one he'd considered many times. He said, "You mean, has being a pianist helped me be a better detective?"

"Exactly," she said, leaning in to hear him better, to be closer. "Most detectives don't have your background. They didn't go to Juilliard."

"My background is weird," he admitted, "but I think it's helped me. I know it has. The hours, the practice, the attention to detail—in the case of music, the attention to every note and phrase and melody and counterpoint. Now I try to see everything. To notice everything. Back then I worked to figure out what the composer was trying to hear, trying to make *me* play. Now it's figuring out what the victims are telling me. Not like they're ghosts or anything," he'd said quickly, and shrugged.

Although he thought briefly of Lauren.

Mei said, "You must work long hours."

He sat up a little straighter. "Yeah, I do. And"—here he held up a hand—"there's one other thing that's the key to being a good pianist and a good detective."

"What's that?"

"Obsession," he said. "Relentlessness."

She stared at him and nodded slowly.

Realizing his mistake, he said, "But I'm not obsessed about women. Just about work."

"You don't want me to think you're a nutcase?"

"That's right."

She only laughed. And then moved even closer to him, kissing his cheek.

The elevator chimed, the door opened, and he walked into her—*their*—foyer.

At the sound of the chime, Ben ran along the hallway toward him, his bright eyes focusing on Buddy, his face lighting up with a smile. And then Ben stopped abruptly.

"Hello," he said, suddenly shy and uncertain.

"Come here!" Buddy said, getting down on his knees and extending his arms. "Give me a hug."

Ben ran toward him and fit himself within Buddy's arms, pressing his face against Buddy's neck. Buddy squeezed him tightly.

The boy took comfort and then loosened his grip. They separated. Buddy looked him in the eye. "You all right?"

Ben considered this for a moment. He stared at his feet and said, "If I can't have my mom and dad and Ellen-Marie, I want you and Mei to be my family."

Buddy didn't know how to go forward, whether to turn, or if they could go backward. He was stuck. Looking up as if for help, he saw Mei.

She was standing in the hallway, still in her work clothes. The black silk dress with raspberry-colored designs and high heels made her seem very dressed up, but she held two red oven mitts in her right hand. Tilting her head, she waited to see what he'd say to Ben.

He felt his face warm, but he didn't smile or joke or shrug off the moment. He looked at Ben and touched his shoulder. "We'll find a way for you to be safe," he said. "We'll find a way for you to be happy. I don't know exactly how it will happen, but it *will* happen. Do you trust me?"

Ben remained motionless for a long moment, and then he nodded. Buddy stood and said, "Good. Now, I need to ask Mei a question." Mei walked into the foyer, closer to him.

After unbuttoning his coat, he slipped his arms free of it and sent it in a short arc over to the back of a chair in the living room. Then he put his right hand in the left breast pocket of his suit coat. As he removed his hand and the box he'd hidden there, he got down on one knee, hoping he wouldn't topple over.

Landing solidly, he held out the small box trimmed in black velvet. He looked up at Mei. She'd dropped the oven mitts. Her mouth was open in surprise.

He said, "Mei, I love you more than anything on earth. Will you marry me?"

He heard Ben gasp, but he kept his eyes on Mei.

Her hand dropped from her mouth to her chest. She breathed quickly. Tears ran down her cheeks.

For a moment he feared he'd done the wrong thing. That he shouldn't have asked.

But he held aloft the small velvet-lined box, waiting for her answer.

Ben stood beside him, his head about the level of Buddy's. He blurted out, "Mei, what are you going to do?"

"Yes!" she cried, looking at one and then the other of them. "Of course! *Yes!*"

Ben clapped excitedly.

Mei took a step closer to Buddy. She leaned over and reached for the box. "May I?"

"It's yours," Buddy said.

She took it in her slender hands. Holding her breath, she opened it. And smiled.

Chapter Fifty-Eight

When Ben had gone to bed, Buddy and Mei walked into the master bedroom and closed the door.

Buddy took off his tie. He was thrilled that Mei had accepted him, but more than anything he felt relief. She was his, forever.

Smiling at him, she said, "I'm so happy, so glad you proposed."

He grinned. "I'm relieved you said yes."

"You knew I would."

"I didn't know. I wasn't sure."

"Well, you should have been sure." She closed the blind, blotting out the lights of the city. "I'm surprised by how happy it made Ben. He's really a wonderful boy, great to have around."

Buddy didn't react.

"What about . . . ," she began. Her face flushed as she turned away.

This was another hint he'd ignore. Ben had asked outright. He'd tried not to consider it, and he'd argued with Ward. He shook his head, exhaled. "One thing at a time, okay?"

He knew she understood him to mean they'd be married first, before more discussions about children. The idea of Ben's joining their family, he couldn't get his head around. He liked Ben, liked him a lot. But further than that, he couldn't go. At the same time his own mind had begun daydreaming of the possibility, even as he pretended these rosy images were nothing but fantasies.

As they were changing, she said, "Did I tell you?"

Buddy piled up three pillows and climbed into bed. He got comfortable and said, "Tell me what?"

She'd gone into the closet and come out wearing cream-colored sheer satin panties and a matching camisole. He could see her nipples and through her panties a tidy patch of dark hair.

She said, "That I was thinking about you?"

"Just now?"

"When I was away in Greenwich."

He said, "It was only for a couple of nights."

She stood by the foot of the bed and faced him. "So you didn't think about me?"

"Sure I did." But he'd replied too quickly, automatically.

She shook her head. "That isn't want I meant." She went over to the bedroom door and pushed the button to set the lock. Then she returned to the middle of the room.

Now he understood what she meant.

He watched her take the narrow straps of the camisole in her fingers and lift it over her head, revealing her lovely firm breasts. Even in the low golden light of the bedside lamp, he could see her erect nipples. Then she pushed her panties down to her ankles and stood straight, hands on her hips.

In that moment he wanted her more than he'd ever wanted any woman.

Very softly she asked, "Are you thinking about me now?"

Chapter Fifty-Nine

The solitary figure crouched by the parapet of Time Warner Center. He looked north over the city at the lights bordering Central Park, his feet planted firmly on the roof. He needed to keep his center of gravity low, as the sheer force of the wind at the skyscraper's crown could easily knock him over, if he weren't careful.

But he was careful. He wouldn't have come this far without expertise.

He huddled between two enormous ventilation fans as shelter from the constant winds and from observers.

Two hours before dusk and a mile away, he'd climbed into a commercial laundry truck that jostled through the Midtown streets and pulled into the building's service bay. As the truck had backed up to the loading dock, he rolled up the cargo door, jumped onto the edge of the dock, and walked a short distance to the service elevator. He wore a uniform from the laundry company, dark makeup, sunglasses, and a Yankees cap.

Using a wire he'd brought, he tricked the fire-suppression system into thinking the door from the fire stairs to the roof remained closed even when he'd opened it. Most condo owners in the tower would be safe, but not Carl and his family.

They were rich and lived in the penthouse. The top floor.

With two skylights.

He'd stood on the roof three times before. He'd used the laundry truck four times. While the family had been out for the day, he'd talked a maid into allowing him into the apartment. He knew the layout of every room.

He was careful and methodical.

But would all the planning and practice make the actual event dull? Never.

He saw himself as a great Olympian whose years of anonymous effort were leading to surging triumph. Since he began this work to redress old grievances, he'd made only one mistake: the boy had survived. But he'd remedy that mistake.

And soon.

He checked his watch.

Chapter Sixty

Ariel Brook yawned as she sat on a barstool in her family's kitchen. Her mother and father were standing nearby, drinking wine and discussing a ski vacation over the upcoming spring break. Her brother, John, was watching ESPN from a lounge chair in the great room.

"I'd like to bring a guest," John called over to them.

Ariel turned to him. "You have a girlfriend?"

"Mind your own business," he told her.

Ariel smiled. She looked at her mother and father.

Her mother shook her head and said, "Best not to fight over it. You can bring a friend, too, if you'd like."

"A boy?" Ariel asked.

Her father said, "No. Not a boy."

"But John can bring a girl."

"John's older."

Ariel flushed hot. She'd no intention of bringing a boy, but she didn't want to be treated differently than her brother. She said, "That's not fair."

"When you're John's age, you can bring a boy," her mother said.

Ariel slipped off the stool and marched out of the kitchen and into the hallway that led to the bedrooms.

"Good night!" her father called after her.

She didn't reply, just continued into her bedroom and locked the door behind her. How *annoying* all of them were. And how unfair!

After changing into her pajamas, she padded into her private bathroom and brushed her teeth. Then she pulled down the blinds—she'd seen the spectacular view from her windows so often she no longer noticed it—and climbed into bed.

After setting her glasses on the night table, she lay on her back. Holding up her phone, she pressed the Netflix icon and began watching an episode of *Cupcake Wars*.

But she was too tired to learn who won. She muted the phone and set it facedown on her night table. Then she lay back, pulled the down comforter up to her chin, and sighed once. As she fell asleep, she thought she heard footsteps on the roof above her. She imagined the sound to be not one but hundreds of pigeons. The birds waddled about, pecking at the roof for seeds and other food, and finding none, rose all at once in a flock that wheeled away over the Hudson River and up into the black sky.

Chapter Sixty-One

In the night Buddy heard a scream.

He sat up. Mei woke.

She said, "What is it?"

Another cry.

She recognized it. He didn't. Not right away.

She whispered, "It's Ben. Another nightmare." She pushed down the duvet and swung her legs out of the bed.

Buddy touched her back. "I've got it. You should stay here."

"You're sure?"

"Yeah."

Buddy got out of bed and, in the dark, put on his bathrobe. He went out into the hallway and the few paces to Ben's door. He entered the smaller bedroom quickly, sat on the side of the mattress, and put his large hand on Ben's chest.

The boy was breathing rapidly. His body was rigid. His legs jerked as if he were trying to run.

Buddy saw the outline of Ben's face, just a little darker than the white of the pillow. Ben stirred under his touch.

"Ben," he said. "Ben, wake up. You're having a bad dream."

Ben was still.

"Ben?" he repeated. "Are you okay?"

The breathing halted. In one motion Ben sat up and put his arms around Buddy. He held on tightly, pushing his face into Buddy's chest. Yet he said nothing. He whimpered once and held on. For several minutes.

At last Buddy said, "It's all right. Just a bad dream. I have them all the time. Usually they're about . . ." He stopped. He wouldn't tell Ben about his own nightmares. Instead he offered, "Why don't I grab the checkerboard and we can turn on the light and play a few games? Would that be okay?"

Ben nodded against him.

Buddy gently disengaged and went out to the living room. Under the bar in the corner of the room, he found the checkerboard and pieces and carried them back to Ben's room.

But Ben was lying on his side, the covers pulled up around him. Buddy approached the bed and stood there, watching the portion of the boy's head that wasn't under the duvet. Ben was sleeping peacefully, though Buddy didn't know for how long. He listened to Ben's regular breathing and stepped back toward the chest of drawers. He set the checkerboard on the chest and returned to the side of the bed. The room was pitch black. The blinds were drawn snugly against the windows, and either there wasn't a moon or it was hidden behind thick clouds. He could barely see his own arm. And yet Ben had known he was there and been comforted.

As he stood vigil, he realized he'd been thinking too much about himself and not about what he could give Ben. He thought maybe he did have things to give. Maybe not as much time as he should, but some time. Some evenings. Most weekends. A wealth of knowledge of the world and how it worked, although he didn't want Ben to learn much of what he'd discovered as a detective. He also realized that he had an odd sort of role model in his own father. Yes, he resolved to treat Ben in the opposite way his own father had treated him. Time and love, these he might be able give Ben. Money? He didn't have any. But maybe time and love were what mattered most.

After a while he left, closing the door slowly behind him. In the master bedroom he took off his bathrobe, climbed into bed next to Mei, and lay awake. He thought about the bills of sale Carl had sent him, could picture them lying on the kitchen counter, waiting to be looked at. His curiosity needled him. He couldn't stifle it.

There was something in those documents. Perhaps a name. Perhaps something else.

Chapter Sixty-Two

He'd look at the bills of sale now. He didn't care that it was the middle of the night.

Quietly as he could, he dressed in street clothes and left the bedroom.

He padded into the kitchen and made coffee. Mei had one of those coffee makers in which you inserted a plastic capsule, pressed a button, and the machine would brew a single cup. So he'd brought over the Mr. Coffee from his old apartment. He wanted a pot of coffee, not a cup. Plus, he preferred the taste of the Mr. Coffee. He measured enough Dunkin' Donuts coffee for ten cups, filled the machine's tank with water, and switched it on. A moment later he heard the coffee dripping through the filter into the pot.

He listened to the coffee brew. He liked the sound, even liked the wait, the anticipation. He saw the manila envelope at the end of the granite counter by the phone. He reached for it, pulled open the flap, and withdrew the papers. He counted eight of them, and spread all eight across the counter.

All used the same form, printed in a language he assumed was German.

All included the name Gerhardt Bruch halfway through.

There was less than a page of writing on each sheet.

Leaning closer, he studied the documents. At first he couldn't make out any of the language, not even the names above Gerhardt Bruch. They were foreign and handwritten in an ornate cursive that made it difficult to know where one letter ended and another began.

But looking more carefully, he saw names he could decipher and did recognize.

One of those names was Rembrandt.

Hadn't Carl pointed out a Rembrandt self-portrait as he'd stood with Carl and Rebecca in the family's gallery?

Less than a page of writing to transfer ownership of a Rembrandt that was worth millions today. It seemed to Buddy there should be more—more documentation and a photograph.

The coffee maker beeped. He poured himself a large mug and set it on the counter above the bills of sale. Steam rose, curling out of it. He lifted the mug, brought it up to his nose, and inhaled deeply. His eyes misted over, just briefly, and he thought he could make out an unusual name—Ranem Baum—on the bill of sale closest to him.

Ranem Baum, he thought. *What can you tell me?*

Setting down the mug, he hurried into the living room, found Mei's laptop, and brought it into the kitchen. He set it on the counter to the left of the photocopies and opened a browser. He typed "lists of Holocaust victims and survivors" into the browser window and clicked the "Search" button.

At the top of the results was the US Holocaust Memorial Museum in Washington, DC.

He clicked on that link, which took him to the museum's website. He clicked again on a link that led him to the Survivors and Victims Resource Center, and found the Survivors and Victims Database with a search feature by name.

Clicking on that link led him to a search feature with fields for exact name, details around birth, death, places of birth, places prewar and during the war and at death, prisoner number, and nationality.

His heartbeat jumped.

He stepped to the side, leaned down, and studied one particular bill of sale further. Then he filled out the search fields, to the extent he could, for Ranem Baum. For "places" he listed Berlin. He left "death place" empty.

He clicked on the search bar.

He sipped his coffee.

The results showed on the screen.

He narrowed his eyes and read that Ranem Baum had lived in Berlin and been sent with his family to Auschwitz-Birkenau in February 1944. He'd died there in November 1944, yet he'd had a child or children—the database didn't specify—and one or more of them had survived the war and now lived in places unknown.

Places unknown, Buddy thought, his eyes lingering on the phrase.

Europe?

Or America?

Or New York City?

He straightened and refilled his coffee mug. He needed to focus his search.

Victims, he reasoned, wouldn't be relevant to his investigation, as long as they had no offspring or surviving relations. The family line, and any claims on family property, would have ended in a horrific way.

But this wasn't the case for survivors. If any of the sellers had descendants who'd survived Auschwitz, those descendants might have reason to take revenge and even to claim some of Carl Brook's paintings.

And the art of Alton Brook and Bruno Brook as well, if not their lives.

He drank more coffee. He thought that in his career, he'd never come across a motive that extended over so many years but was so completely, utterly understandable.

Yes, understandable.

But leading to a horrifying evil.

Chapter Sixty-Three

The solitary figure standing on the condominium tower pressed the crown button on his wristwatch.

It was 2:24 a.m.

He'd be in position by 3:30.

He'd strike by 3:35.

Using gentle footsteps, he circled the skylight above the room the family used as an art gallery. From his black backpack he removed two large sharp anchor screws, a hammer, and a vise grip. On one side of the skylight, he set the sharp end of an anchor screw. He took up the hammer and swung it hard—once, twice—driving the screw through the roof membrane. The sound of metal on metal was drowned out by the wind whipping around the tower.

Wearing form-fitting climbing gloves made of goat leather, he used the vise grip and turned the screw tighter and tighter, until it held and didn't give when he pulled at it.

After repeating the process three more times—on the three other sides of the skylight—he removed three short ropes from his backpack and a stainless steel ring. He tied one end of three of the short ropes to the anchors and one end to the center ring.

Then he laid the ropes off to one side and pulled out the same glass cutter with the diamond tip he'd used in the attack at Greenwich, and set it on the skylight. Just as he'd done at Ward Mills's mansion, he used the diamond-tipped blade to cut a wide circle.

He lifted a single disc of cold glass and set it on the roof. But as the skylight was a double-pane, he repeated the process for the interior pane, and set that one beside the first. Reaching through the opening, he used a short knife to cut the fabric of the interior louver.

Then he attached one end of the fourth short rope to the fourth anchor screw and the other end of that rope to the center ring, and shifted the ring into the center of the hole in the skylight.

From his backpack he removed a black twenty-foot rope. After attaching one end to the center ring, he slowly eased the rope into the condominium below. He looked through the hole, listening, watching.

But he heard nothing, saw nothing.

At last, it was time.

He felt infinite calm, as if nothing could slow or distract him. His concentration was total.

Looping the straps of the pack over his shoulders, he stepped through two of the short ropes, lowered himself through the glass hole, and slid on the black rope almost noiselessly into the living room.

Landing, he crouched low. Felt the warm air of the room loosen his muscles.

He had no exposed skin. His hair was under a tight-fitting nylon cap. His face was hidden by a mask. From his forehead he pulled down night-vision goggles—goggles with lenses made by Brook Instruments—that made the condominium and everything in it different shades of green.

He stayed there, listening, watching.

He was a ghost. He was the angel of death.

Slowly he rose, standing to his full height. Without removing his backpack, he reached behind his neck, unzipped the flap of the largest compartment, and withdrew the hatchet.

Chapter Sixty-Four

Buddy stood in the dark living room, looking out at the lights in the buildings on Central Park South and all the way to Time Warner Center. He saw that many windows in the hotels still glowed and wondered if the guests were awake. Or if the bright rooms were empty.

He considered the town houses owned by Ben's parents and by Bruno Brook and his wife. They must be heated and perhaps cleaned and repaired by staff, and yet the families that had lived in them were gone forever. They'd be silent tonight, cavernous and dark.

He breathed out, turned from the windows, and went over to the small bar in the corner of the room. He saw the bottles arranged in neat rows. Below them, the crystal tumblers Mei preferred. Taking one, he held it up and watched the faint light from the kitchen refract in colorful jags. *So many ways of seeing,* he thought.

Setting the tumbler on the bar, he poured two fingers of whiskey and gulped it down.

As his stomach warmed, he thought about emptiness and the lost, the missing, the destroyed. Of the more than seventy years since the most terrible crimes ever committed. So much time for the desire for revenge to cool—too much time for what he'd seen since his visit to Camp Kateri.

The killer wasn't angry only about events in the distant past, Buddy had come to believe, but about events today. Motive might include the deaths at Auschwitz and possibly the theft of paintings, yet there must be a recent wrong, still new and raw—a wrong the killer witnessed frequently, perhaps each day. Only that strange combination of the past and the present could explain the calculated, deliberate planning and the hot fury of the hatchet.

He set the tumbler on the bar and poured another ounce. Drank it quickly.

He didn't need to look outside to see the gathering storm. He could sense it. The electricity in the air—the current he'd sensed in the lobby of Ray Sawyer's building—had descended over the entire city, infesting everything with a tang of dread.

Before the storm hit, he needed to find a single family with three characteristics. First, it had sold—under duress—paintings to Gerhardt Brook. Second, it had suffered Auschwitz but in part survived. Third, at least one survivor was now in New York City.

Yes, Buddy thought, setting down the tumbler. *Here.*

Chapter Sixty-Five

Ariel Brook woke. A strange noise came from the other side of the wall.

She sat up in bed, rubbed her eyes, listened.

It sounded like people were wrestling in the bedroom next to hers. Grunting. Threatening.

Now someone was thrown against the wall.

She heard a groan.

She heard a shout. "No!" Her brother's voice.

Then his scream.

A cold terror filled her chest. She knew that what had happened to her uncle Alton, aunt Brenda, and cousin Ellen-Marie was happening to her family tonight.

Her hands began to shake.

She held her breath and heard the clicking noise of someone trying the handle of her bedroom door.

Her throat seemed to close up.

She saw the dark outline of her mobile phone on the night table. Crash! *Crash!*

Someone was trying to kick in her door. She had so little time.

She grabbed the phone and darted around the bed to the armoire on the other side of the room. She opened the two large doors above the four drawers. Putting her toes on the edge of the front of the drawers, she climbed up, gritting her teeth. When she was standing on the shelf on which the television sat, she swung a leg onto the top of the armoire.

For a moment she clung there, almost falling. Her arms hurt. Her heel was hooked over the edge, slipping on the smooth wood.

She dug her heel in, hurting herself, but she didn't cry out.

Pulling hard as she could, she curled her body over the edge to the top.

Sitting, she reached down with both hands and closed the armoire's doors.

Now standing, she touched the ceiling. But it was drywall, and there was nowhere to go.

She was caught and could do nothing but hide.

Quietly she lay curled up on the top of the armoire, hoping to be invisible, her back against the wall. She sensed dust on the wood near her face, but tried not to sneeze.

She unlocked her phone and dialed 911.

The dispatcher came over the line. It was a woman with a friendly voice.

Crying silently, she whispered, "Help me. Please help me! I think I'm going to die."

Chapter Sixty-Six

Buddy returned to the kitchen, found a pad of paper, and set it below the eight bills of sale.

Though unable to read the documents, he did his best to decipher the handwritten names of the paintings' sellers. After entering into the database of the US Holocaust Memorial Museum those names and any information he could assume, he studied the results.

Of the eight sellers, or "grantors"—which seemed to be the same word in English and German—five appeared to have perished at Auschwitz along with every member of their families. Not just immediate family members but *all* members.

Buddy shook his head and breathed deeply, trying to tamp down the beginnings of nausea.

For a moment he turned away and poured another mug of coffee.

Then refocused.

The lines of five families broken by the Nazis.

But that meant that in three families, at least one member had survived.

Their names?

Ranem Baum, Yetta Morgenstern, Nessa Meyer.

The database indicated they'd remained in Poland. They hadn't returned to Germany. The families of these three might have died out over time, after the war. But the museum's database lost track of them after Auschwitz was liberated by Soviet troops on January 27, 1945.

Buddy wished something about the names was familiar to him, but there was nothing. He'd never heard these last names before.

He stared at the names. "Tell me something!" he said aloud. *"Tell me!"*

But they didn't resonate. He couldn't make the connection.

He knew he needed help.

Waking the laptop, he opened another browser window. He searched for information about Holocaust survivors in Poland, and in the search results, found the Polish Institute for Holocaust Studies in the Bronx.

He'd contact the institute after it opened for business later that morning. He'd ask Ward to accompany him to a meeting. Ward spoke Italian and maybe knew some German, and was always reading books about European history.

He looked at the time on the top right of the laptop screen: 3:40 a.m.

He was tired now. His mind buzzed with information and possibilities but also fears that he'd chosen the wrong path, one that would take too much time and lead him away rather than toward the killer. But there was no more he could do tonight.

He closed the laptop and carried his mug out into the living room. He stared unthinkingly at the darkness of Central Park.

Chapter Sixty-Seven

Ariel's teeth chattered as someone kicked in her bedroom door. Lying on her side, only her left eye could see over the lip on the top of the armoire. She saw a figure clad in black. The figure wore a black mask and goggles.

She held her breath.

Clenched her jaws together.

She pressed the button on her phone to end her 911 call. She clutched the phone screen to her chest to hide its white light.

She lay perfectly still.

The figure circled the room and knelt down, checking under the bed. Then it stood and moved with a faint swoosh of fabric into the bathroom.

She heard the cabinet doors under her vanity open and close. Two soft sounds.

And then she saw the figure return.

The figure turned toward the armoire, toward her. The goggles rose until they were looking directly at her.

Chapter Sixty-Eight

The solitary figure regarded his work.

Let the air out of his lungs.

His pulse remained steady and slow.

The boy had been unexpected. A light sleeper who'd come to the door just as he was opening it. Others might have panicked because the boy was strong. But he'd remained cool. He'd put enough distance between them, shoved the boy against the wall, and swung.

He'd been colder with the girl. He'd seen her fearful shivering on the top of the armoire. Yet he'd felt no pity.

Now in the hallway, he listened. Heard nothing. No sirens, yet. He'd seen the girl's cell phone and assumed she'd called 911.

He had three or four minutes, no more.

As he'd practiced so many times, with one motion he put the hatchet back into the largest compartment of his backpack and zipped the compartment closed.

Rapidly he retraced his steps.

Standing in the picture gallery by the rope, he recalled all he'd done. Every step, every door opened and closed, every swing of the hatchet. Satisfied he'd made no mistake, he saw the object that was his—his family's—and moved toward it.

Moments later, his feet and his leather-gloved hands wrapped around the rope, and he slithered up until he reached the skylight. Grasping its stainless steel frame, he hauled himself up and into the cold and the churning winds outside.

Nearly tripping, he moved his feet outward. Got purchase on the roof. Regained his balance.

Then he brought up the rope, coiled it, and stowed it in his backpack. Went down the interior roof-access stairs to the freight elevator. In the elevator he removed his nylon clothing to reveal the uniform of the laundry company. He put on the Yankees cap. In the loading bay he walked purposefully toward the laundry truck, stepped off the dock and into its rear compartment. Picking his way past white bags of now-dirty linens and towels, he hid.

Sometime later the truck driver rolled down and fastened the cargo door, climbed into the cab, and drove the truck out of the loading bay and into the street.

From the rear the figure heard sirens grow louder and louder and then pass the truck on the way to the condominium tower.

Chapter Sixty-Nine

At four in the morning, Buddy's phone rang. He ran into the kitchen to answer it.

Worry slid into his chest. Calls at this hour meant bad news.

"Yeah?" he answered.

It was Chief Malone. "Buddy, I need you at Carl Brook's place in Time Warner Center."

"No," Buddy said.

The chief sighed into the phone. "I'm sorry."

"Goddammit," Buddy said. "Goddammit."

Twenty minutes later he joined Chief Malone in the penthouse's elevator lobby. Malone wore a rumpled suit without a tie. His typically ruddy face was ashen. He handed Buddy a pair of booties.

Neither man spoke.

Buddy put the booties over his shoes and then pulled on latex gloves he'd taken from the side pocket of his suit coat. Two cops stood like sentries on either side of the elevator. Buddy glanced at them and then at Malone.

Buddy said, "CSU?"

"On their way. Vidas, too. So for a while you've got the place to yourself. I'll wait here and give you some time."

Buddy nodded, pulled open the door to Carl's condominium, and walked inside.

A warm glow illuminated the living room where he stood. Everything appeared as it had when he'd been here before. The kitchen and great room, too. Nothing out of place. Two empty wineglasses on the counter by the sink, a few drops of red at the bottom of each.

He checked the dining room. Nothing.

Then he went along the hallway to the den where he'd interviewed the family. He flicked on the light switch. The room was exactly as it had been when he'd spoken with John and then with Carl and Rebecca and Ariel.

Leaving the light on, he returned to the hallway. He stood there on the handsome maple floors and stopped.

He didn't think he could go any farther. He'd seen enough death. Any more and he'd be damaging himself.

Fuck! he thought. *I can't do it.*

He squeezed his hands together, trying to make the blood move, trying to see if he could keep going. In response he felt his own strength. He breathed deeply, squared his shoulders. Took a step forward.

He came to a doorway on the right. In this room the responding cops had switched on the light. He saw two figures on a large bed. The bed's sheets and duvet had once been white but now were red. Carl lay collapsed over Rebecca. He'd been trying to protect her when one of his hands was cut off and his neck severed. He hadn't lived to see his wife die. A hatchet blade had split her head in two uneven pieces. Her nose was gone. One eyeball clung weakly to one side of her skull. The other eye was missing, revealing a spongelike gash that stared at him.

To avoid the blood on the floor, he didn't go closer.

Backing out into the hallway, he turned and walked to the next doorway. A bedroom illuminated by a black floor lamp. On the desk were John's schoolbooks and his phone. The north wall had suffered a rose-colored indentation. Below the desk, against the baseboard, lay

John's body. The area between the shoulders had been hacked at, so chunks of the spine lay like oddly sized dice in the lake of blood on his back and also on what had been tan carpeting.

Feeling dizzy, Buddy backed out of the room and into the hallway. He leaned against the wall and listened to his breath. It was coming too fast. Forcing the air in and out at a much slower pace, he felt the light-headedness begin to fade.

He pushed off from the wall and approached the final bedroom door on the left side of the hallway. The responding cops had turned off this light. He stood in the doorway, reached along the wall for the switch, and flicked it up.

Almost immediately he turned away. His eyes stared at the white doorframe. Something was caught in his throat, as if he might vomit or cry. Opening his mouth wide, he took in a mouthful, a gutful, of air, before letting it out in a rasping, nearly silent wail.

Here was another girl he hadn't saved.

Forcing himself to straighten and to look once more, he saw the top of the armoire, crushed and with parts of a young girl's body dangling through the splinters. He turned away. He couldn't do it anymore. Not tonight.

Rapidly he left the bedrooms and back hallway and emerged into the great room and kitchen. He stood at the sink and turned on the cold water and let it run for a long moment. Then he leaned over, angled his head, and drank. He drank as if he'd been in the desert for a year without water. And then he shut off the tap, turned, and wandered through the living room and into the picture gallery. All the lights had been switched on by the responding officers. The paintings shone under the lights as if alive.

Hearing the wind rushing above, he looked up and noticed the circular hole cut in the skylight. Staring up through the missing disc of glass, he could see only darkness. No moon or stars were visible, but of course he was in the city, and so much of the universe was obscured by the ambient light. All at once he felt overwhelmed and exhausted.

He sat down on one of the wooden benches in the middle of the gallery. He knew he wasn't supposed to do it, that it would annoy CSU or worse, yet an unexpected faintness had come over him again. He bent over, lowering his head between his knees until his head began to clear. After a while he placed his latex-gloved hands on his knees and sat up.

He'd thought, as he'd worked in Mei's kitchen that night, that he was on to something—some clue that would guide him to an answer. Yet his confidence had been misplaced. He was as lost as ever, working feverishly in the wrong way, while not a mile from him another family was being murdered. As he recalled what had been done to Ariel as she'd hidden on top of the armoire, his hands began to shake and he closed his eyes. In his memory he saw what was left of her, and the image wouldn't go away.

Opening his eyes, he blinked at the gallery walls. He didn't see the large painting of Napoleon astride a white horse, only recalled the horrifying image of Ariel.

As if from a great distance, he heard the CSU detectives arrive and begin their examination of the scene. When Malone's voice, issuing an order or two, boomed from the kitchen and great room, he made no move. He didn't think he could. The gallery around him was bathed in the shine of the lights—they must have been specially made and located to exhibit the paintings—yet the room itself remained cold as the warm air rushed out through the hole in the skylight. The bracing cold kept him vaguely aware of his surroundings, of the room and the lights and the polished teak bench on which he was sitting. But he could do no more than stare straight ahead.

Yet his mind hadn't entirely closed down. It was like he was hearing a melody emerge from silence. First an illusion. Then a fragment. Finally, a more definite sound.

He noticed something.

Not what was in the room but what wasn't.

What the hell?

He reached into the breast pocket of his suit coat and pulled out his phone. After unlocking it, he pressed the photos icon and saw stills of the videos he'd taken recently. The last video was of this very room, when Carl and Rebecca had shown him their paintings.

He touched the video and began to watch.

He turned off the volume so he could ignore the conversation he'd pretended to have, and focused on the images. The video played, all fifteen seconds of it. When it ended, he played it again.

He was right.

He stood and held up the phone so he could watch the video and also see the wall directly in front of him. He played the same video a third time and confirmed his observation. Tonight, on the wall in front of him hung the large painting of Napoleon leading his army. In the video taken only yesterday, the large painting of Napoleon hung just as it did now, but in the video there was a second painting, a small one about the size of a sheet of letter paper, hanging just to the right of the large painting.

Buddy played the video again, this time pausing it for the two seconds it lingered on the wall opposite him. With thumb and forefinger he pulled apart the image to enlarge it. He squinted at the phone screen.

He wasn't sure of the small painting's subject matter, but it looked to him as if it showed a bowl of fruit. Or was it a wreath of fruit on a boy's head? The boy had pale skin, black hair, and resembled Ben.

Buddy stared at the image. Then he shut off the phone, dropped it in his suit coat pocket, and approached the wall where the small painting had hung. The white paint was just a shade darker than the paint around it—the paint around it had been exposed to sunlight and artificial light. An imperceptible difference, unless you knew a painting had been there. He moved closer still and saw in the plaster a tiny pinprick where a picture hanger and nail had held the diminutive painting. The painting had had a narrow frame, and the frame and canvas must have weighed very little, and so the nail and picture hanger used must also have been small.

Had he not been working this case, the small painting wouldn't have been noticed. Not by CSU. Not by anyone.

He thought rapidly now. He asked himself, *Did the killer make a mistake? Does the painting have any particular meaning to the killer, or did he take it because it was small and easy to conceal?* His energy and resolve returned. He faced the room. Saw the priceless works of art. Suspected the paintings weren't a sideshow to his investigation but *the* show.

The killer had departed from his executions and perhaps on impulse taken something. That in itself meant something.

Buddy would ask Mei about the missing painting. And then he'd work to determine who'd sold it to Carl's grandfather in Nazi Germany. That information might tell him nothing, but on the other hand, it might tell him everything.

Chapter Seventy

When Buddy returned through Carl Brook's living room to the kitchen and great room, he saw half a dozen men and women wearing CSU windbreakers. They were setting up their lights and cameras to document the state of the condominium.

Malone paced back and forth in the kitchen, talking quietly with Vidas.

Vidas had arrived and put on booties. He came up to Buddy, touched his shoulder, and said, "I'm sorry, boss."

Buddy nodded in silent thanks, then stood in the center of the great room. He had a view of the hallway to the bedrooms, but he wouldn't enter that hallway again.

He looked through the oversized windows at the dim outlines of the buildings on Central Park West. He checked his watch. It was so late—or so early. He couldn't call Mei, as she and Ben would be asleep for another couple of hours. And what would he say? How could he tell Ben *this* news?

His reverie ended as he heard calls from two detectives down on their knees in the hallway. Chief Malone stopped his pacing in the kitchen and hurried over to them, joined a moment later by Vidas.

Buddy didn't move.

Vidas broke from the group and hurried over to Buddy. His face showed excitement. He held up an evidence baggie and said, "CSU found a contact lens. Just one, torn along one edge."

Buddy shrugged.

"Boss, it's *still* damp."

Buddy felt a hit of adrenaline. He knew a contact lens outside the body would remain moist for thirty minutes, maybe less.

He took the baggie from Vidas, held it up to the kitchen light, saw the lens.

DNA, he thought.

Did it belong to one of the victims, or to the killer?

He thought he might be lucky in this respect. During the killer's brief struggle with John, the lens might have come out and fallen as he'd left the boy's room—fallen onto the hallway floor.

"Run it down," Buddy told Vidas. "Did any family member wear contacts, and what were their prescriptions?"

Vidas said, "There aren't many family members left, just Dietrich Brook, Lydia Brook, and Hayley Brook."

"Check on those three, plus the four who died tonight."

"Sure, boss."

Vidas turned and hurried off to assist the CSU detectives.

Buddy looked over at Malone, who was on his mobile phone and pacing back and forth by the kitchen island. He watched the chief's heavy black shoes striking the maple floors. It was then he saw it.

He walked into the kitchen, leaned down, and picked up a slender attaché case made of leather so black it shone under the lights. He laid it sideways on the marble countertop, unbuckled the flap, and opened it.

Pens, eyeglasses, a calculator, and a sheaf of papers.

With his latex gloves he withdrew the papers. They were held together by a metal binder clip and appeared to be legal documents of some kind.

He set the papers on the counter and removed the binder clip. Then he leaned over and began to read.

Before he'd gotten to the end of the second page, he realized that more had been going on among the four Brook brothers than he'd been told. For this wasn't an agreement to sell the company to GE, it was an agreement among Alton, Bruno, and Carl—a majority of the company's board of directors—to remove Dietrich Brook as vice president of European sales.

The agreement referenced mismanagement, bad faith, and breach of fiduciary duty on the part of Dietrich Brook. Buddy didn't know what "breach of fiduciary duty" meant, but he got the gist.

He flipped to the signature pages. Two brothers had signed: Alton and Bruno. The signature line for Carl remained blank.

Dietrich's brothers had been about to cast him out of the family business, something that would cause him to lose his salary and position. Buddy wondered if Dietrich had fought back.

Chapter Seventy-One

Mei was running through shadows. Pale stone walls rose on either side of her. The stone overhead lowered and lowered the farther she ran. In front of her was only darkness. But she couldn't turn around or go back. Not with the footsteps behind her, moving faster and faster, sounding louder and louder on the floor that was so dark it must be onyx.

Now her head bumped the rock above. It was hard and hurt her. She had to crouch down to keep going. The walls angled inward, and as she stuck out her arms she could touch both of them. She shrank as she moved forward. She was afraid to turn back. She had to get down on her knees and scuttle. Now the walls brushed her shoulders.

She could hear the footsteps behind her, the rustling of clothes.

The shadows had become pitch black. She could see nothing, could sense nothing of her surroundings except the cold stone pressing against her on four sides.

The ceiling grew lower still. She had to lie on her back and go head-first into the ever-shrinking passageway. The stone around her smelled of moisture, dampness, minerals. The stone above touched her nose, her forehead. She could go no farther.

She stopped her frantic motion.

She lay still.

Listened for the footsteps.

But there weren't any. She was alone. Yet she couldn't move, couldn't get out. She began to push at the stone, to pound at it with her fists. But it remained immovable, silent, vast.

Almost without noticing, she realized the air had grown thin. She was breathing quickly, but her consciousness was fading. She fought it as long as she could. She pounded the stone, tried to turn and go back the way she'd come. But she couldn't move or breathe.

A tomb, she thought. *My tomb.*

She punched the stone as hard as she could.

And woke.

In her bedroom she sat up. Saw that Buddy was gone when she most wished he were here. She looked around the quiet room, then rubbed her eyes.

Sighing, she turned to sit on the edge of the bed and looked at the clock on her night table.

Eight o'clock.

Shaking off the dream, she padded into the kitchen where she saw Buddy's note on the counter saying he'd left for work, and he was sorry.

She hoped he was all right, but she didn't look at the photocopies of the bills of sale spread across the kitchen counter. There wasn't time.

When she checked her phone, she saw that Anta Safar, Porter Gallery's assistant director, had sent her an e-mail urging her to be at work promptly that morning. Anta Safar and Jessica would be at an all-day client meeting in East Hampton. Mei had to hurry, but she'd comply. She'd never been one of those rich women who couldn't keep a job because they wouldn't work hard.

Knocking on Ben's door, she woke him and asked him to shower and dress. He barely moved under the covers.

"Come on, Ben. You're really late for school."

He groaned. "I don't want to go. Not today."

"But you shouldn't miss class. You'll fall behind."

"Just tell them I'm sick."

She was going to be late to the gallery. She didn't have time to take him to school, and he'd be afraid of being accompanied by one of Ward's bodyguards. Despite the precedent she might be setting, she said, "All right. But you have to go with me to the gallery."

"Fine."

"We have to go now, Ben."

Slowly, he sat up and pushed aside the covers. His hair was disheveled, his cheeks pink with the warmth of sleep.

She thought he was the most adorable boy she'd ever seen.

"Hurry," she told him.

In her bedroom she put on a black dress of heavy silk and a pearl necklace with matching earrings. She packed high heels in a tote bag, put on a pair of L. L. Bean boots, and walked out of her bedroom. As she met Ben in the foyer, where he was putting on his New Balance sneakers and navy-blue peacoat, she thought of the small revolver Ward had given her. She reached to press the button for the elevator—and then paused.

Recalling the attacks here at her home and at Ward's house, her chest tightened. Going outside, out into the streets, and walking or taking a taxi to her gallery filled her with anxiety.

"Just a minute," she told Ben, and hurried back down the hallway to her bedroom.

After closing the door, she took the nylon case holding the revolver from the closet shelf, together with the box of bullets, and set them on the bed. Then she unzipped the case and took out the revolver. It took her a moment to remember how to work the cylinder, but eventually it popped open. She didn't think she needed to fill the entire cylinder, so she took only three bullets from the box and inserted them into the revolver. Once she'd snapped it closed the way Ward had shown her, she thrust it into the bottom of her handbag and left the room, the nylon case and box of bullets remaining on the bed.

At 8:25 a.m., the elevator door opened in the lobby, where they were met by one of Ward's security guards.

He didn't smile.

Mei turned to her left and saw the second security guard by the fire stair door. She said good morning to both guards.

They nodded.

The guard by the elevator said, "Where are you going?"

"Work," she told him. "Porter Gallery, on Fifty-Eighth just east of Fifth."

"We'll get a cab."

"No," she said. "Ben and I have heavy coats and hats. We'd like to walk."

The guard shook his head. "I'd advise against it, ma'am. I can't cover you when you're walking, not as well as if we're in a car."

She said, "Thank you for your concern, but we've been cooped up for a day and we need to be outside for a while."

"It's very cold, ma'am."

"We don't mind, do we Ben?"

Ben was already walking toward the door. He liked Mei's apartment, but he felt restless. The cold air outside gave him energy. Running would be best, he thought, but he'd walk quickly, if Mei and the bodyguard could keep up.

He headed right out the door, toward Fifth Avenue.

He heard the soft rubbery sound of Mei's boots behind him. He saw people walking to work and strolling with their dogs. He saw older people using canes with one hand and clutching their coat collars closed with the other. He looked up, exhaled, and watched his breath form a cloud above him.

And then he no longer heard Mei's boots.

Suddenly worried, he stopped and turned around.

She was ten yards behind him, smiling, waving.

And just behind her was the big bodyguard. He didn't have a hat and seemed like he was in a bad mood. The guard met Ben's eyes but didn't smile.

Ben was reassured by the bodyguard's presence, but he didn't fully trust him. He allowed Mei to catch up to him, then walked beside her. In a low voice he asked, "Did you bring it?"

She looked at him. "What?"

"Did you bring the gun?"

"Yes," she told him. "Yes, I brought it."

Chapter Seventy-Two

Late morning, Buddy sat in his cubicle drinking from a large Dunkin' Donuts coffee cup. He tried to get his mind cranked up again, but the fatigue had him in its grip and was slowing him down. He stood up, circled the bull pen, and tried to shake it off. Yet even when he felt sufficiently awake to continue his work, he realized the deaths of Carl Brook and family had convinced part of him that no matter how hard he tried, he couldn't solve the case.

But the other part of him was royally pissed off.

Now he knew he was being played.

In the foyer of Bruno's town house, he'd discovered the bullet from the antique Gaston. That clue led right to Carl Brook—until Vidas had confirmed Carl's innocence through DOT video footage.

Now Buddy was presented a second time with physical evidence—the contact lens. Was it authentic, a mistake by the killer? Or was it another plant?

He didn't point out these things to Malone or Vidas. He figured they already knew he'd been played. That they'd also been fooled brought him little satisfaction. He resolved again to press on, to be as relentless and focused as he'd ever been.

Sitting in his desk chair, he called the attorney Robert Kahler.

Kahler's secretary put him through immediately.

Buddy said, "Mr. Kahler, I'd like to know if your client, Dietrich Brook, wears contact lenses. And if so, would you give me the prescription?"

Kahler said, "No words of condolence for my other client, Carl Brook, and his family?"

Buddy was silent.

Kahler added, "You're not doing your job."

Buddy wanted to reach through the phone line and throttle the guy, but he kept his emotions in check. "Just call me with the information. Thank you, Mr. Kahler."

He put down the phone and rolled back his chair so he could see Vidas. Hearing him, his partner turned around.

Buddy said, "Did you get the prescription on the contact lens CSU found in Carl's hallway?"

Vidas nodded, reached for the small notepad on his desk, and looked at it. "Greek to me, boss," Vidas said, holding it out for Buddy.

Buddy glanced at the numbers. "Makes no sense to me, either. Is that prescription strong or weak?"

"CSU said it was average."

"Average," Buddy echoed. "Except it was moist, so it had to belong to a family member or the killer. Unless . . ."

Vidas asked, "Unless?"

"Nothing," Buddy said. He didn't want to highlight the embarrassing notion that the killer was fucking with him.

His desk phone rang. "Lock here," he said.

"Detective, this is Robert Kahler."

"What do you have for me, Mr. Kahler?"

"My client, Dietrich Brook, does in fact wear contacts. He has provided me with his prescription."

Buddy picked up a pencil and grabbed a Post-it note. "Would you read it to me?"

He wrote as Kahler spoke. Then he read it back to Kahler, who confirmed it was correct.

Buddy said, "Hang on a minute, would you?"

He muted the phone and rolled his chair back. "Vidas," he said, "show me the prescription you got from CSU."

Vidas ripped off the sheet of notebook paper and handed it to Buddy.

Buddy compared them carefully, but it was clear the prescriptions matched. He returned the notebook paper to Vidas. Vidas nodded at him encouragingly.

Buddy rolled back to his desk, pressed the mute button again, and said, "Mr. Kahler, may I send a team over to collect a DNA sample from Dietrich Brook? It's an easy thing, just a cotton swab to the mouth. Doesn't take long and it's painless."

A pause on the other end of the line. Then Kahler said, very crisply, "No, Detective. You may not have a DNA sample or anything else. Goodbye."

Buddy hung up and considered Dietrich Brook. The man probably had the ability to commit the crimes. He'd no alibis, other than his wife, for any of them. He had motive—his brothers were trying to force him out of the family business. He likely knew of Carl's antique pistol. And early this morning CSU had discovered a single contact lens with a prescription that matched his own. For most detectives this would be convincing, yet Buddy wasn't convinced. He couldn't put his finger on exactly why, but he believed two connections existed. The first between the murders of the Brook family and the paintings that were essentially stolen in Nazi Germany. The second between those paintings and the most notorious of death camps.

As he thought about the case, he heard Vidas answer his phone, then hang up. "They're at the lab," Vidas told him, standing outside Buddy's cubicle. "Dietrich Brook's prints. From the SEC."

Buddy felt his body warm. "Did the lab scan them so we can compare them to the prints from the Carlyle Residences' lobby and elevator, plus Mei's apartment?"

"They're doing it now, but there are hundreds of prints. It might take a while."

Buddy followed Vidas down the hall and to the small lab at the back of the precinct offices. A young male technician—short, thin, pasty skin, large glasses, flannel shirt under his white lab coat—was scanning in the print card from the SEC.

Once the prints were scanned, the technician turned to them and said, "Thank you, Detectives. The prints are in the queue, and we'll get to them as soon as we can."

Vidas asked, "How long?"

The technician raised his eyebrows. "I'd say a week. Maybe a week and a half."

Buddy shook his head. "You'd say wrong. I'll give you an hour. You come to me with results in more than an hour, and I'm going to Chief Malone."

The technician stood and backed away. His face went from pale to pink. He seemed unused to being challenged. He said, "We have a system. Everyone waits his turn."

Vidas said, "What about priority? We're working a murder here."

The technician's eyes narrowed and his voice developed an edge. "Everyone's working a murder. Or a rape. We have limited staff." He waved his hand toward the room where a few others were bent over computers, lab tables, and equipment.

Buddy took a step forward. He knew he shouldn't be antagonizing anybody in CSU. He needed them today and he'd need them in the future. But in this moment he didn't care how many bridges he burned. He said, "We're dealing with twelve murders, including two cops. Do you want to be responsible if he strikes again?"

"No, sir."

"That's what I thought." Buddy looked at his watch. "Detective Vidas and I will be back in one hour."

But they didn't need to return. The technician called Buddy thirty-seven minutes later.

"It's Michael in the lab. I have a three-point match. Out of a possible twelve points to feel good about your guy. Not great, I'm afraid. Pretty tenuous, and it wouldn't stand up in court."

Buddy gripped his desk phone. "Where did we get the print that matches the SEC print?"

"From inside the Carlyle Residences."

"Which residence?"

"Nobody's residence. It came from the elevator cab that serves the residences."

Buddy thought about the path Dietrich Brook—if it had been Dietrich Brook—would have taken after attacking Mei and Ben at the Carlyle. Walk out with everyone else evacuating the building. Nab someone else's wallet. Go through the queue on Seventy-Sixth as that person. Or make up a name, address, and telephone number. And walk free.

Buddy hung up the phone. He sat quietly in his cubicle, glanced at his computer screen, and then turned away from it, instead staring blindly at his dented and coffee-stained desk. The bullet from Carl's Gaston had matched the bullet in Bruno's foyer, linking Carl to those murders, if only weakly. A bad set of fingerprints linked Dietrich to the Carlyle Residences elevator, but not conclusively.

Closing his eyes, he breathed deeply. He admitted to himself that he might be wrong. Perhaps things were as they seemed and Dietrich Brook was guilty. And yet he sensed the killer was near but faintly obscured, that his adversary was an ever-present but malevolent spirit rather than an ordinary man.

◆ ◆ ◆

Half an hour later the bull pen grew quiet. Buddy heard Chief Malone's booming voice. Just like the other detectives, he stood to see why the chief had come to the Nineteenth Precinct. In an instant he knew. Malone's huge figure bore down on him.

Buddy didn't move.

Malone, who looked no different than he had at four in the morning, other than his face having turned purplish red, planted one foot on Vidas's side of the cubicle wall and the other on Buddy's side. Malone pointed at both of them. "Time to poke the hornet's nest, gentlemen."

Buddy acted like he didn't know what Malone was urging him to do. Vidas looked at Buddy yet said nothing.

Almost panting, Malone said, "The lab told me what they found. You didn't think to call me? Not even as a *courtesy*?" Malone spit out the last word.

Vidas said, "It's only a three-point match."

Malone leaned forward. "What about the contact lens CSU found?"

Vidas shifted his weight from one foot to the other. "Same prescription used by Dietrich Brook, but we don't have DNA to compare."

Malone shoved his hands into his trouser pockets. He lifted his fleshy chin and glared at Buddy. "So what do you need, Detective? A video of Dietrich Brook killing everyone? Or having him do it in a theater with a thousand witnesses? How much before you get off the pot?"

Buddy knew he'd lost the argument, but also that Malone could be right. He might have his man, and moving now would take Mei and Ben out of danger. He turned to Vidas and said, "Go meet with Judge Conrad. Request a search warrant for Dietrich Brook's place in SoHo."

Chapter Seventy-Three

Late afternoon, Mei worked at her desk at Porter Gallery. She was alone, except for Ben, who was playing in Anta Safar's office behind the exhibition space. Mei was writing her essay for the Joshua Reynolds catalogue to be issued in connection with the show in September, when she received an e-mail from Peter Armitage. She clicked on it and read:

> Thanks for having drinks with me the other day. You asked me not to contact you for three months, but here I am doing just that. You're very beautiful and I think we'd have a good time together. Some friends and I are off to Ibiza on Saturday. Travel is private, of course. Would you join me? Best, Peter

Her face grew hot. Peter had assumed her relationship with Buddy would falter. Peter had ignored her request to leave her alone for a mere ninety days. And that *of course* irritated her, as if one simply didn't and wouldn't travel on commercial airlines.

She deleted Peter's e-mail and continued working for another half hour. When she heard a metallic noise from the rear of the gallery, she realized it had been nearly an hour since she'd checked on Ben. Concerned that he'd left Anta Safar's office and gone to explore the large storage room at the rear of the gallery, she slid her chair back from her desk. The storage room, she knew, contained vertical racks holding million-dollar paintings. It wasn't a playground for a ten-year-old.

Then she heard another noise. It sounded like the rear gallery door between the back hallway and the alley.

As she stood, she noticed her handbag and remembered the revolver inside it. Shaking her head, she began to leave her desk. She glanced at the front door, to be sure no visitors had entered the gallery, but Ward's guard wasn't there. She didn't know if he'd stepped away for a coffee, walked ten feet beyond her vision, or gone.

Returning to her desk, she grabbed the handbag and looped its straps over her left shoulder. Then she walked slowly into the hallway leading to the offices and the storage room, her high heels clicking on the polished concrete.

Chapter Seventy-Four

Buddy sat in his cubicle and called the Polish Institute for Holocaust Studies in the Bronx.

When the receptionist answered, he said, "This is Detective Lock with the New York City Police Department. I'd like to meet with someone who can help me trace survivors of Auschwitz who lived in Poland after the war."

"Good afternoon, Detective," the woman replied. "There are two gentlemen who work as researchers and scholars in your subject area. The first is a young man who did excellent work at Oxford University. He's bright and very pleasant."

Here the woman stopped.

Buddy said, "And the other researcher?"

"Ah. Well, that would be Dr. Kosmatka."

Again the woman paused.

Buddy said, "What are Dr. Kosmatka's qualifications?"

"He's . . . he's a linguist, Detective. Speaks many languages. But he's older now, a bit frail, and hard of hearing. I'm surprised he's still with us, after surviving the death camps as a boy."

Buddy felt his pulse quicken. "Is Dr. Kosmatka available to meet with me tomorrow?"

There was a pause during which Buddy heard the rustling of papers.

Coming back on the line, the receptionist said, "Dr. Kosmatka is available anytime after three o'clock tomorrow afternoon. But are you sure, Detective?"

Buddy ignored her question, saying only, "Please tell him I'll be there at three p.m."

As he hung up, he noticed the desk sergeant standing by his cubicle. He stood.

"Buddy, there's some confused kid here to see you. Says he wants to confess, but that he didn't do it."

Buddy winced. "Didn't do what?" he asked.

"Wouldn't say anything more than 'Bruno Brook.' Want me to send him away?"

"No," Buddy said, jumping up. "Put him in the interview room."

Minutes later Buddy sat across a scratched and gouged metal table from a high school kid. The kid wore a navy-blue sport coat with his school's crest embroidered on the breast pocket of the jacket. He had a few pimples but was otherwise handsome, with fair skin, dark hair, and a mole to the left of his nose.

Buddy set his digital audio recorder on the table and said, "What's your name?"

"Mark Rydell." The kid's voice was in the middle range, a little nasal.

"You're in school?"

"Dalton."

"Why are you here?"

"To tell you what I know."

"About what?"

"About what happened to Lucy Brook. Well, to her entire family."

Buddy leaned back, crossed his arms. "What do you know?"

"Lucy was my girlfriend."

Buddy didn't say anything.

Mark Rydell stopped, waited for Buddy to do something, and then continued. "I saw her on New Year's Eve. Up at Camp Kateri."

Buddy said, "How'd you get to Camp Kateri?"

"There's a road a half mile away. I borrowed my uncle's Jeep and drove up there to be with Lucy. But I left before the police arrived."

"Did you?"

"Yes, sir. Lucy kicked me out."

"Why would she do that?"

"We had an argument. And that's . . . that's why I'm here, sir. She had something going with John Brook. He's her cousin."

Buddy kept a poker face.

The kid nearly stuttered, "I just want . . . wanted you to know. Because John Brook found out about us—about Lucy and me. And he threatened to kill her."

Buddy said, "So you think John Brook might have taken revenge on Lucy by killing her and her family?"

Mark Rydell nodded. "Isn't it possible? I mean, I just thought I should tell you what I know."

Buddy uncrossed his arms and leaned closer to the kid, who obviously didn't know that John Brook was dead. Buddy thought the kid was telling the truth, but he had the chance to confirm his story and also John Brook's veracity. "Mr. Rydell," he said. "When you found out about John and Lucy, were you angry?"

"Yes."

Buddy waited a moment and then asked, "Did you hit Lucy?"

The kid's eyes wandered down to the table.

"Did you hit Lucy?" Buddy asked again.

Mark Rydell nodded.

Buddy said, "Yes or no, please. Did you hit Lucy?"

"Yes."

"Where?"

The kid looked up at him. "At Camp Kateri."

"No," Buddy said. "Where on her body did you hit her?"

The kid pointed to his chest.

Buddy said, "Will you hit a woman ever again?"

"No, sir."

"Then get the hell out of here."

Chapter Seventy-Five

A solitary figure waited in the storage room at the back of Porter Gallery. He stood in the high-ceilinged space with white walls and concrete floors, behind a rack that held a large painting upright. He didn't move. He breathed silently. A few moments ago he'd intentionally banged two large racks together to create a fierce metallic sound. He wanted to draw Mei away from the exhibition space where anyone might enter, where the security cameras recorded everything, where the bodyguard waited out on the sidewalk. He'd been here before, having visited the gallery on Mei's day off. He'd seen the security cameras in the exhibition space and then asked to use the restroom and come back into the hallway that ran between the offices and the large storage room. He'd found the locked door between the end of the hallway and the alley outside. In the hallway he'd seen no cameras, and his plan had taken shape.

He heard the click of Mei's heels on the concrete. The sound grew nearer, sharper, louder. He fastened more tightly the Velcro of his leather gloves. To an art gallery open to the public, he hadn't brought his favored tool. Instead he'd rely on his hands. It would be a more immediate, a more direct pleasure to watch Ben's life squeezed out of him like nectar from a peach. And the attractive woman approaching him along the hallway? Well, it couldn't be avoided. Her crime had been offering help to the doomed boy.

Chapter Seventy-Six

Mei continued along the back hallway. She glanced through the window into Anta Safar's office and saw Ben watching a movie. He was so intent on his laptop screen, he didn't see her. Remaining in the hallway, she stopped and listened but heard nothing. She was being silly and worrying too much, she thought. Nobody would try something at a Midtown art gallery on a weekday. She smiled as she walked into the office. Now Ben noticed her. He looked up, paused his movie, and removed his headphones.

He said, "Hi, Mei."

"Everything okay?"

"Yep."

"Do you need anything?"

"No."

"You're sure?"

"I guess I'm thirsty."

She said, "Don't tell anyone I did this," and then went around Anta Safar's desk, opened the small refrigerator behind it, and took out a lime mineral water for him and another for herself.

He opened it and sipped. In his right hand was Anta Safar's cigarette lighter. He was playing with the wheel, making the flame shoot out.

"Let's put the lighter in the top drawer, all right? It's not a toy."

He looked at her, hesitated, and complied.

"I'll be up front," she told him. "Come get me if you need anything."

"Okay," he said, and put on his headphones.

She opened her water and began walking toward the door.

Then she heard another clang—similar to the one she'd heard a minute ago but louder. It sounded as if one of the storage racks was rolling around the storage room. Her body flooded with heat. Her hands began to shake.

She reached into her handbag for the revolver. Touching it, she found it heavy and its metal cool. Her hand was steadied as she took hold of the gunstock and lifted the revolver out of the handbag. She dropped the handbag on the floor, set down her can of water, and moved to the doorway.

"Hello?" she called. "Ms. Safar? Jessica?"

But there was no answer.

She stepped into the hallway. Looked right toward the exhibition space and left toward the storage room. Saw no one.

Reaching down, she removed the sling back off one of her heels, then the other. Now that she stood in bare feet, she could move quickly on the concrete.

"Mci?"

It was Ben's voice from behind her. He must have seen her take out the gun and drop the handbag. But she didn't look back at him, only put a hand behind her to indicate he should stay by the desk.

He obeyed, slipping out of view.

Slowly she proceeded down the hallway, keeping the gun at her side. She didn't want to shoot Anta Safar or Jessica by accident. On the right side of the hallway was the door to the storage room. She approached it cautiously, her right hand gripping the revolver tightly.

The storage room door was open. She peeked into the opening, but she couldn't see much. The room was dark, the lights out.

Reaching her hand around the door, she switched on the lights.

Immediately the entire room was illuminated.

She saw that one of the large racks had rolled into the center of the room. It held a large canvas that hid most of the room from view, but otherwise nothing seemed wrong.

Standing very still, she heard nothing, saw nothing.

Sighing, she relaxed and reasoned the rack must have drifted into the center of the room, as there was a gentle slope toward a drain in the floor slab. She entered the room and walked around the rack holding the canvas that blocked her view. Behind it she saw only more racks of paintings, all in their proper places. With her free hand she grabbed the rack's side bar and pulled it against the wall to the left.

The door to the storage room slammed shut.

She jumped in surprise. She moved around the rack, rushed to the door, tried the handle.

Locked.

"Ben?" she called. *"Ben!"*

She heard nothing on the other side of the door. She was locked in the storage room while Ben watched a movie in Anta Safar's office. But he wasn't alone. Someone else was out there in the hallway.

Beginning to panic, she realized she couldn't protect Ben. Couldn't save him. And if he were cornered in Anta Safar's office, he'd have no way to escape. He'd be killed.

No! No. She'd find a way.

But the storage room locked from the outside. She knew she had one option. It might not work yet she'd try.

She stepped back eight feet, and with both hands, aimed the gun at the door lock. Remembering she had only three shots, she held her breath and pulled the trigger.

Chapter Seventy-Seven

Ben stood when he heard the gunshots.

Bang! Bang!

Guessing they'd come from Mei's revolver, he feared someone had taken her gun and shot her. For a moment he didn't know what to do. He'd run or hide, he thought. But he didn't trust the hallway. Someone must be waiting for him just outside the door, ready to grab and kill him if he left the office.

Yet he moved toward the door. One step. Two.

He listened. Heard nothing except Mei's faint voice calling for him, urging him to run just as his mother had urged him to run on New Year's Eve.

He saw the lock on the office door. He reached out and pressed the button to set it, then pushed the door with all his strength so it slammed shut.

On Anta Safar's desk was a telephone. He could call the police, but they wouldn't be here soon enough. Looking around the room, he searched for another way to stop the killer. But he saw nothing except a smoke detector on the ceiling.

This gave him an idea.

He grabbed Anta Safar's cigarette lighter and a piece of paper. After climbing up on the desk, he flicked the lighter's wheel and held down the button to keep the flame going. Then he held the flame to the piece of paper.

The paper ignited.

He held the burning paper up to the ceiling.

Five seconds later a piercing siren rang out through the gallery.

Dropping to his knees, he climbed down, stamped out the paper on the floor, and knelt behind the desk.

Knowing he couldn't be seen from the office window, he didn't look up. He tried not to move, but he trembled. He hoped Mei was all right, but he believed she'd die and the killer would search for him.

The siren wailed. It hurt his ears. He wanted to cover them, but he needed to hear Mei if she came for him.

He didn't look up. He put his hands together as if in prayer.

Chapter Seventy-Eight

She'd fired two shots, but the lock held. Each second mattered. Each second she was stuck in this room, Ben was unprotected.

The siren shrieked. She didn't know if it was the security system or a fire alarm.

Oh, God!

She tried to think clearly: two shots, one shot remaining.

Taking a step forward, she crouched to lower her center of gravity. She slowed her breathing and counted to five. Then she squinted, aimed the barrel of the revolver at the stainless steel lock, and fired.

Bang!

A crisp, overwhelmingly loud noise.

The lock blew apart.

Ears ringing, she jumped forward and pulled away the lock's remnants. Once again she raised the gun and with her free hand opened the door.

The siren was louder. *Screeching.*

Carefully she looked out into the hallway. To her right, disappearing through the door into the back alley, she saw a figure in black wearing a black hat. And then the figure was gone. She thought she was too late, but still she rushed to her left to find Ben.

Looking through the window into Anta Safar's office, she couldn't see him. Her heart was in her throat. She tried the handle but it wouldn't move.

She pounded on the door.

No response.

Again she knocked, this time calling his name. "Ben! Are you there? Ben, it's Mei. *Ben!*"

A shock of black hair rose above Anta Safar's white desk, followed by Ben's eyes. He saw her, stood, and ran forward. After he'd opened the door, she put her arms around him and drew him close. She inhaled the clean smell of his hair mixed with the mint shampoo he'd used.

Thank God, she thought.

He didn't let go immediately, just held her.

The siren stopped abruptly. They heard voices in the exhibition space. One of them sounded like Ward's guard.

In the office she could hear both of them breathing.

Her pulse beat so fast she felt weak.

Now she recalled the figure in black. Had it been only a delivery guy? She tried to compare the figure with the one she'd glimpsed at Ward's house, but her memory of the man she'd seen vault through her bedroom window was too fuzzy. At least this time she'd a sense of the man's shape, if not his face or any other characteristic. She thought she might have seen him before. Perhaps he wasn't someone she knew, but someone not entirely unfamiliar.

And yet she wasn't sure she'd been attacked, not sure she was in any danger at all. Perhaps she'd been spooked by the door closing in the storage room, and the man who'd disappeared was only a deliveryman. Disengaging from Ben, she looked once again out into the hallway. There by the alley door was a package from FedEx.

"I think I overreacted," she said aloud.

Ben looked up at her. "But you fired the gun," he said. "Three times."

"I was stuck in the storage room and I thought we were under attack, but maybe there wasn't any danger. Maybe my brain is playing tricks on me and I'm seeing things."

She walked barefoot back down the hallway to the alley door. It was locked.

"See," she said, "nobody could have gotten in."

But as she said this, she wondered how the FedEx guy had entered the gallery.

Chapter Seventy-Nine

Buddy pulled the Charger in front of Porter Gallery. He climbed out, ignored the bodyguard Ward had posted by the door, and walked inside.

Mei and Ben were standing behind her desk at the far end of the exhibition space. When they saw him, they rushed over.

After kissing Mei's cheek, he knelt and gave Ben a hug.

"You all right?" he asked.

Ben said, "I think so." But his voice was tentative and small.

Buddy stood and looked at Mei. "I'm glad you called. Sounds like the revolver saved you. Or the fire alarm."

Mei said, "I don't know. Maybe he didn't expect me to have a gun. Or maybe it was only the FedEx man and we weren't in any danger."

Buddy shook his head. "It wasn't FedEx. Not if things happened the way you told me. So I'm having CSU come over here, but we're leaving."

Lines formed on Mei's forehead. "I can't leave. Anta Safar and Jessica aren't back yet."

"We're leaving," Buddy insisted. "Ward's guard can watch the gallery until whoever gets back. Don't argue about this—Ben isn't safe here."

Chapter Eighty

That evening Buddy forced normality on them, and they ordered Chinese. Although Buddy was exhausted from not sleeping the night before and deeply disturbed after seeing the brutalized bodies of Carl Brook and his family, he tried to be upbeat. He couldn't let them see how he felt. He couldn't let them know. He needed to be the rock for their little family.

After dinner he avoided switching on the television, in case there was news about Ben's family. Instead he got behind the piano and began to play Bach's Fantasia and Fugue in A Minor. It wasn't long before he was lost in the music, almost forgetting the woman and boy who'd come to mean more to him than anything else. From the corner of his eye, he saw Ben slide over toward Mei, lie down on the sofa, and rest his head on her leg. She ran a hand through his hair. He closed his eyes.

Buddy thought he'd failed as a concert pianist before he'd even started, but maybe those years of practice and stress had been worth something if the music would soothe a traumatized boy.

At the end of the piece, he stopped for a moment and then began Chopin's Nocturne no. 18. Yet just as his mood regained some buoyancy, he felt anew the anguished loss of Carl Brook, Rebecca Brook, John Brook, and Ariel Brook. It took all his concentration just to continue playing. He closed his eyes and tried to think of something better: Mei's happy tears as she'd accepted his proposal, Ben's clapping in that moment. But when he'd finished the short piece, he realized he couldn't keep going. The darkness had lodged in his soul and wouldn't release him.

He got up from the piano, went over and knelt by Ben, and embraced him. Briefly. Firmly.

Then he left the room. Went to the kitchen for a beer. Didn't return.

The photocopies of the bills of sale remained spread out on the counter. He separated from the others the three bills of sale he'd marked as having sellers who'd survived Auschwitz or had children or relatives who'd done so, but who also had family members who'd died at the death camp.

He studied them. And waited for Ben to go to bed.

After a while he heard Mei and Ben leave the living room and go into the hallway. A few minutes later she returned.

She said, "He's in bed. You won't say good night to him?"

Buddy nodded but didn't move. "I can't tonight."

Her face showed disappointment, confusion. "Why not?"

"I'm struggling," he told her. "It was a bad night."

"What happened?"

"At about three thirty this morning, the killer struck again."

Mei put her hand to her mouth.

Buddy said, "Carl Brook, his wife, his two children."

Her eyes watered. "No!"

"Yeah. The worst thing I ever saw. The daughter . . ."

He turned from her, stared at the papers on the counter.

She touched his shoulder but didn't speak.

He sensed that he was about to double over in grief, but he placed his palms on the counter and clenched his teeth until the feeling passed.

She watched him but was quiet.

After a long breath he said, "Don't tell Ben. Not yet. We're keeping it out of the news for a couple of days."

"All right."

"And Mei, I need your help."

"Whatever I can do."

Spreading the three bills of sale over the counter, he said, "Tell me about the paintings described in these. And then"—he took his phone out of his pocket, found the video he'd taken in Carl's gallery, and pressed "Play"—"tell me who made this small painting at the six-second mark."

She took the phone from him, held it close, and watched the video. When it was finished, she played it a second time. And a third. Then she played it a fourth time before stopping it at the six-second mark.

After squinting at the half-blurred image, she returned the phone to Buddy. Bending low over the counter, she studied the bills of sale. "They're in German," she said.

"Yeah. That's what I assumed."

"One of them is for a Michelangelo. Wow. I didn't know anyone actually owned a Michelangelo. The other is for a Rembrandt. The third is for . . ." Her voice halted. "May I see the image on the phone?"

He handed it to her. She watched the video a fifth time.

"This one," she said, pointing at the bill of sale in her hands, "is for the small painting in the video."

"Who painted it?"

"Caravaggio."

Buddy said, "How valuable?"

"Priceless, really. Extraordinarily rare. Caravaggio is considered one of the greatest painters in history. It's a version of Bacchus, the god of wine, similar to the one that hangs in the Borghese Museum."

Buddy nodded. He took the bill of sale from her and slid all the papers into the manila envelope. "Thank you."

She faced him and put her hands on her hips. "But I also need your help."

He sipped from his beer. "What can I do?"

"Take Ben to school tomorrow."

He considered all the arguments for keeping him home, but home hadn't turned out to be safe—and it wasn't even his home. Today they'd learned the gallery wasn't safe, either. CSU had spent hours there and turned up nothing. At the school there was tight security, children were never alone, and adults other than teachers and staff were prohibited. "All right," he said. "I'll drop him off on the way to searching Dietrich Brook's home."

Her eyes widened. "You're going after Dietrich Brook tomorrow?"

"Malone's orders."

"You don't think he's guilty?"

"I'm not sure."

"But you think there's something to do with the paintings."

"It's only a hunch."

She caressed the back of his neck. "Be careful."

Later, as Buddy lay in bed, he knew he'd sleep deeply. He had the premonition that tomorrow he'd break the case wide open. He'd need to be mentally sharp and physically strong. It would be a day not for mercy but for agility and relentlessness. He'd have to match his adversary in every way. No, not match. He'd have to destroy his adversary, or everyone he cared about would be taken away.

Chapter Eighty-One

At 7:50 a.m. Buddy pulled his Charger into the loading zone in front of Vista School. He got out and walked Ben inside.

The headmaster himself greeted Ben by the security turnstile. "Welcome to Vista, Ben!"

Ben gave Mr. McConnell an uncertain smile and shook his hand. He turned to Buddy and waved.

Buddy said, "You'll be all right?"

Ben nodded. "Will you pick me up?"

"Mei or I will be here at three o'clock."

Ben waved forlornly. "Bye."

Buddy's heart felt like it was cracking. He tried to smile. He hoped nothing would happen to Ben today at school. He said, "Goodbye, Ben."

He watched the headmaster lead Ben to the security desk and help the guard issue him an identification badge. Ben turned around, watched him for a moment, then followed the headmaster through the turnstile before disappearing into the hallway to the classrooms.

Chapter Eighty-Two

Twenty minutes later Buddy joined Vidas and knocked on the door of Dietrich Brook's condominium, a CSU team in tow.

The door opened.

Buddy placed his hand over his chest, two inches from the Glock in his shoulder holster. Then he dropped his hand when he saw the beautiful Lydia Brook.

"Mrs. Brook," Buddy said. "Detective Lock, NYPD. Here's a warrant allowing us to search your home. Please step aside."

Vidas held up the warrant he'd picked up from Judge Conrad an hour earlier.

Buddy expected Lydia Brook to complain or show anger that her privacy was being invaded. But instead she nodded and moved away from the door. He watched as she strode into the kitchen, picked up a mobile phone, and pressed two buttons. She whispered briefly into the phone, and didn't look at him again. She just turned and disappeared farther back into the condo, away from the search team.

Buddy guessed they had ten or fifteen minutes before Brook's lawyer, Robert Kahler, found another judge to halt the search. His problem was that a textbook search of Dietrich Brook's enormous condominium would take two or three days rather than thirty minutes. They had almost no time to find Dietrich Brook's mistake—if, that is, Brook had made one.

"You take the common areas," he told Vidas, "I'll do the bedrooms."

Vidas nodded, slipped on a pair of latex gloves, and charged into the great room and kitchen.

Buddy hurried toward the master bedroom. He moved deep into the condominium, the way Lydia had gone. He looked around. Large room, floor-to-ceiling windows looking out over SoHo. Wood floors partly covered by a Persian rug. Large paintings on the two walls without windows. Lydia was there, standing by the windows, staring outside. She started when he entered the room, but she didn't turn toward him or leave.

Ignoring her potential objection, he took out his phone and photographed the paintings. He went into an enormous walk-in closet with built-in cabinets and drawers. He opened the cabinet doors and saw more clothes hanging in perfect order than he'd ever seen outside a department store. He didn't search further. Dietrich Brook wasn't stupid. He wouldn't have hidden incriminating evidence in his closet. He'd have known it was the first place Buddy would search.

Buddy walked through the closet and into the bathroom. All white. A large window overlooking the neighborhood with a sheer blind lowered. His and hers sinks. Spotless. He opened the drawers under the vanity, saw Lydia's hairbrushes, creams, and perfumes. He went to the next column of drawers and saw Dietrich's hairbrush, comb, toothbrush, bottle of Advil, and bottle of cologne.

He picked up the cologne. It was Zizan, made by Ormonde Jayne of London.

Chapter Eighty-Three

Buddy's chest tightened. He held up the bottle and saw the bourbon-colored liquid inside. He pulled off the cap and sniffed. *The scent.*

A mistake, but not enough for court or to forge a connection to the murders. Yet his internal compass pointed closer to Dietrich Brook.

After replacing the cap and setting the bottle in the drawer, he closed the drawer and glanced at his watch. Five or ten minutes remaining.

Within the vast condominium, where would someone hide the tools of murder?

He hadn't seen all of the condo, but he'd seen enough to know there would be closets and drawers and hundreds of hiding places. He considered all those places, and then he decided.

Leaving the master bathroom, he walked out through the closet, past Lydia Brook, and out into the hallway. He returned to the great room, passed Vidas and some of the CSU team, and kept going. He entered the second, narrower hallway he'd used when he interviewed Dietrich Brook in the office. He passed the office and came to another open door. He looked inside. Here it was.

A girl's room. Must be Hayley's. He walked in and saw a cream-colored rug over the wood floors. Large windows. An expensive-looking duvet on a queen-sized bed. Modern and old-fashioned European paintings on the walls. A corkboard with ticket stubs and playbills for shows on Broadway. A signed and framed Vampire Weekend poster on the wall. He looked more closely. A lift ticket for Buttermilk in Aspen, Colorado. Photographs of Hayley and her family. Of Hayley and friends.

Nothing to arouse suspicion, he realized. But wasn't that the point?

Whatever Dietrich had hidden would have to be out of Hayley's reach. She couldn't discover the tools of murder or she'd know the truth about her father.

Beyond her reach, Buddy thought. And looked up.

The condominium was a converted industrial building. Brick exterior walls, thick wooden beams extending across the rooms, exceptionally high ceilings with exposed ductwork painted black as the metal ceiling. A maze of wires and track lights and lights suspended on wires.

He walked out into the hallway and called for CSU.

"Yes, sir?" asked a young man of about thirty. Clean cut with brown eyes behind thick eyeglasses.

"You don't have a ladder, do you?"

"We don't. Why do you ask?"

Buddy pointed skyward. "I wanted to get up near the ceiling."

"I'm sorry."

"Think there's a utility closet?"

The young man's eyes widened. "I don't know. If there is, it would be toward the core of the building."

"The core?"

"The center. Where the elevators and the plumbing run from the basement up to the roof."

Buddy said, "Help me find it. We have five minutes or less."

The CSU guy shook his head. "I don't understand. We'll be here for a couple of days at least."

"Nope. Our warrant will be thrown out. You don't think a billion-aire under suspicion of murder hasn't lawyered up?"

Now the CSU guy understood. "It would be this way," he said, motioning Buddy farther along the hallway, which turned right and dead-ended at two large doors.

Buddy opened the first door, but it was a gym. Which told him something. The man who'd killed and broken into Ward's house and escaped from the Carlyle couldn't have been frail. Not even out of shape. Dietrich Brook was thin but strong.

The CSU guy opened the second door. They looked inside and saw an eight-by-eight-foot utility room. Electrical systems, security-system control panel, telephone riser, audio system, and leaning against the far wall, a tall stepladder.

Buddy charged into the room, picked up the stepladder, and carried it out through the doorway and into Hayley's bedroom. He set up the ladder in the center of the bedroom, looked at the junior detective, and said, "Stay here, by the base, okay?"

"Um. Okay."

Buddy gripped each side of the ladder and climbed as fast as he could, the ladder swaying under his shifting weight. At the second-highest rung, his feet were nearly ten feet above the cream-colored rug. The ladder was unsteady, but he wanted to have the best view.

He found patches of light mixed with shadows. He couldn't see clearly and had no flashlight to point into the shadows. With a gloved hand he grasped and angled one of the pendant lights hanging by a wire from the metal ceiling deck. Turning it almost horizontal, he aimed it at a patch of shadows. *Shit!* The light was too hot to hold. He let it drop and it swung helter-skelter to his left.

He looked down at the junior detective. "Take off your windbreaker and hand it to me."

"What?"

"For Christ's sake. Do it now!"

The guy unzipped his navy-blue CSU windbreaker and handed it up to Buddy. Buddy took the jacket, folded it, and put one hand on each side of the fold. Then he took hold of the same pendant light and aimed it into the shadows above the room. He saw, brightened by the light, aluminum ductwork painted black, PVC pipe painted black that surely held the electrical wires that coursed around the ceiling of the giant condominium. He saw dust on all of the foregoing. He saw the tops of the wooden beams that crossed the entire living space and rested atop the wooden columns and the brick exterior walls and the interior walls. But he saw nothing suspicious.

After easing the pendant light down, he turned the opposite way, in the direction of the windows, and used the windbreaker to cradle another pendant light. He picked it up and aimed it toward other shadows and other darkness. He saw more ductwork and PVC pipe suspended by wires extending from the deck above. He saw fabric above the beam where the beam met the exterior brick wall. Straining to see, Buddy held the light up and over, as far as he could. The light wouldn't quite reach.

A duffel bag and . . . rope? Climbing gear, maybe. He wasn't exactly sure what climbing gear looked like, but was it something a teenage girl would hide on a structural beam directly over her bed?

They heard shouting coming from the main part of the house. He thought he heard the word *quashed*.

Time was up.

The CSU guy was perspiring. He'd heard what Buddy heard. He said, "Someone's shut down our search."

Buddy said, "Not yet."

"They're calling us to the elevator. They're saying we have to leave. Immediately."

"Then do what you're told."

267

The guy looked at him, pushed up his eyeglasses, and left the room.

Buddy ignored the people calling for him. He thought if he got his hands on the duffel before he had actual notice his search warrant was quashed, the duffel's contents might be admissible in court. His blood boiled through his body. If he could just . . .

He dropped down the ladder, then moved it to the side of the room. He pulled at Hayley's bed, yanking as hard as he could, one end of it and then the other, to the center of the room. He picked up the ladder and carried it around the bed until it was stationed beneath the stash. He began climbing the ladder.

"Stop right there, Detective." A loud, deep voice.

He ignored the command.

He heard Vidas's voice say, "Leave Buddy alone, for Christ's sake!"

The deep voice came again: "Stop now, Detective! We're NYPD, just like you."

Buddy continued climbing.

"Get him down!"

Buddy reached up into the ceiling space, hands probing the shadows for the stash.

Then they grabbed his legs.

He tried to pull out his phone and take a photograph of what he'd seen, but he was unsteady up that high. He reached for the ceiling beam, but two NYPD uniformed officers pulled him off the ladder as if he were some kind of heavy package.

"Let go of me!" he yelled, thrashing at them.

The two officers half dropped, half set him on the floor. One of them—a boy cop with acne—laughed.

Vidas stood by, red-faced. He made a fist and was about to hammer one of them.

Buddy caught his eye and held it. He didn't need his partner arrested.

Buddy got to his feet and turned on the two cops. "Do you know what you've done?"

"NYPD," said a voice behind him. "The court of appeals quashed your search warrant. You're done here, Detective."

Buddy swirled around and saw a middle-aged captain. The name on his left breast pocket read "Copley." Short graying black hair, skinny build, thin lips.

Buddy pointed up at the ceiling. "Know what's up there, Captain Copley? Maybe all the evidence we need to convict the owner of this condo for murder one. Murder one for multiple victims. But what do you do? You hurry over here to fuck with my search warrant."

The captain shifted his weight from one foot to the other. "You going to be insubordinate?"

"You're not in my chain of command."

"You want me to take this up with the commissioner?"

Buddy raised his chin. "I wish you would. You can explain how you let a serial killer go free."

"I don't see a serial killer here, Detective," the captain replied, looking around the bedroom before taking hold of Buddy's upper arm.

Buddy shrugged him off, more violently than he intended. Buddy walked through the doorway, out into the hallway, and into the great room. He turned and made no eye contact with members of the CSU team. He went out into the foyer and pressed the button for the elevator. As his temper cooled, he asked himself if there'd been anything important on the beam over Hayley's bedroom. Maybe. But maybe the duffel had been filled with old clothes or drugs. Or the contractor who'd remodeled the space for the Brook family had forgotten it.

A gold mine or a dead end.

He heard a chime and the elevator doors opened.

"You're following the wrong leads, Detective." It was Dietrich Brook, dressed in a long gray overcoat and black leather gloves. Brook's voice rose. "Find the killer! My God, what's the matter with you?"

Buddy stared at him.

Shaking his head angrily, Dietrich Brook walked out of the elevator and past Buddy.

Buddy got into the elevator. He smelled vetiver.

Chapter Eighty-Four

At two thirty that afternoon Mei began to put her desk in order. She was going to leave the gallery and take a taxi downtown to pick up Ben from Vista School.

But at that moment Ms. Anta Safar emerged from her office behind the exhibition space. Ms. Safar was dressed as usual in tight black pants, black boots, and a black blouse.

Mei smiled at her.

Usually Anta Safar returned her smile, but not today.

"You'll need to stay late," Anta Safar told her. "You'll be meeting with a potential client."

Mei tensed. "But I have to . . . I have something I need to do. In a few minutes I—"

Anta Safar didn't blink. "You must attend, Mei. Jessica is on vacation for the next week, and I have a conflicting meeting with a curator at the Met."

Mei nodded, realizing she had no choice. She hadn't told Anta Safar about the attempts on Ben's life, or even that Ben had come to live with her. She also hadn't told Anta Safar about the bullets she'd fired into the door of the storeroom, and her often scatterbrained boss hadn't noticed the damage. Mei said, "Who's the potential client?"

Anta Safar said, "A rich collector named Dietrich Brook."

Mei tried to hide her shock. To be sure they were discussing the same person, she asked, "We're meeting with the Dietrich Brook whose relatives were recently killed?"

Anta Safar nodded. "Yes, that's right. Have you read about them in the *Gazette*?"

Realizing she'd been holding her breath, Mei exhaled, then took in another gulp of air. Her face was flushed. Her heart pounded. She clasped her hands together and asked, "When is our appointment with Dietrich Brook?"

"He'll be here soon," Anta Safar said curtly before disappearing into the hallway that led to her office.

Mei pulled out her mobile phone and called Buddy. He picked up immediately.

She said, "Where are you?"

"Almost at the Polish Institute for Holocaust Studies in the Bronx. Ward and I are meeting with a researcher who might tell us if the killer is related to one of the Nazis' victims."

Mei pushed the phone tightly against her ear. "I have to meet with Dietrich Brook in a few minutes."

"What?"

"He wants to discuss buying or selling paintings—I'm not really sure which."

"You okay?"

"Yes," she lied. "It's the middle of the afternoon and there are lots of people out on Fifty-Eighth. Security cameras cover the exhibition space, and I'll call 911 if necessary, but I'm sure everything will be fine."

Buddy didn't respond.

She continued, "So I can't pick up Ben from school. Should we have him take a cab?"

"No," Buddy told her. "I'll have Vidas do it. But you should know that Dietrich Brook won't make your appointment."

"You're going to arrest him?"

"Maybe soon. But right now Ward's goon is watching him. Won't let him near you."

This made Mei feel better. Her meeting, she realized, wouldn't happen, no matter what Anta Safar wanted. Relief filled her.

Buddy said, "When you leave the gallery, go straight home and wait for Ben. Okay?"

"I'll be there," she promised.

Chapter Eighty-Five

Ben watched through the large plate glass window of the Vista School lobby. He looked out on to West Twenty-Eighth Street, afraid that instead of Mei he'd see Uncle Carl or Uncle Dietrich or someone else from his extended family. He checked his watch. It read 3:05 p.m. He sensed someone behind him and turned around.

"Ben? Ben Brook?"

It was the security guard, who'd walked around the front desk and approached him.

Ben said, "Yes?"

"I have a call for you over at the desk."

Ben nervously followed the security guard, who went behind the desk, picked up a telephone, and handed it across to him.

Ben held the phone up to his ear. "Hello?"

"Hi, Ben. It's Mei."

His voice brightened. "Hi, Mei."

"Everything all right at school?"

"Yes. Will you be here soon?"

"Something's come up, Ben. I'm stuck at work. So Buddy's sending his partner—you remember Detective Vidas, don't you?—to pick you up."

Ben sighed and said, "Okay."

"You'll be safe with Vidas, Ben. He carries a gun just like Buddy."

For a moment Ben was quiet. Then he said, "When will I see you?"

Her voice was cheerful. "I'm going to have a quick meeting at work, and then I'll go right home. Vidas will drop you off as soon as I get there, and then we can have a snack and maybe decide whether Buddy will let us take a walk in the park. So I'll see you in an hour or so, all right?"

"All right."

"Don't worry about anything."

"I won't."

The line went dead. Ben listened to it for a few seconds longer before handing it across the desk to the security guard. He returned to the window on Twenty-Eighth Street. And soon he saw a black Ford Fusion pull into the loading zone along the curb in front of the school. The driver's door opened and Detective Vidas, tall and thin and with a pale face, climbed out. Ben watched Vidas look right and left as he closed the driver's door, walked the few steps to the building, and pulled open one of the school's glass doors.

Ben left the window and walked over to meet the detective.

Vidas saw him and smiled warmly. "Ben, how are you?"

Ben instantly felt better. He wished Mei could pick him up but knew he was safer with Vidas. He said, "Pretty well."

"Good! Buddy asked me to give you the special police-car ride home today. Ready to go?"

"Ready," Ben said, and followed Vidas out onto the sidewalk.

Before getting into the Ford, Vidas gripped Ben's shoulder and said, "Hang on, Ben."

Ben looked up at the detective's face. They were standing just outside the school doors. He saw Vidas scanning the street and the sidewalks, Vidas's right hand up near his chest so he could grab his gun if necessary. Ben said, "Are we safe?"

Slowly Vidas nodded. "Yeah, we're good. Let's get in the car. Quick."

Chapter Eighty-Six

"Mei?"

It was Anta Safar calling out from behind her.

Mei turned in her desk chair to face the assistant director. She forced herself to smile. Antagonizing Ms. Safar would only bring more trouble.

Anta Safar was dressed in her black coat with the shawl collar and a black scarf. She was carrying her usual black quilted Chanel handbag and walking briskly toward Mei. "I need to run, Mei, but I'm sure you can handle the meeting. I'm sure Mr. Brook will be along shortly."

Mei couldn't maintain the smile, even though she knew Ward's bodyguard would keep Dietrich Brook out of the gallery.

Anta Safar passed her and said, "Treat him *well*, Mei. It would mean a fortune for all of us if they used our gallery to sell his paintings."

Mei said, "Sure, that's just fine."

And then Anta Safar was gone. A few minutes later the gallery doors swung open again. But it wasn't Anta Safar returning for something she'd forgotten, it was Dietrich Brook.

He stepped into the gallery, stood very still, and glared at Mei.

Chapter Eighty-Seven

Buddy parked in front of the Polish Institute for Holocaust Studies. He grabbed the manila envelope containing the bills of sale Carl Brook had sent him, got out, and looked up at the old Gothic-style building in limestone with an ornate slate roof and narrow but tall windows. Then he turned and saw the campus of the Horace Mann prep school. A single flag flew at half-mast, drooping and still on the windless day. Buddy remembered now that John Brook and Ariel Brook had attended the school until their deaths yesterday. He watched as students left the campus after their last classes of the day, some with sorrowful expressions, some red-faced and weeping, none with smiles.

Hearing a large but quiet engine approaching, Buddy turned to see Ward's silver Range Rover drive up behind the Charger, Brick in the driver's seat.

As soon as the car stopped, Ward jumped out. He wore a dark suit under a light-gray overcoat with a black velvet collar. Buddy's practiced eye noticed a bulge under Ward's left arm and an irregular metallic shape at his right ankle. He didn't know if Ward had a license to carry these weapons, but he wouldn't object.

Buddy didn't greet Ward or shake his hand, just nodded toward the double front doors of the institute and walked inside, Ward following.

They passed through a vestibule and into a cavernous hall with a multivaulted ceiling like that of an old church. There were no security measures. In the middle of the hall was a low wooden reception desk with a middle-aged woman in an ivory-colored blouse and a periwinkle cardigan sitting behind it.

The woman smiled at them. "Good afternoon, and welcome to the Polish Institute for Holocaust Studies. May I help you?"

Buddy recognized her voice. "Thank you, ma'am," he said, and held up his opened badge wallet. "I'm Detective Lock with the NYPD. My associate and I are here to meet with Dr. Kosmatka."

The receptionist nodded and stood. "As I mentioned on the phone yesterday, Dr. Kosmatka is somewhat frail and has asked me to show you to his office."

She led them down the length of the hallway to a single honey-colored door at one end. The door had no window or name on it. After she'd knocked twice, they heard a muffled response. She opened the door and stood aside. "Dr. Kosmatka," she said, "the detectives are here to see you."

"Come in, please," came a low voice.

Buddy entered a large office with high ceilings. It was filled with books on shelves and piles of books on a large table and on the floor. To his left stood a metal filing cabinet with drawers five feet wide, to his right a large oak desk. Behind the desk sat an overweight man well over eighty years old who had thick white hair neatly parted. Dr. Kosmatka's skin was dark and mottled with age spots, and he held an unlit cigarette in one hand. He wore a wrinkled blue shirt and didn't stand up from behind the desk. He just stared at Buddy.

Buddy introduced himself and Ward, not bothering to badge the old man or explain Ward's status.

Dr. Kosmatka nodded but didn't ask them to sit down. Ward removed his overcoat, as if he meant to stay a while.

Buddy began to doubt this meeting would lead anywhere, but he'd see it through. He said, "Dr. Kosmatka, in the early 1940s in Berlin, some wealthy Jewish men and women sold extremely valuable paintings to Gerhardt Brook, an industrialist cozy with the Nazis. The paintings were sold under duress, probably for far less than they were worth. Gerhardt Brook's grandchildren inherited the paintings. But in the past few days nearly all the Brook family has been murdered."

Dr. Kosmatka's expression was inscrutable. He moved the unlit cigarette to the other hand.

Unsure if the old man was hearing him, Buddy spoke more slowly and louder. He said, "I believe the killer might be a descendant of one of the Jews who sold the paintings and were sent to Auschwitz. While there, some might have worked as slave labor for Gerhardt Brook's company. But some of those prisoners survived the war. And some may be living in America."

Dr. Kosmatka's voice rumbled, "I can't help you."

Buddy didn't move. He wasn't going to give up. Not when he'd come this far.

Dr. Kosmatka's eyebrows rose. He coughed once and said, "I can't help you, not without more."

Buddy opened the manila envelope with the bills of sale. He removed the three having sellers who had family that survived Auschwitz, and placed them in front of the old man.

Dr. Kosmatka picked up a pair of half-moon metal reading glasses and bent over to read the three bills of sale. He studied them for several minutes.

Buddy related how for these three families, the trail had gone dry upon the camp's liberation.

Dr. Kosmatka didn't look up at him, but said, "I was there."

Buddy was quiet.

Dr. Kosmatka unbuttoned his left shirt cuff and pulled up his sleeve.

Buddy saw a tattoo on the old man's forearm. He made out an *A* followed by five numbers.

Dr. Kosmatka said, "I was there that cold day in January. I met the Red Army soldiers. They gave me kasha, a porridge. Three years later I get to America." He refastened his shirt cuff.

Buddy nodded. He shifted his weight from one foot to the other. He took off his overcoat and draped it over the chair behind him, but he remained standing.

Dr. Kosmatka peered over his reading glasses at Buddy. He said, "Famous paintings, yes?"

Buddy nodded. "And one in particular, a Caravaggio of Bacchus, was stolen yesterday from the scene of a multiple homicide."

Dr. Kosmatka gave no response for a moment. Then he said, "Famous sellers, yes?"

"Are they?" Ward asked.

Buddy said, "I don't recognize them."

Dr. Kosmatka said, "Famous names before the war that ended those names, you understand? Prominent families. But it's unlikely any of them survived, as people this grand would have used their influence to make connections outside Poland after 1945."

Buddy asked, "Would you help us?"

Dr. Kosmatka stuck the unlit cigarette in his mouth. He put his hands on the armrests of his chair and with great effort, stood up. He shuffled around the desk and over to the metal filing cabinet with the unusually wide drawers. Bending over to peer at the labels of the drawers, he grunted and then straightened up. He pulled open one of the large drawers and looked into it.

Buddy turned and moved a step closer to Kosmatka. He could see the drawers contained thousands of papers of various sizes, many of them quite large. The papers were of different quality, some brown and flaking with age, some newer and a crisp white. Drawn on the papers— by hand or by computer—were family trees.

Dr. Kosmatka lifted several large sheets of paper, some as wide as a fully opened newspaper, and carried them a few paces to the book-filled table. He stopped near the table and looked at Buddy and Ward.

Ward hurried over and cleared the table of books, setting them off to the side on the floor.

A scrap of paper fell from one of the larger pieces, drifting like a leaf onto the floor.

Ward picked it up.

Dr. Kosmatka grunted his thanks as he laid the large yellowed papers on the table.

Ward fit the scrap into the correct area of the family tree as if he were doing a jigsaw puzzle.

Dr. Kosmatka picked through several other metal drawers, and pulled out more large papers with drawings of family trees as well as other official-looking documents marked by embossed stamps in black, blue, and red.

Buddy said, "Are you seeing something—something that will help us?"

Dr. Kosmatka ignored him.

Hurry, for Christ's sake! Buddy thought. He knew he was being unreasonable, but he wanted to squeeze the old man until he gave up the answer—if there was an answer.

Dr. Kosmatka took the cigarette from his mouth and bent over the table. He studied an extensive family tree before turning the top paper over to the side of the table.

He studied the second sheet and the family trees drawn across it. He turned that paper over to the side and studied a third.

And then a fourth.

A fifth.

A sixth.

Buddy felt like he was going to jump out of his skin. He began pacing to the side of the old man.

Dr. Kosmatka turned toward Buddy.

Buddy stopped pacing.

Dr. Kosmatka said, "You're searching for the wrong names."

Buddy's spirits dropped. "The wrong names?"

Dr. Kosmatka nodded.

Ward asked, "What do you mean?"

Dr. Kosmatka turned to Ward and said, "This is my life, see? I study the families who suffered. Sometimes, an entire month on a single family. So I've learned how the survivors adapted so they could live. After the war it was difficult time, you understand. And relatives of the sellers listed on the bills of sale—they changed their names by marriage, by other means. And who could blame them? They were German Jews and they wanted to become Polish Catholics."

Buddy sensed that in the next few minutes, he'd either solve the murders or be lost forever. His stomach tightened and his breath came in short bursts. His hands turned rigid. He stepped closer to the old man. "Can you help us find the new names—the *right* names?"

Dr. Kosmatka returned his gaze. After a moment he nodded. "Yes, I can help you. I have the right names."

Chapter Eighty-Eight

Mei walked gingerly toward Dietrich Brook. She recalled Buddy telling her that Dietrich Brook's eyes were dead. Now those eyes watched her as if they were made of synthetic material. They showed no emotion or expression. They weren't cold, the way some people's eyes were described. They were dead.

Mei looked into those eyes and found herself unable to speak or move. This was the man, she thought, who'd twice tried to kill her and Ben. And he had her alone in the gallery. There were security cameras, but they didn't give her much comfort. She knew Dietrich Brook could do anything he wanted, including making the camera footage go missing.

Brook had dressed all in black, just like the figure that had climbed into the bedroom at Ward's house where she was sleeping. Five feet from her, he folded his arms across his chest. He was much taller than she, thin and muscular and hard looking, with a body like a blade. She saw a red mark that looked like blood on the back of his right hand. His voice, when he spoke, was precise and uninflected. "We need to make a deal," he said flatly.

Mei swallowed and tried to relax, but she was calculating how long it would take her to run to her desk at the far side of the gallery, pick up her desk phone, and dial 911. Eight seconds? Twelve seconds? She'd never reach the phone. Dietrich Brook would grab her and take her into one of the conference rooms behind the main gallery, rooms invisible to the street. And if he got her there, she wouldn't survive. He'd have more blood on his hands, and it would be hers.

Her only hope, she decided, would be to remain out here, in the main gallery where passersby on the street could see through the large windows into the brightly lit gallery. She must remain here, delay, and pretend to make a deal, as he'd suggested.

She said, "You're considering selling artwork through Porter Gallery?"

"Yes," Dietrich Brook replied. "I'm considering it. If things work out."

Mei nodded. "Porter Gallery has long been a leader in the Old Master, Renaissance, and European paintings markets. To be sure we obtain the highest prices for our clients, we also have branches in London, Dubai, and Hong Kong. And we place the work in the best collections, public and private."

Dietrich Brook said, "Why don't we find a more private place to meet?"

"No," Mei said abruptly, dropping the veneer of professionalism. "We'll meet right here and nowhere else."

Dietrich Brook lifted his chin and looked down his nose at her. Very slowly he said, "Who do you think you are?"

Mei remained silent.

He continued, "You think you can take my nephew from his family? I won't allow such a thing. Not at all, Miss Adams."

He turned so quickly that Mei took a step back. But instead of moving toward her, he moved away, in the direction of the street. There, he pushed open the door, allowing a younger man with a messenger bag over one shoulder to enter the gallery. Dietrich Brook then locked the door.

The young man had a shaved head and wore jeans and strange shoes that looked like they might clip into bicycle pedals. He walked right up to Mei.

Utterly confused, she took a step back.

"Mei Adams?" asked the young man.

"Yes?"

The young man thrust an envelope into her hands and said, "You've been served."

She looked at the envelope. "I don't understand."

He sidled next to her, held up his mobile phone, and took a photograph of them as she held the envelope.

Stunned by this surreal turn of events, she didn't move or even look at the phone camera.

Without another word the young man returned to the gallery door, turned the lock, and exited out onto the sidewalk.

Dietrich Brook again locked the door and returned across the polished concrete floors toward her. His face and eyes had no expression.

Mei held up the envelope. "What is it?" she asked, unable to keep anger and fear out of her voice.

Dietrich Brook said, "A lawsuit. Actually, a motion for an emergency custody hearing in which I'm asking a judge to return Ben to us within three days."

"Three days!" Mei blurted. "That's impossible."

Dietrich Brook smiled for the first time, his thin lips barely parting. "I assure you, Miss Adams, it's quite possible. In fact I expect to prevail over you and your bottom-feeding boyfriend. What judge in the city would award custody of a boy not to his family but to a childless woman? What judge—"

"Ray Sawyer is Ben's legal guardian," Mei interrupted. "He'd never agree to give you custody. Not after what you've done. If Ben goes to live with you, he's as good as dead."

Dietrich Brook said, "Ray Sawyer is a senile old man who can't function since his wife died. He'll be no problem."

"But he has legal guardianship of Ben," Mei argued.

Dietrich Brook shook his head. "Not for long. The judge will make things right. You won't win, Miss Adams. You'll lose. And Ben will be ours."

He'll be mine! Mei wanted to shout at him. But she said nothing. Her cheeks inflamed, she sensed tears about to form in her eyes. She sensed her own desperation. Yet she knew these were the very reactions desired by Dietrich Brook. So she dug the tips of her fingernails into the palms of her hands until the pain sharpened her mind and she could feel only resolve. Trying as hard as she could to keep her voice calm, she said, "Ben will not be yours. And *you* know why. If you don't leave immediately, I'll call the police."

Dietrich Brook chuckled. "But I'm here to discuss selling paintings worth hundreds of millions of dollars through your gallery. What would the gallery owner think if you turned me away?"

Mei said, "I don't care."

"I have every right to sell the paintings."

"I don't believe you."

Dietrich Brook said, "And I don't care what you believe. I'd like to sit down with you, have you study the images of the paintings I might sell, and provide me with an estimate of their fair market value."

Mei stared at him. Was he serious or was this further intimidation? Or was he suggesting a quid pro quo—her agreement not to object to their bid for custody of Ben in return for her directing the sale of paintings whose commission to the gallery would be many millions of dollars? Maybe all of these things.

She pointed to the door and said, "Please leave this gallery immediately."

Dietrich Brook stared at her, before reaching into the breast pocket of his coat. She could see a bulge there that seemed to be in the shape of a gun.

She turned and ran across the polished concrete floor. In heels she couldn't move quickly. She heard footsteps behind her. They were gaining on her, faster and faster they came, louder and louder.

She saw the black telephone on her desk and lunged for it.

And slipped.

And fell to the concrete floor.

Chapter Eighty-Nine

Ward checked his watch. He thought Buddy was wrong and this was a wild goose chase with a doddering old researcher. He feared Dietrich Brook, who remained at large and who could do more damage to Mei and Ben.

Withdrawing to the far corner of Dr. Kosmatka's office, he held up his phone and dialed.

"Huh?" A deep voice with attitude.

"Is Dietrich still at his place?"

"Hasn't left."

"You're sure?"

"Fucking sure."

Chapter Ninety

Mei looked up, expecting a terrible blow. She cringed at the dark figure above her. Tall and lean and muscular. His expression superior but puzzled, as if he were observing a roach in distress. His large hands were closed into fists. He brought one of them down near her chest. She squirmed backward on the concrete floor, trying to get away from him. But he moved faster, leaned over her, suddenly opened his hand.

She wanted to scream, but what good would it do? She was alone in the gallery with Dietrich Brook. She'd bend, break, or die at his will.

In his hand was a small white card. He held it three inches from her breasts, then dropped it onto her dress.

"My business card," he said quietly. "Call me after you've determined the value of the paintings. And don't for a moment think of obstructing my taking custody of Ben." Then he set a green folder beside her.

She watched as he walked to the gallery entrance, paused to unlock the glass door, then opened it, and stepped outside onto East Fifty-Eighth.

Mei didn't get up. She lay on the floor and began to shake. *So close,* she thought. So close to being killed. Dietrich Brook had pursued her, chased her across the gallery. And then for a reason she couldn't fathom, he'd let her go. Rather than the gritty death she'd expected, he'd offered her a bribe.

Nothing about the last few minutes made sense to her. Nothing. As she stared up at the lights in the ceiling, the panic and tension of the encounter eased, and she began to cry. Her tears weren't from physical pain, although her right hip ached from the fall and her right hand hurt so badly she thought it might be broken. Her tears were for Ben. She believed that Dietrich Brook had been right about no judge allowing her and Buddy to keep him. What had she been thinking? Their wonderful life—a life with Ben so filled with danger but nevertheless enchanting—would end. During her few days with him and with Buddy, she'd been happier than she'd believed possible. Their status as a family had begun to seem permanent, although she knew it might not be. She didn't think she could endure losing the boy but didn't know how to prevent it. If she lost Ben . . . her mind traveled along that terrible path and she wept.

A moment later she used her left arm to push herself up. She looked across the empty gallery and saw the lights of cars pass by on the street outside. She heard herself breathing and was grateful to have lived. She'd survived, but she didn't know why.

Chapter Ninety-One

Dr. Kosmatka said, "Bring me the bills of sale."

Buddy went over to the old man's desk, picked up the three papers, and brought them to the table.

Dr. Kosmatka set them beside the family tree diagrams and the official documents. He put the unlit cigarette in his mouth and bent over until his eyes were very close to the bills of sale. He looked at one, compared it with the diagram of a large family tree, and glanced at an official document.

Buddy watched him, trying to be patient. The old man straightened, pointed at the first bill of sale. He said, "At age forty-four Ranem Baum sold a painting by Michelangelo to Gerhardt Bruch. Baum was soon thereafter condemned to Auschwitz, along with his wife, his son, and his daughter. The only survivor was his wife. When Auschwitz was liberated she remained in Poland, perhaps voluntarily and perhaps not, and in 1946 married a Polish Catholic, at which time her name changed to Nowak. They had one child, in 1947, and the couple died three months apart, in 1968. The child married but had no children. According to our records that child is a widow named Agata Nowak. She's approximately sixty-eight years old and lives in Krakow."

Buddy nodded and glanced hopefully at the two remaining bills of sale.

Dr. Kosmatka took up the second bill of sale. He again studied it carefully, peered over at a different family tree, and checked an official document.

Buddy glanced at his watch and asked, "Same result with this one?"

Dr. Kosmatka cocked his head for a moment, and said, "No, no. This bill of sale"—he pointed a large walnut-colored finger at it—"is for a painting by Rembrandt, sold to Gerhardt Bruch by a woman named Yetta Morgenstern. She was condemned to Auschwitz along with her mother, father, husband, three sons, and one daughter." Dr. Kosmatka straightened, looked up at Buddy, and said, "Only the daughter, Olinda, survived."

Buddy lowered his eyes and shook his head. "Terrible," he said.

"Terrible," Dr. Kosmatka agreed, and turned back to the family tree atop the papers. He breathed deeply and then continued. "Olinda married a young man called Daniel Roth, who'd also survived Auschwitz. They immigrated to Israel and had three children, two of whom died in infancy. Daniel and Olinda Roth died in 2002 and 2005, respectively. The surviving child, Adon, is alive and living in Israel, where he has two children of his own."

Buddy said, "Do they all have Roth as a last name?"

Dr. Kosmatka nodded. "Yes."

Buddy pulled out his notebook and pen and jotted down the names. He'd follow up late tonight or tomorrow. He'd call Jerusalem or Tel Aviv or wherever they lived. He'd talk with them and see if any of Adon Roth's children were in America.

"But this one," Dr. Kosmatka said, pointing to the third bill of sale, "is a different case from the others."

Buddy saw Ward move closer and stand on the other side of the old man.

"This is the bill of sale for the Caravaggio, the painting you told me was stolen last night."

"Yeah," Buddy said. "Sold to Gerhardt Brook by Nessa Meyer. What happened to Nessa Meyer?"

Dr. Kosmatka shook his head. "Very bad, I'm afraid. She was sent to Auschwitz with her grandmother, grandfather, mother, father, husband, three sons, and two daughters. As in the previous case, only one son survived." He sighed and shook his head slowly and with great sadness.

Buddy watched him, sensed his deep emotions.

Dr. Kosmatka continued, "The son remained single for a long time. At thirty years of age he married a Polish Catholic woman. And here's where this case is different." Dr. Kosmatka picked up the copy of an official document and said, "By some method, the son took his new wife's name. At the time that was impossible without intervention from the courts. Perhaps a bribe was paid or a favor done, I don't know."

Buddy grabbed the edge of the table, held it tightly. "What was the name?" Buddy asked.

"It doesn't matter," Dr. Kosmatka replied, waving him off.

Buddy stared at him.

Dr. Kosmatka continued. "After the wedding, this man and his wife had two daughters. The man died in 2012 and his wife last year, both in Krakow. One of their daughters died five years ago in Gdańsk. But the other daughter married a Lithuanian and, according to these records, is alive."

"Where?" Buddy said. "Where does she live?"

Dr. Kosmatka looked up at him. "Here, in New York."

Buddy felt a chill come over him. He nearly shivered in the warm room. He removed his hand from the table and clenched it between him and the old man. He said, "Did she and her husband have children?"

Dr. Kosmatka turned back to the table and studied the family tree. "Yes," he said. "One son."

"How old is the son?"

Dr. Kosmatka squinted at the family tree. "He's twenty-six or twenty-seven."

"Does he also live in New York?"

"Yes."

For the first time Ward spoke. "The *name*, Dr. Kosmatka. What's the young man's name?"

Dr. Kosmatka checked his papers once more, straightened, and removed his reading glasses. He held the unlit cigarette in his left hand. He said, "The young man's name is Jonas Vidas."

Chapter Ninety-Two

Ben peered out the window of Detective Vidas's car. He didn't like the way the car seats were low and the side of the door high. It was hard to see out. He couldn't see the people on the sidewalk, though he had a view of shop signs lining Tenth Avenue and the upper stories of the buildings they passed. Not that it mattered all that much. He told himself that soon Detective Vidas would drop him off at the Carlyle Residences where Mei would be waiting for him on the sidewalk. She'd take him upstairs to her apartment, and they could talk and have a snack and maybe he could goof around on the piano. He listened in the car but didn't recognize the song playing over the radio. Then he heard Vidas's mobile phone ring.

Vidas took the phone out of the breast pocket of his suit coat and glanced at it. He frowned and pressed the button on the side of the phone to make it stop ringing. Then he returned the phone to his breast pocket.

Ben felt the car accelerate through the traffic. Vidas honked once, and the Ford gained speed.

Ben said, "Was it Buddy?"

Vidas looked at him and smiled. "What?"

"Was it Buddy on the phone?"

Vidas laughed. "No, no. It was just my mother. She forgets that I work and can't listen to her talk about her dinner plans or her hair appointment. No, when Buddy calls I answer. Don't you worry about that." Vidas smiled a second time and then faced forward.

Ben turned to see out the passenger window.

Vidas's phone beeped twice, in rapid succession, the notification of a new voicemail.

Vidas took the phone from his suit coat, pressed a couple of buttons, and held it up to his left ear.

Ben couldn't understand the voicemail, not even a word of it, but the voice on the recording sounded a little like Buddy's. It didn't sound like a woman's voice, unless Detective Vidas's mother had a strangely deep voice.

Ben looked over at Vidas, whose expression had become anxious. Vidas glanced at Ben but didn't smile this time.

Vidas said, "Yeah, that was Buddy. Didn't realize when the phone rang a minute ago. He said Mei's appointment is running longer than she expected, and he wants us to hang out together until Mei can get over to her apartment. Once she's back at her place, she'll call me, and I'll drop you off then. But in the meantime we should grab a snack, all right?"

Ben said, "Mei was going to make me a snack."

Vidas nodded. "Yeah, I hear you. But Mei isn't around, so I'll have to do. Just this once. Now, what sounds good to you?"

Ben shrugged. "I dunno."

"Pizza?"

"No."

"Tacos?"

"No."

"Donuts?"

For a moment Ben stared out the window, not really seeing anything, only wishing he could be with Mei and that she didn't have a meeting. Then he said, "I'm not hungry."

"Come on, Ben!" Vidas said. "My mom always gave me a snack after school. I'm sure you're hungry, so I'll think of something. Maybe I'll even make you something myself, at one of my apartments. I rent two of them. They aren't far."

Chapter Ninety-Three

Buddy rushed out of the Polish Institute. He stood on the steps above West 246th Street and felt the cold air of dusk.

He recalled Ward's description of the killer. *Omniscient* was the term his brother had once used. It meant "all knowing." Now he understood how the killer had discovered Ben's whereabouts at any given time.

He'd told the killer.

He'd hidden nothing.

He'd trusted.

And Ben would die because he hadn't seen what had been right in front of him.

Jesus.

He felt panic take over him. His stomach roiled. His chest felt hollow, and the cold air he drew into his lungs hurt bitterly. He felt his hands begin to shake. He knew he needed to do something, but what? He could put an APB out on Vidas, but on what evidence? Vidas could just disappear with the boy. And what if he were wrong? What if Vidas meant no harm?

He turned to Ward. "Call your guy. Make sure he's still watching Dietrich Brook."

Ward nodded.

"Where?" Buddy asked. "Where the hell would Vidas take Ben?"

Ward didn't move. He thought for a while, staring into the middle distance toward the Horace Mann School. He said nothing.

Buddy grew impatient. "Ward? Hey, Ward? We've got to *do* something!"

Ward turned and looked straight at him. His expression was hard and cold, his voice flat. "He'll take Ben somewhere private, somewhere he can do his work quietly and without notice."

Buddy said, "That could be anywhere."

"No. Not anywhere. He'll go to an abandoned building or his apartment or . . . or there's another option. He could—"

"By the river?" Buddy interrupted. "He could . . ." Buddy went silent. He couldn't say "dump the body," couldn't say that Ben's body would be "wiped clean and without prints."

Ward shook his head. "Too many people. Too big a chance of being seen."

"Fuck!" Buddy said, making fists with his hands. He wanted to jump out of his skin, but he had no idea where to go.

Ward said, "He could go to Ben's parents' town house. Has it sold?"

"I doubt it's even on the market," Buddy said. "There's no way Ray Sawyer sold it this fast."

"If he goes there, Ben would be killed in his own house, just as Ben's and Bruno's and Carl's families were killed in theirs."

Buddy said, "Let's roll."

Ward didn't move. "But what about Vidas's apartment? He'd feel safe there, wouldn't he? He'd think he could deal with Ben on his own terms."

Buddy nodded. "Yeah, he could take Ben there. He has the top floor, so he could escape by the roof to the roof of the next building if he got cornered."

"Maybe that's where he's gone," Ward said. "I'll go there and you go to Ben's family town house."

"Deal."

Buddy used his phone to look up Vidas's address in the East Bronx, gave Ward that information plus the address of the town house owned by Ben's family on East Seventy-Fourth Street, and jumped in the Charger.

Ward hurried toward his waiting Range Rover.

Buddy considered the fastest way to get to the Upper East Side. Then he made a U-turn on 246th and headed west to Waldo, then wound south and west until he could merge onto the Henry Hudson Parkway heading south.

For seven or eight miles.

In rush hour traffic.

Fuck!

He punched on the siren and drove dangerously fast, as if Ben's life depended on his reaching the town house rapidly. Because it probably did—if Ben wasn't already dead. He thought of Vidas laying a hand on Ben, and something in him reacted in a way he'd never felt before. It was like a knife cutting into his own body. He saw Ben's light-brown eyes and black hair, his boyish smile, and the way he'd clapped when Mei had accepted his proposal, and he instinctively wanted to protect and even to love him. Yes, in that moment he knew he loved Ben. He loved him as if Ben were his own son, loved him in a way that was different from how he loved Mei, but just as insistently, just as completely. He must save his boy—*his* boy—he thought. Some way. Somehow. There must be time.

Yet he worried he'd be too late. That he'd fail Ben as he'd failed Lauren.

He sensed a sliver of hope, but that hope was fading by the second.

Chapter Ninety-Four

Ward climbed into the plush back seat of the Range Rover, nearly shouted Vidas's address to Brick, and told him to step on it.

Brick turned around the big but powerful car and headed north on Tibbett Avenue. The heavy SUV leaned right and left as he sped over Broadway and got onto the Mosholu Parkway that carried them south and east toward the Bronx River Parkway.

Ward pulled out his phone and called the man watching Dietrich Brook.

The line rang and rang, rhythmically and seemingly forever. Ward stared at the back of Brick's head as he listened. His heart began to pound. Another ring and another.

And then the line went to voicemail.

Ward ended the call and dialed a second time. With the same result. The line rang eight times, then went to voicemail.

He didn't want to alarm Buddy. Not unnecessarily. Not when the goon might have been using the restroom or talking on the other line with his girlfriend. So he decided to wait a few minutes and try again. If he still got no answer, he'd warn Buddy that Dietrich Brook might be in motion.

Ward ended the call and looked out the window as they sped through the city. *We're too late,* he decided. *We won't get there in time, even if we've guessed Ben's location.*

Chapter Ninety-Five

Ben thought it was strange that Detective Vidas knocked on the door of his own apartment. When they'd climbed out of the unmarked Ford and walked up the five steps to the ground floor of a ramshackle apartment building, Vidas raised a hand and pounded on the gray metal door.

From inside came the sound of a television. And footsteps. Ben looked at the mail slot and saw the name Vidas in faded lettering. He didn't feel right in this neighborhood. The street, the buildings, and the small shops were unfamiliar and he didn't know anyone. He wished Detective Vidas hadn't brought him here. Why hadn't he told the detective he wanted a hot dog or something near his school or near Mei's apartment?

The door opened and an old woman was standing there. She smiled at Detective Vidas and invited them in, waved them in, but she didn't speak English. It was a language Ben didn't recognize. It wasn't French or Spanish, because his mother had spoken French and his former nanny Spanish. This old woman smiled at him. He followed Detective Vidas into a dark and dingy room. And the apartment was really just one room: living room, galley kitchen on the interior side, and a white sheet hung to separate a tiny bedroom.

The tan-painted walls were nearly barren, the ceiling stained and caramel colored, the furniture old and brown and sunken. On the living room sofa lay an old man. His legs were frail and too thin, like those of a bird. His blue plaid pajamas couldn't hide his emaciation. The old man frightened Ben. He didn't move, except that he held an oxygen mask up to his mouth. His eyes saw Ben and then searched upward for Detective Vidas. Then the old man extended his free hand.

Vidas grasped the old man's hand and bent forward. He kissed the old man on the forehead and spoke to the old man in the strange language.

Vidas straightened and seemed as large as a giant in the small room. He turned to Ben and said, "These are my parents. They're poor, and my father is sick. He worked for Brook Instruments for many years. You've heard of the company?"

Ben nodded. "My family's company."

"That's right," Vidas said. "Your family's company." In a low but angry voice, he continued, "My father swallowed his pride and ignored what your family had already done to mine. He worked for your family for thirty years because they needed his expertise in chemical engineering. And then last September he was in an accident at the factory upstate. Your company refused to help when the insurance didn't cover all the surgeries he needed. He had to leave the company and his health insurance ran out by Thanksgiving. All you gave him was a set of military binoculars."

Ben looked down. He put his hands in his coat pockets.

Vidas continued, "My parents had to sell their house upstate and now they rent here, although I pay for everything. But their money's almost run out—and mine, too. When my father goes, my mother will have to move in with me, at my apartment a few blocks from here. Do you see her? She's a broken woman with bad health. It's been a shitty decade for them. And every day I have a reminder of what your family did to mine. Every fucking day."

Vidas glowered at him.

Ben said, "I'm sorry."

Vidas snorted. "It's too late for that."

The old woman mumbled in the language Ben didn't know. Ben turned and saw that the old woman was offering him a dark-brown cookie on a small plate. He wanted to shake his head and tell her he wasn't hungry, but he decided he wouldn't refuse. He feared insulting the old woman and further angering Detective Vidas. So he nodded, tried to smile, and took the plate and the small cookie on it.

She watched him expectantly.

He picked up the cookie and took a bite. It was a ginger snap. He murmured, "Very good."

She grinned and turned to her son.

Detective Vidas spoke to her in the strange language.

They seemed to be arguing, yet Ben understood none of it. He'd finished the cookie and was holding the plate, unsure where to put it.

Detective Vidas turned to him and saw it. He took the plate and handed it to his mother. Then he said to Ben, "Let's go."

Ben walked to the door, Detective Vidas's heavy footsteps behind him.

Detective Vidas said, "See the walls, Ben?"

Ben stopped and looked. The walls were bare except for the small painting that hung on the wall over the sofa, above the old man with the oxygen mask. It was of a young boy with black hair and a fruit-filled wreath on his head.

"See the walls?" Vidas repeated.

Ben said, "Yes."

"Anything on them?"

"Just the one painting." Ben's eyes stayed for a moment on the canvas, which seemed familiar, but he didn't remember where he'd seen it.

"Yeah, Ben. Just the one," Detective Vidas said in a strange voice. "But there should be more. The paintings at your house should be here."

Ben didn't know what to say.

The detective reached around him, grabbed the door handle, and jerked the door violently open.

Chapter Ninety-Six

Ward told Brick, "When we're a block away, pull over. I don't want him to see the car—or me."

Brick nodded almost imperceptibly. A block west of the address, Brick slowed the car and double-parked. He said, "Where do you want me?"

"Here, or as close to here as you can get," Ward replied, opening the right rear door.

A moment later he was walking down Beach Avenue. The area once had a fearsome reputation but now was solidly middle-class with all kinds of ethnicities. A Lithuanian wouldn't have stuck out. Instead of walking to the front of the building where Vidas lived, Ward first jogged around it. He saw no backyard or alley, only more apartments. Then he doubled back.

The modest building was red brick and had small windows. It would be dark or at least dim inside, and it wouldn't have a modern security system, let alone a doorman. Ward strode along the street and then turned left onto Beach. He approached the steps that led up to the building's ground floor entrance. He reached into his left coat pocket. Sprinting up the steps, he tried the door handle, but it was locked. He brought out a small nylon bag. He unzipped the bag and removed two delicate metal tools. With one hand he used a torsion wrench, with the other a hook pick. A moment later the door's lock drew back. Ward dropped the tools and the nylon bag in his pocket.

With his left hand he pushed the building door open. His right hand gripped his Desert Eagle.

He went inside quickly, quietly, closing the door behind him. He was glad it didn't squeak or jangle. He glanced at the directory to the left of the door, and moved like a cat up the terrazzo staircase covered with a dirty maroon-colored runner. Two or three steps at a time. He turned on the first landing but saw no sign or Vidas or Ben.

He climbed another flight.

Nothing. The building was quiet.

He moved up to the third floor, but there was nobody there.

Up again to the fourth floor.

He stopped, listening. He heard nothing but his own breathing, which spiked along with his heartbeat.

He took a deep breath and ran up to the fifth floor.

Three doors, each with a name in gold block lettering in a small holder in the middle of each oak door. Vidas's door was the one in the middle. It was scuffed and battered and old, but also thick and solidly made. Ward doubted he could kick it open. He moved to the side of the door and carefully, silently, placed his ear against the wood. Holding his breath, he remained still and listened.

He heard something.

Chapter Ninety-Seven

Ward listened at the door to Detective Vidas's apartment. He heard what seemed to be the muffled sounds of a child. Definitely not a man's voice. He also thought he heard light footsteps. In his mind he pictured the detective standing silently and unmoving on the other side of the oak door, listening for *him* and aiming a sawed-off shotgun at groin height in the center of the door.

He looked around the small landing with three nearly identical doors, one to the left of Vidas's door, one to the right. He looked down at the maroon carpeting. But there was no table or chair he could use as a battering ram. He'd have to kick in the door, or shoot off the lock. Both approaches would be loud and dangerous. Both would give Vidas time to kill Ben.

But he had no good alternative. Picking the lock would take too much time and be too much of a risk.

Quietly Ward positioned himself in front of the door. He held his arms out on either side for balance, his right hand gripping the gun. He raised his left leg and kicked the oak door panel near the lock.

Smack!

The door splintered, but the lock held.

Angry now, Ward raised his leg and kicked at the door as hard as he could.

Still, it held.

He was out of time. He kicked again, aiming his heel near the lock. Now it was coming loose.

He held his breath and bashed at the door.

At last it flew open, banging against the interior wall to Ward's right. He crouched in combat position and aimed the gun into the center of the opening, ready for the assault or the bullet that would surely come from the dimly lit room.

Yet no assault came. No bullet flew. He listened in the sudden silence and heard only the same faint cries from within the apartment.

Trying to remain calm, he moved swiftly to the side of the doorway. He dipped his head into the opening. Once, twice, he peeked in.

It was a small living room. Nondescript black leather sofa. Flat-panel television set on a low wooden stand. A bookshelf. Nothing on the walls. The blinds were open, and the gray dusk came weakly through the windows.

To the left of the living room was an opening.

Ward stepped through the doorway and against the wall to his left.

He crept toward the opening, tense and prepared to shoot. As he neared it, he saw the faint glow from a light. The same muffled, high-pitched voice grew louder. It sounded like someone attempting to speak.

At the opening Ward bobbed his head at the edge of the open space. Once. Twice. But again there was no assault, no bullet. He saw only a small kitchen and beyond it a bedroom. The bed unmade. The yellow glow of a lamp near the windows but outside his view.

And the sound of a voice mixed with anxious movement.

Crouching down, he stepped through the kitchen and leaned against the wall to the right of the opening to the bedroom. To his left he saw a small room with a white tiled floor. The bathroom.

He took a deep breath, moved across the opening to the bedroom, and leaned against the wall to the left.

No new sound.

He dipped his head and glanced into the room.

Chapter Ninety-Eight

To be sure the detective was out of the apartment, Ward slid around the bedroom wall until he reached the bathroom door. It was narrow, white, and half-closed. He stood by the opening and pushed the door open with his foot. He remained alert and kept his weapon up, but he'd become close to certain he was alone. Yet always careful, he bobbed his head into the doorway. He saw nobody, only an empty shower stall, toilet, vanity. He flicked on the light and walked into the bathroom.

Nothing unusual that he could see. Nothing pointed to the apartment's occupant as anything at all. There'd been no attempt to make this a home. It seemed completely anonymous. But he'd look a little further.

He opened the doors under the vanity. They rattled open and contained nothing odd, except the middle and bottom drawers to the right of the sink. The middle drawer was . . . filled with bottles of cologne. Perfectly organized, alphabetized, in neat rows. Cheap bottles and expensive ones, their tops gleaming brightly. He saw Tom Ford and Ralph Lauren, Creed and Dior. He held up an unusual-looking bottle and read the label: Zizan, by Ormonde Jayne. Looked expensive, but he didn't recognize it. He sniffed. A pleasant scent. He thought the collection a strange fetish for a police detective.

After replacing the bottle and closing the middle drawer, he opened the bottom drawer.

And drew in his breath.

He knew what this was, but he didn't touch it.

He thought of the death of Bruno Brook and his family, of the Zyklon B. Of how they'd died but someone else in the room had lived.

Lying in the drawer was a black gas mask, the nylon mesh straps loose, the plastic eye coverings clear, the filter canister at the end of it frightening even in repose.

Now it all made sense, but he was too late.

He slid the bottom drawer closed and returned to the bedroom. Near the window but not too close to the floor lamp was a cage made out of bamboo. And within the cage were two small white birds. They watched him warily, silently.

He pulled his mobile phone from the breast pocket of his suit coat and hit the speed dial for Buddy.

When the call went to voicemail, he said, "Nobody at the apartment, but Vidas is your target. Leaving now to back you up."

After ending the call, he dialed 911 to report a suspected kidnapping at the town house owned by Ben's family. Then he put away the phone, thrust his gun into the side pocket of his coat, and ran down the stairs, out of the building, and onto the sidewalk.

His silver Range Rover was idling half a block away.

He sprinted toward it.

Chapter Ninety-Nine

Ben knew the town house. Knew it better than anyone, for it was his family's and he'd lived there all his life. But he didn't understand why Detective Vidas had pulled his car alongside the curb on East Seventy-Fourth Street. Or why they hadn't gone directly to Mei's apartment, where she'd told him she'd wait for him. He wanted to be with her, to be having an after-school snack in the kitchen while she made dinner and he told her about his new school. She was his family now, and being here only made him sad and fearful, but not afraid of Detective Vidas, who'd always been kind to him and who'd even taken him to meet his parents. He hadn't understood the detective's reference to the walls of the dingy apartment they'd just visited. What could art have to do with him? He knew nothing about paintings, even if he liked those his family owned. He'd grown up with them, and so he accepted them as part of his life, of his family's life. They didn't seem extraordinary in any way, except that some of them were large. His friends had paintings in their houses as well, sometimes even with naked women. Yet he was more interested in his friends' games and toys than in their parents' art collections. He didn't know why the detective knew or cared about paintings.

Vidas said, "You have the keys?"

Ben looked over at him. Vidas was sitting behind the wheel, his face calm and almost friendly. Ben said, "They're at Buddy's."

Vidas glanced past Ben at the town house's wide front door. It was up four wide stone steps and had so many coats of black paint that it gleamed under the streetlight. Men and women passed by on the sidewalk, some talking to companions, others with their dogs, and a few by themselves.

Ben waited.

Vidas said, "Well, we won't let that stop us." He unbuckled his seat belt, glanced at his side mirror, and opened his door. "Come on," he said. "Let's take a look around."

Ben wasn't going to disobey a police officer, especially not Buddy's partner. And at least he wasn't with one of his uncles. With Vidas he felt safe, although the detective was acting differently from what he'd expected. So he unbuckled his seat belt, opened the passenger door, and stepped out of the car.

The cold braced and startled him fully awake. A west wind had picked up and swept through the street and between the town houses and apartment buildings. Suddenly he was alert. He held his hands at his sides, ready to move. He was ready to go home to be with Mei. With Buddy. He looked around, hoping to see someone he recognized. Maybe Buddy would appear. Maybe he'd arranged to meet Vidas here. Maybe they needed something from the town house.

He heard another car door opening and saw Vidas lift a black duffel bag from the back seat. Vidas closed the door, smiled at him across the roof of the car, and walked around to the sidewalk where Ben was standing.

The detective said, "Let's go inside. I'd like to check on the property."

Ben didn't want to go into his former home. He pursed his lips and didn't respond. He hunched his head down into his shoulders and wished he'd brought a hat. The cold was biting.

"Come on," Vidas said, ushering him up the wide steps.

Ben followed obediently.

"Stand by the door."

"Okay." Ben moved where the detective indicated, to the left of the handle.

Vidas pulled something out of his coat pocket and leaned close to the silver lock. Ben didn't look at him, only listened to the slight rasping of metal on metal. A few moments later the lock drew back.

Vidas pressed down on the handle and the large black door opened into the house. The alarm system began to beep.

Vidas stepped over the threshold and into the dark foyer. He turned back to Ben and said, "Come on. Why don't you show me around your house? I've never seen the inside."

Ben hesitated. He didn't like the way the detective had gained access to his house. *My house,* he thought, but it wasn't really his house, not anymore. Vidas hadn't used a key but something else, something that made him uneasy. And so his trust in the detective waned a little more.

Vidas stood in the doorway and offered his hand. "You can turn on the lights, show me the kitchen, show me your bedroom."

Ben didn't like the idea of showing the detective his bedroom, but the kitchen would be all right. The ginger snap the detective's mother had given him had made him hungry. And he knew the very kitchen cabinet where his mother had kept the Lindt chocolate bars. He could have one now, a large one of the milk-chocolate variety, or maybe one with milk chocolate and almonds. Then he could show the detective the house and they could return to Mei's apartment at the Carlyle Residences.

He reached out, took the detective's hand, and stepped over the threshold and into his family's town house.

The hand was warm but firm—unexpectedly firm and hard. The arm pulled him past the door. He heard the door close.

Vidas said, "Turn off the alarm, would you?"

Ben entered the code. The beeping stopped.

"Where's the light?" asked the detective.

Ben was paralyzed with sudden fear. Being in the house frightened him. And there was something about the detective that he didn't understand, that put him on edge.

"Turn on the light," ordered the detective, his voice no longer so friendly. "Do it now."

Ben swallowed and went over to the wall in which the door was set. The switch wasn't near the door, as in many houses, but in a recessed box a yard away. He lifted the box's plastic panel, found the correct button, and pressed it. He looked up at the bright crystal chandelier, at the fourteen-foot ceiling and the large paintings that had greeted him upon his return home every day of his life. He looked down and saw the gray marble floors, still polished as they'd been before his mother and father had taken him and Ellen-Marie to Camp Kateri for the New Year's holiday. The house appeared to be the same as it had always been, and yet everything had changed. At the rough sound of a zipper, he turned toward the detective.

Who'd somehow put on black leather gloves and was withdrawing from the duffel bag a coil of thick rope.

His eyes met Ben's.

And Ben took off, running across the marble floor in the direction of the grand staircase that wound upward to the second level. He held his breath and leaned forward, going as fast as he could, his legs charging and his arms swinging wildly. His back tingled with the fear and expectation that Vidas would strike him there, although at first he heard no footsteps behind him. In a few seconds he made it to the foot of the wooden staircase, leaped up to the second stair, and began climbing two steps at each stride, faster and faster. The steps were wide and high, but he kept going, two at a time, trying to go faster, but the climb became more difficult the higher he got.

Now he heard footsteps behind him. The rustling of clothing. The heavy breath of a man rushing after him.

At the turn of the staircase, he suddenly lost his footing. He felt something clamp around his right ankle and pull at him. Setting both hands on the wooden tread, he tried to kick his right foot loose, but then his left foot was clamped at the same time. And slowly, slowly, he was yanked downward, one step, two steps. The edge of the stairs digging into his stomach. With both feet he kicked but he couldn't break free. He tried to crawl up to the next step, clawing with his hands. But he couldn't escape. He was stuck. He looked over the staircase's railing to the gray marble floor below him. It was a long way down, but maybe he could break loose, climb over the railing, and jump. Maybe he wouldn't die if he jumped. Maybe he could jump and land, and then run or crawl out the front door. Just maybe. Because there wasn't any other way out of the town house, except for the doors from the kitchen downstairs to the small garden behind the house. There was no other way out.

He heard rapid movement behind him. He turned and looked back over his shoulder.

He screamed, as loud as he could. He began to cry.

The detective was lifting a knife over him.

And then he felt a sharpness drive into his right leg, into the side of his thigh. The sharpness was cold and hard. The pain was so great that he felt himself choking. His body tensed and he couldn't breathe. He felt himself falling down the stairs, one by one, each time screaming, and falling onto the marble floor. The world fell with him and his mind went black.

Chapter One Hundred

Buddy was snarled up in rush hour traffic. Fading light, cold weather, slippery pavement, and cars and taxis and buses slowed to a steel-and-glass centipede that seemed to move no faster than that creature. As he'd rushed from the Polish Institute for Holocaust Studies in the Bronx down the Henry Hudson Parkway, he'd run the siren and the light bar. At least then he'd moved, and pretty quickly until he reached the spaghetti junction near West One Hundredth Street. He'd been tied up there, no matter how much he honked and how loud the siren. There just wasn't anywhere for anyone to move in order to get out of his way. He'd cursed and begun sweating.

He banged on the steering wheel, all the while counting the minutes Ben had been with his partner. He guessed he had very little time to save the boy. He feared he might already be too late. But maybe not. Maybe he had a chance.

As he drove, he considered calling it in. Having another cop check out Ben's family town house. But what did that cop know about the situation? Anyone else would defer to Vidas. Would be sweet-talked and then killed. And so would Ben. No, this was something he had to do himself.

He feverishly envisioned what he'd do when he pulled up to the town house on Seventy-Fourth. How he'd burst through the door and what he'd do when he was inside. He'd never been there, but tonight, as he eventually turned east on West Seventy-Ninth Street and made his way to the Seventy-Ninth Street Transverse, he wished he'd taken the time to visit the town house and understand its layout.

If Ben were even there. If Vidas hadn't taken him to an abandoned building or under a bridge by the Hudson. Because if Ben weren't at the town house, Buddy knew there was no hope. He had to be there, Buddy told himself. Just *had* to be. Otherwise . . .

But he couldn't let himself think about otherwise. He had to remain focused, relentless.

Now he was moving. He crossed Central Park. He turned right and barreled down Fifth Avenue, the park to his right, the stately residential buildings a blur to his left. But he wasn't looking at the buildings, he was swerving around cars. He reached to the dash and hit two buttons. He knew the light bar had switched off. The siren stopped abruptly. Except for the sound of the engine as he accelerated through openings in traffic, everything outside of him was quiet. But his heartbeat sounded in his ears like a drum.

Seventy-Eighth Street.

Seventy-Seventh Street.

Closer.

A city bus pulled out in front of him.

Shit!

He didn't honk. It wouldn't help.

The bus moved forward, turning in a wide arc into Fifth Avenue. But the driver hadn't gauged the turn correctly. The bus stopped. The white reverse lights came on.

"You're kidding me!" Buddy shouted.

He pulled left and did a one-eighty. The right front tire hit the curb and the car bounced roughly as he brought it back onto the pavement. He headed north, against the one-way traffic, stomping on the accelerator, making a screeching turn east on Seventy-Seventh. But Seventy-Seventh was one-way going west.

Immediately the westbound cars were honking at Buddy.

He ignored them, weaving left and right, driving on the north sidewalk. He took out the pedestrian canopy of one building, his front bumper tearing its poles out of the sidewalk. He didn't look at it in the rearview mirror. Focused on what was coming at him. He didn't slow, only went faster. Didn't slow much at Madison. Executed a right turn, wheels squealing, and headed south on Madison.

But Madison was a busier street, and it ran one-way northbound.

Here the cars, buses, and trucks came at him at thirty miles per hour. He was going fifty.

They didn't honk. There wasn't time.

Some of them angled off to the east or west side of Madison.

He bore down in the middle of the street, straddling two lanes, flooring the gas the entire way. The Charger's big engine thrust the car south, the steering got looser, the buildings on either side whished past. One block. Two. Three.

His eyes were on the intersection of Madison and Seventy-Fourth.

He took a wide turn and headed west on Seventy-Fourth.

A third time it was one-way and he was driving straight into traffic.

But except for two black Mercedes sedans and three trucks making deliveries, the street was clear.

He shoved his foot into the accelerator and held on.

Passed one truck.

One car.

Second truck.

Third truck.

Second car.

His phone rang, but it was in the breast pocket of his suit coat. He couldn't answer and drive. And it didn't matter who called or what they said. He was committed. More committed than he'd ever been in his life. And he'd be more lethal. He wouldn't hesitate if he had to choose between Ben and anyone else. He'd choose Ben over his partner. He'd choose Ben over himself.

He spotted it. His partner's car parked in front of the town house. He parked nose-to-nose, jumped out of the car, and then all his plans vanished as he ran headlong toward the wide black door.

He didn't attempt to hide himself or to be quiet. He passed an older couple that glanced at him with surprise and fear.

He leaped to the fourth step and the door, stopping long enough to grasp the stainless steel handle. He pressed down and it moved. He pushed on the door and it opened.

A break at last.

A mistake by his opponent who'd remained camouflaged for so long.

For too long.

Buddy pulled the Glock from his shoulder holster. Gripping it firmly, he crouched down, raised the gun, and stepped silently through the door.

Chapter One Hundred One

Ben awoke. He was on his back, staring at the ceiling. But he wasn't on the staircase. He didn't know where he was, at first. Softness beneath him. He figured his head was on a pillow. He was in a bed. He looked around and recognized the black lamp with the brilliant halogen bulb on a desk in the corner of the room. *His* desk. And he was in *his* room. Yet he couldn't move. He tried to raise his arms, but they were pinned under something. He thrashed around but his right leg suddenly hurt so badly he cried out. It was as if someone were pounding a spike into his thigh until it split apart.

In the torment he writhed uncontrollably and wept and remembered—the drive here, the way he'd fled up the staircase, his capture, and the knife raised and plunged. He remembered the rope and understood why he couldn't move. Why he couldn't escape. And he knew he'd die here, in his own bed, in his family's house. Just as his mother and father and sister had died at their house upstate. Just as his aunt and uncle and cousins had died in their house not far from here. There was nothing he could do except cry and hope and wish for a miracle or at least for the agony to end.

"Shut up, would you?"

The voice was from behind him, and he recognized it. He cringed, expecting a blow to fall. Or another cut of the knife, but this one to his throat or his chest. He felt himself tense, but then he thought to calm himself. To consider what he could do. Searching his memory, he hit upon Buddy's advice the night Buddy had taken him home to meet Mei, the night he'd begun to feel safe and protected. He and Buddy had carried the antique medicine cabinet in Mei's foyer over to block the elevator door. Buddy had knelt down and told him what to do if he were ever again in danger. Ben couldn't recall . . . *yes, I can.* Buddy had told him that if he could run away, he should. If he couldn't run, he should hide. And if he couldn't hide, there was one other way to fight. But it would only work if the danger were close to him, so close to him it would take the person by surprise. He considered his options and decided he had only one.

So he began to talk. Very quietly. About the paintings and the little he remembered about them. He didn't know why the detective cared, but the reason didn't matter now. He described the painting hanging in the stairwell where he'd fallen, the portrait of the knight with the suit of silver armor, the black beard and flowing black hair, the red sash, the battle scene in the distance. He spoke about the painting, even about its frame.

The voice behind him didn't tell him to shut up. Instead he saw the figure move around to his side where he could see it. Vidas had removed his winter parka and now wore a black shirt, black pants, and black gloves. Ben saw the pale, angular face, the angry eyes.

"What are you saying?" Vidas asked.

Ben kept babbling, most of his words nonsense but not all of them. He stared at Vidas but didn't address him or cease his description of the painting and what it meant.

"Yes," Vidas interrupted, nodding. "The Goya over the staircase. It was bought by my great-great-grandfather in the 1890s. He was a grain merchant and then a banker. German through and through but also Jewish. Your family swindled my family out of it. You paid almost nothing. So it's *my* family's—mine, not yours. Your family stole that painting and four others, and mine got a one-way ticket east. My family worked as slaves. They got typhus and dysentery, and nearly froze and starved. Then they were gassed. Yeah, you have it easy, Ben. Your family got Camp Kateri and mine got a camp called Auschwitz. How's that for a bargain?"

Ben didn't recognize the word, Auschwitz, or know what it meant. Yet he understood some fundamental unfairness must have occurred in the past that had damaged or ruined the detective's family. He also believed that what had happened wasn't his fault and that he shouldn't have to answer for it. He should live and so should Detective Vidas, but he knew both of them would die and everything would end.

Once again he began speaking of the painting of the knight with the silver armor and the red sash. But then he stopped. He waited to see if the detective had noticed what he'd noticed, but the detective only turned aside and pulled the gloves more tightly onto his large hands.

Ben had lived in the town house all his life. He'd slept in that bed for most of his ten years. He'd learned to hear things in the kitchen when his mother was cooking and in his father's study when his father was watching a Yankees game after Ben had gone to bed. He'd also learned to sense small changes in the house, the silent movement of air when doors opened and closed. A moment ago he'd sensed just such a small change.

He knew that someone had entered the house.

Chapter One Hundred Two

Buddy stood in the foyer and listened. He heard nothing at first, only the sound of cars on the street outside. Slowly, silently, he closed the wide black door. He listened again, straining to hear something, anything that would tell him Ben's location. The town house was silent as a tomb, yet Buddy knew he wasn't alone. Ben and Vidas were somewhere in the vast space with high ceilings and many rooms, the hundreds of millions of dollars of paintings and their ghosts which could never be vanquished.

Buddy moved across the foyer in combat position, relieved he didn't have nice leather-soled shoes like his brother's. They'd have clicked on the marble floors. His cheaper rubber-soled shoes gave him traction on the smooth stone and, more importantly, silence. He held the Glock steady, the pad of his right index finger on the trigger, and slid against the right wall of the foyer. There was an opening. He bobbed his head into it, but found only an empty study.

His heart pounded. Boom! Boom! *Boom!*

Sweat formed on his forehead and his palms.

He lifted his left forearm and wiped off his face. Brushed one hand and then the other on his pants.

Then he had the Glock in both hands and began to move urgently, not caring about his own safety.

Next room. Deeper in the house. On the right a living room, also vacant. Farther, a formal dining room. Next, a great room and kitchen with a large island and bar. Glass doors gave onto a small garden and backyard. There was no one. He felt out of place in such a formal house, but he wouldn't be here long. He'd either save Ben or he'd take a bullet himself—or maybe both.

He spun around and retraced his steps, hurrying now, almost running, realizing the house's silence might be telling him Ben was dead and only his partner lay in wait.

Back in the foyer he eyed the grand staircase that wound up the left wall to the second level. He charged up the stairs, raising his gun at whatever came at him from the better-positioned higher ground.

At the turn halfway up the stairs, he saw a dark stain on the cherry wood. He glanced at the large painting to his left and saw it was smeared with blood.

Ben's blood.

The Glock wavered and shook. Buddy felt the adrenaline surging through him. He took a deep breath to calm himself, and then raced up the staircase, three steps at a time, until he reached the top.

In the near darkness he stopped. Before him was a hallway with a pair of French doors at the end and three doors on either side. All the doors were open. He crouched down, making himself a smaller target, lowering his center of gravity. He waited, expecting to be shot at.

Yet nothing happened.

Then something did.

He heard whispering, very faint, almost inaudible. He couldn't make out the words. Nor could he tell if the sound came from one of the doors on the right or the left side of the hallway. Yet from the third door on the left came a faint yellow light.

Caution told him to approach each doorway methodically, that the lamp switched on in one of the rooms might be a decoy or a distraction and he'd be a moth to the flame. But instinct told him he was out of time. He'd either get to Ben in the next few seconds, or be too late. Caution wouldn't work. Holding his breath, he steadied the Glock and went for the doorway with the yellow light.

But he didn't step inside. His training held him back. He stood against the wall by the doorway. He dipped his head into the space.

He saw a desk lamp that lit two figures on the bed, one of them Ben and the other Vidas. Vidas was dressed entirely in black and wore black gloves. Ben was lying on his back, his head on a pillow. In the instant of his glance, Buddy had seen no weapon, though he was certain there were many. From his vantage point twenty feet away—it was a large bedroom—the figures provided a blended target. If he fired he'd probably hit Vidas, but then again he might hit Ben. He didn't have a shot. He wouldn't make that mistake twice.

As he stood there, he heard Ben talking, or at least whispering. He bobbed his head into the doorway a second time.

Vidas was moving closer to Ben, trying to catch what the boy was saying.

Now Buddy knew he couldn't shoot. Vidas had brought his head and shoulders over Ben. Buddy had planned to charge into the room, but what if Vidas picked up Ben and hid behind him with a knife to the boy's throat?

Again he bobbed his head into the doorway, this time more slowly. He paused, watching the large man and the small boy in the grayness, just outside the golden halo spread by the desk lamp. He held his breath, listening for Ben's words, yet he couldn't quite hear them.

"You're going to die." This was his partner's voice—strong, calm, clear. "Just like your mommy and daddy and your little sister. She was the best of all. In a little party dress for New Year's Eve. Until I put my hatchet between her ears. Nice little girl, but you'll top her. And who'll be blamed for your death? Your uncle, of course," he sneered. "Just like he's to blame for everyone else's. Wasn't hard to do. A push here and there. I lifted your uncle Dietrich's prints from a glass at a restaurant and pasted them into the elevator at Mei's building," he bragged. "Could have put them in Mei's bedroom, but that would have been too obvious. Fired your uncle Carl's antique gun in Bruno's foyer. Left one of your uncle Dietrich's contact lenses at Carl's house. And my moron partner will never figure it out. I moved him around like a piece on a chessboard."

Ben shrunk away from him.

"Yes, little Ben," the man above him snarled, "one by one all the Brooks will die, out of prison or in prison, it doesn't matter, so long as you're all gone. And when I walk out of here today, I'm taking some paintings. They're mine, you know that, don't you? They're mine. You and your shit family murdered my family, and now I'm paying you back. An eye for a fucking eye."

Ben continued to whisper, but he also shrank from Vidas. Attempted to move across the bed, away from the figure in black.

As Ben tried to slide his body, his head tilted back. Buddy thought it was involuntary but it wasn't. Ben's eyes were open and he was looking right at Buddy.

Buddy read the look, and nodded.

And then the whispering ceased.

Ben jerked his head upward like hammer, driving his forehead into Vidas's face, up into his nose.

Vidas lurched off the bed. He screamed. He brought one hand up to his newly crooked and bloody nose. His other hand held a hatchet.

Rising to his full height, he lifted the hatchet, whose blade glimmered in the light. Vidas said nothing else. He didn't hesitate.

But neither did Buddy.

When Buddy saw the hatchet raised for the fatal blow, he knew he'd have to go for the headshot. A bullet to the chest or stomach or leg wouldn't stop Vidas, who was likely wearing body armor. Even if his partner fell, gravity would pull the blade down until it was stopped by something soft or solid. He knew it would kill Ben. He had to take the risk of all risks.

Buddy planted his left foot and swung his right one hundred eighty degrees until he was centered in the bedroom doorway. He held his breath, didn't blink, aimed carefully, pressed gently on the trigger of the Glock. Once, twice.

Crack! Crack!

A burst of sound in the silent bedroom.

Brains and skull sprayed onto the walls.

Vidas stared at Buddy, his eyes vacant, a gaping hole in his forehead. He toppled, the weight of the hatchet he'd raised pulling him backward like a diver going off a board. He dropped almost soundlessly to the floor, the blade making a dull thump.

Ben screamed louder than ever before. "*Buddy!* Help me! *Help me!*"

Buddy ignored the boy.

He charged into the room, circled the bed, Glock steady in both hands, and came upon his partner lying on his back with blood bubbling from his forehead, the hatchet on the floor beyond. Buddy felt his partner's neck.

A faint pulse.

Unbelievable.

Buddy moved between the bed and the figure on the floor. Ben had seen enough—he didn't need to see this.

Buddy aimed at his partner's forehead. He wanted to fire again, to be sure, but he waited. He slowed his breathing, counted to five. Then he let go of the gun with his left hand and again felt for a pulse.

This time there was nothing. It was over.

He shoved the Glock into his shoulder holster and turned to Ben.

Who was sobbing uncontrollably.

Buddy saw why the boy had used the head butt. He was trussed like an animal, crudely and so tightly the rope was digging into the boy's arms and legs, swelling them, turning his hands blue. He also saw Ben's leg. Blood had soaked through the khakis and stained the duvet cover. Buddy noticed his face. More pale than he'd ever seen it.

Jesus.

How much blood had Ben lost?

He heard sirens. More than one.

He lifted the knife off the floor and cut the rope, freeing Ben.

Ben reached for him but couldn't sit up, instead falling back onto the bed, lying in a daze, quiet and distressingly still.

Buddy said, "Stay with me. Please stay with me, Ben. Don't leave me now."

Chapter One Hundred Three

Three days later Buddy sat in an aisle seat in the second row of a courtroom. He'd come down to New York County Family Court on Lafayette Street in lower Manhattan. He saw the blond wood behind and in front of the judge's bench, maple pews and wainscoting and white walls—all the décor an attempt to make the ugly things that happened here seem pleasant. Though Buddy didn't want to be in this place, he had no choice. But at least he wasn't alone.

To his right was Mei, one wrist sprained but not broken, and to her right, Ward. To Buddy's left, partly blocking the aisle, he'd positioned Ben's wheelchair. Ben sat with his right leg wrapped in thick bandages, the chair's hanger adjusted to support the leg extending outward. His typically bright eyes dulled by painkillers, he held tightly to Buddy's hand. He'd been in the hospital all weekend, and Buddy and Mei hadn't left his side.

Buddy listened to Robert Kahler, the lawyer for Dietrich Brook, argue before Judge Sylvia Miles, a middle-aged woman whose dark hair was streaked with gray. Kahler wore a solid navy-blue suit, white shirt, light-blue tie. His silver, wire-rimmed eyeglasses reflected the overhead lights. Before Kahler spoke, he turned around and nodded silently at the first two rows on the other side of the room. There sat Dietrich, Lydia, and Hayley Brook, all conservatively dressed.

Without using notes Kahler said, "Ben Brook is a wonderful boy who should be living not with the esteemed older gentleman, Ray Sawyer, but with his aunt, uncle, and cousin, all of whom adore him."

Buddy looked over at Ben, who was slowly shaking his head.

Kahler continued, "And Mr. Sawyer's recent loss of his wife in tragic circumstances will make it impossible for him to provide the kind of warm and supportive family environment a ten-year-old boy needs."

As Ray Sawyer was sitting directly in front of him, Buddy couldn't see the older man's face. But Sawyer's body wasn't straight. He was hunched over his table, writing. Today he wore the same clothes as when he'd greeted Buddy and Ward at Camp Kateri the first week of January: dress trousers and a tweed sport coat.

Kahler stood at the lectern and raised a hand. "And finally, there has been some discussion recently that Detective Cyrus Edward Lock, with the New York City Police Department, and his girlfriend, Mei Adams, who live together, should take custody of my clients' nephew. This option should not be considered for one moment. Mr. Lock and Miss Adams have been dating for less than a year, and during the week they've had custody of Ben, there have been three—*three*, Your Honor— attempts on Ben's life. Fortunately all were unsuccessful, although the poor boy has suffered a major knife wound to one of his legs in addition to possible psychological trauma. If only, Your Honor, Ben had been with his uncle Dietrich over the past week, he would not have endured such harrowing experiences." Here, Kahler waved his hand to the side as if brushing away a fly.

Buddy was growing angrier by the second. He wanted to shout: *Ben's uncles couldn't protect him at Camp Kateri, could they? And if he'd gone to live with Dietrich, then surely he'd be dead today!*

But he kept his mouth clamped shut, though he felt his face warm with his temper.

"Even if Detective Lock and Miss Adams have pure motives," Kahler continued, "they certainly know that custody of Ben might lead to gaining control of his parents' trust of which he is sole beneficiary. You'll recall the value of that trust is approximately six billion dollars, with the paintings he's recently inherited being worth about a half billion dollars more." Kahler, after glancing slyly at Buddy and Mei, added, "This is an enormous amount of money to anyone, of course, but it couldn't be a consideration for my clients, who are already billionaires several times over."

Mei turned to Buddy, her face etched with worry lines, and whispered, "What about control of Brook Instruments? That's what they really want."

Buddy tried to reassure her. "Sawyer's time will come."

Kahler added, "And of course I needn't mention that Detective Lock's partner turned out to be a serial killer, with Detective Lock betraying Ben's whereabouts at every turn, and Detective Lock always ignorant of the truth."

Buddy gritted his teeth, determined to hide his emotions even as he raged inside, angry with himself, furious with Kahler. Mei reached over and touched the back of his hand, soothing him.

Kahler concluded, "So my clients submit to this court that it is in the best interests of Ben Brook to rejoin his family, to have daily interaction with his aunt, uncle, and cousin, to have their support and love as he becomes the marvelous young man he promises to be." Kahler paused, half bowed toward the bench, and said, "Thank you, Your Honor."

So many half-truths, Buddy thought. *So many distortions, but maybe not outright lies. Except for the one about Ben's aunt and uncle adoring him. That's bullshit.*

Ray Sawyer stood, a little unsteadily, and shuffled to the lectern. He carried a yellow legal pad, nodded toward Judge Miles, and said, "If it please the court, my esteemed colleague does what he's paid to do, that is, to make his clients look great and me look bad. But allow *me* to submit, Your Honor, that this issue was decided one year ago. Not by anyone in this courtroom but by Ben's parents, who were recently slain. Alton and Brenda Brook knew about the best interests of their son, Ben. They knew about the *supposed* adoration of Ben by his aunt, uncle, and cousin. About the supposedly warm and supportive environment the extended family could provide Ben. And Ben's parents also knew how their son's six and a half billion dollars in assets played absolutely no role"—here Sawyer turned and gestured with an open hand toward Dietrich Brook and family—"absolutely no role in the desire of that aunt, uncle, and cousin to take custody of Ben."

Buddy nodded, silently urging Sawyer on, feeling a flicker of hope.

Sawyer continued, "But understanding what was best for their son, did Alton and Brenda Brook assign custody of the boy to any member of their family? No, Your Honor, they did not. In fact, they specifically state in their wills and trust documents that Ben must never, in any circumstances, be given over to any of his aunts or uncles. Instead, as Your Honor knows from reading those documents, which I've provided to the court and Mr. Kahler, Ben's parents gave custody of Ben to *me*. And it is I, and nobody else, who they asked to make all future custody arrangements for their son, provided that custody arrangement must not—must *not*, Your Honor—involve Dietrich Brook or any member of his family."

Ray Sawyer held up an index finger and added, "And what we haven't heard today is evidence that Ben's parents didn't know his best interests. The fact is they wanted him with me. And yes, my wife was murdered . . ." Sawyer paused a moment, breathed deeply, and continued, "But I'm retired and will dedicate myself to raising Ben. I can give him a safe and supportive environment, the very one his parents wished. It is incumbent upon this court to follow the instructions that Ben's parents gave us. Anything else would be a perversion of the law and of common sense. Anything else would place Ben in an environment not of adoration but of humiliation and danger." With this, Ray

Sawyer bowed slightly toward Judge Miles and concluded, "Thank you, Your Honor."

The rows of reporters behind Mei, Buddy, and Ward began talking immediately. Some typed hurriedly on laptops, others stepped out to make calls.

Buddy watched Ray Sawyer, who seemed shrunken and frail, nearly trip over his own feet as he tottered back to his seat. The older man sat down, his hands grasping the yellow legal pad, and turned to Buddy. He gave a wan smile and then faced the judge.

Buddy turned to Mei and said under his breath, "You see, it'll be all right."

Mei tried to smile, but she looked nervous. Buddy saw her turn her head to Ward. Ward nodded encouragingly and leaned toward her, motioning for Buddy to lean in as well.

Ward said, "Now the judge will take it under advisement. She has ninety days to make a decision."

Buddy relaxed. Ninety days wasn't long but it was better than fearing Ben would be taken away sooner. He sat up and turned to Ben, who was watching him carefully. Buddy squeezed his hand. "I think we'll head home now. Ward says the judge is going to think about it for a few months and then tell us what she wants to do."

Ben's face remained blank. "Will I get to stay with you?"

Buddy thought maybe the doctor had prescribed too large a dose of painkillers for Ben, but then again when it was time for another dose, he began to cry softly from the wound. Buddy said, "Yeah, Ben, don't worry about it. You heard Mr. Sawyer tell the judge about your parents' instructions to have you stay with him, and how he can decide custody arrangements. Mr. Sawyer has already decided he'll have you live with Mei and me. So that's settled."

Judge Silvia Miles banged the gavel and brought the court to order once more. For such a small woman she had a loud voice with a hard edge, a voice with precision and authority but not a hint of warmth.

She said, "Thank you, Mr. Kahler and Mr. Sawyer, for your arguments this morning. I appreciate your and, in the case of Mr. Kahler, your clients' concern for Ben Brook's welfare. Over the past day or two, I've reviewed the short briefs you sent the court. I've also reviewed the will and trust documents signed by Ben's now-deceased parents. Those are very powerful documents, to be sure, but they were written at a different time and in a different situation. By statute it is this court that must determine the best interests of Ben Brook, based on the totality of the circumstances today. And so this morning I've decided to take the decision under advisement and will rule in due time." She banged her gavel twice, stood from the bench, and disappeared into a back corridor.

Buddy got out of his seat and knelt down beside Ben's wheelchair. He put his arms around the boy, covering him as if from a terrible storm. He held Ben fiercely and felt the boy hugging him desperately and sobbing. Still covering Ben, Buddy moved his head close to Ben's ear and said, "Listen, Ben. No matter what happens, you'll be okay. You'll be safe."

Ben cried, "I don't want to go."

Buddy kissed his cheek. "I don't want you to go anywhere." Then he searched for Ben's eyes, all the while fearing that if the judge ruled in favor of Dietrich Brook, there wasn't much he could do. He'd be powerless before the law.

Ben grew quieter. He made no response, nor did he loosen his grip. His eyes met Buddy's. He said, "I love you, Buddy."

Buddy straightened, felt a tear forming. He moved so Ben wouldn't see his face, and wiped it away. Yet his heart seemed to burst. A new warmth flowed through him. Without thinking about it, without regard for the consequences, he turned back to Ben and heard himself say, "I love you, Ben."

Ben smiled at him.

Buddy tousled his hair.

A light hand touched his shoulder. Knowing it was Mei, he moved aside. Mei stepped closer and embraced Ben. She smiled. Then she laughed—and something about her laughter in the face of fear and uncertainty broke the frightening spell of the proceeding.

Buddy felt better, even hopeful.

Ward stood beside Mei and nodded approvingly.

After a moment Ben smiled. His eyes brightened. To all of them, he said, "Can we go home?"

Buddy said, "Damn right we can." He walked behind the chair, took hold of the handles, and pushed Ben down the center aisle of the courtroom, Mei and Ward following them. They went slowly past Dietrich Brook and his wife and daughter, past the reporters and photographers, and out into the cold gray city.

ACKNOWLEDGMENTS

I'd like to thank those who provided early encouragement: John Hatch, Jane Rice, Norma Thomson, Bruce Campbell, Marya Hornbacher, David Lebedoff, Karen Rye, and my mother. And my father for his careful reading. Not least, Will Roberts, my agent, for his brilliant suggestions and always wise counsel. The team at Thomas & Mercer, including Jessica Tribble and Peggy Hageman, whose advice improved the book significantly. And last, thank you to my wife, Megan, for her continuous support and for being the essential ingredient to life.

ABOUT THE AUTHOR

James Tucker has worked as an attorney at an international law firm and is currently an executive managing real estate strategy at a Fortune 50 company, where his work includes frequent travel throughout the United States. Fascinated by the crimes of those in power, he draws on these cases for his writing. He has a law degree from the University of Minnesota Law School and was one of four fiction writers awarded a position at a past Mentor Series at the Loft Literary Center in Minneapolis. He has attended the Community of Writers at Squaw Valley and the Tin House Writers' Workshop in Portland, where he was mentored by author Walter Kirn. He lives near Minneapolis with his wife, the painter Megan Rye, and their family. *Next of Kin* is his first novel.